CROWS ON THE ROOF

ANNA HOUSEGO

This novel was written on the island of lutruwita/Tasmania, on the southern land of the muwinina people and within sight of kunanyi and its mountain power. I pay my respect to the traditional owners and acknowledge the Tasmanian Aboriginal people as the continuing custodians of this land. I honour their Elders, past and present, as the keepers of deep knowledge and culture spanning more than 40,000 years. Their story lives on.

Crows on the Roof by Anna Housego
Published by Anna Housego © All rights reserved
www.annahousego.com

1st edition 2022, paperback
Paperback ISBN: 978-0-6456369-0-1
Ebook ISBN: 978-0-6456369-1-8

For Ned, who always gives it his all.

PROLOGUE

Suppertime, mid-shift on the editorial floor. The night sub-editors leave the mess of papers on their long wooden table to gather around the desk of the day editor, gone hours ago from the newspaper offices.

Murray has worked nights for years and is looking forward to a rare treat. He rips open a loaf of sliced white bread, pulls out a pocketknife and starts piling butter onto every second slice.

'Nothing better,' his colleague Stu announces, slapping down a parcel wrapped in newspaper then pulling a small saltshaker from one jacket pocket and a pepper shaker from the other. He flips the parcel and unwraps it. The light from the fluorescents hits a mound of tiny bodies from all angles, the shine bouncing away in every direction so they seem to tremble.

Stu throws some of the prawns onto buttered bread, salts them generously and wedges them with a second slice. 'Caught 'em up the Swan. You won't get any fresher than pulling them from the river this morning.' He chows down while Murray hands bread to the others.

Still chewing, Stu looks over at the last reporter on the shift, hammering her typewriter towards the final deadline of the day. He fixes his eyes on her, fingers clacking the keys, releasing a fury of letters onto the page.

'Get into it. They won't last long,' he calls over.

It's a kindness, the offer, and nothing more. He'd seen her in the lift when he started the shift, knows better than her that she won't eat; that there's things that will turn a stomach for a long time.

GRAVITY

Tide rising eight metres,
with warning of higher storm surges.

1

LATE IN THE AFTERNOON, THE generator light came on. Bec pulled over and cut the engine. As it died, the silence of the desert forced its way through the vents and pressed in through the open driver's window. She let it come, didn't move an inch, barely breathing. Thought maybe she would stay like that, one hand on the steering wheel, feet flat on the van floor until night drifted in or longer, until the sun rose and the heat kicked in again.

The heat was worse than the silence. Sun blasted through the rear window. With no airflow through open windows, the van's metal roof and sides were hot enough to sear skin. The temperature inside rose rapidly and she flung open the door and bailed out, crouching near the bull bar in one narrow sliver of shade.

She had asked the mechanic, on that final service in Perth, about the possibilities of getting stranded in the Kombi. Like any good journo she knew how to frame the right question.

'It'll be the fan belt, nine times out of ten. Especially as you're getting up around the fifty thousand clicks mark. If it's not that, the engine'll blow up, in which case you'll be buggered because that sort of fire will be the end of it.'

She should have paid more attention when he gave her the demo on how to change the fan belt, what to look for, the importance of getting the tension right. It seemed so long ago, that five minutes in his workshop while he showed her the tools and talked her through it while she tried to hurry him along so she could hit the road.

Was it a month? Two months? She had stopped counting the days, the weeks. All that mattered was to count the kilometres. Two thousand, three hundred and – she got to her feet and checked the speedo – forty-seven. If she could make it to three thousand, she'd stop for a day or two and take a proper rest.

Bec went to the other side of the van and jerked open the sliding door. Inside she found the pouch with the tools. The red dust had worked its way inside the canvas. There was no escape from it. The wheels kicked it up and even when she wasn't on the move the sun acted like a magnet, drawing it into the air around her. It hid in the folds of the van curtains, stuck to the bottom of her feet, was grit in her mouth when she ate.

It had been like that since she left the bitumen and hit the dirt of the Gibb River Road, the nose of the van pointing away from the last town on the coastal edge of Western Australia and into the empty north. The road bleeding endlessly to a horizon that, in a trick of sky and flat scrub, was always out of reach, and everywhere the dust. Before, there had always been a street, a track or at least a tree where her eyes could anchor but out here the sky and the low country kept coming at her from all sides and the road was next to useless in helping get a sense of place.

It had been terrifying at first. Though the Great Sandy Desert was off to the south, this felt like desert country: all the nothing, the featureless immensity and her so insignificant in it. She had debated turning back but then the memory muscled into her mind, an image as clear as the day she had first seen it, and she had gripped the steering wheel and driven on. A woman could lose her way out here, finish the last of the water in the jerry can, let the sun dry her out like the cracked 'roo hide she had passed that morning. She could let the dust have her as its own. It was a strangely consoling thought.

As a kid in school she had drawn maps of the continent where the vast north was merely an arc done with a flourish across the top of the page. It didn't interest her then, the bulky upper part of Australia, so distant from the big cities of Sydney and Melbourne or her country town in Victoria's western corner. Even the trip she and her husband had made the year before across the arid Nullabor Plain to their new jobs in Perth was an extension of the known, a thread of purpose joining Melbourne to Adelaide and on to the final destination.

This was different. It had no bookend, no welcome final point that could be reached with a sense of satisfaction or completion. She was travelling in a void with no sense of its scale or shape, let alone a marker that could tell her how much journeying was enough. Some days she was driving in the void, but on other days all the nothing gathered under her ribs and became a fathomless grey thing that took the wheel. She couldn't afford to sink into it now.

She grabbed the screwdriver and wrench and went to the rear of the van. Tussocks, spinifex and the occasional stunted woollybutt and eucalypt stretched out to the point where the earth curved, with no mountain or hill to hem them in.

Twenty-seven years old and what the hell had she gained, what good had she made in the past decade? The holy trinity of career, marriage, children, had slipped away faster than the rat from her food stash that first night on the road. Ah yes, she could always count on self-pity, the last friend standing. At least it amused her.

Bec knelt in the dirt and undid the three screws to remove the metal grille over the fanbelt pulleys, suddenly conscious that the only tools she had ever used with competence were a knife and fork. She heard a soft shuffling and spun around, jumping to her feet with the screwdriver in her right hand, the screws falling to the ground. Behind her, nothing. She leaned around the van, hoping to see a sand monitor dragging its tail through the dust as it crossed the road, but rows of days-old tyre tracks in the dirt lay undisturbed.

The sound came from the opposite side of the van. She flattened herself against the rear door and slid to the corner, keeping her body concealed as she scanned the surrounds. A pair of round eyes met hers at almost the same height. Three metres away, a feral donkey lowered its head briefly then lifted it to stare again, its steady gaze saying it all. Though it was descended from introduced pack animals, released into the wild after trucks took over the task of hauling supplies long distance, she was the misfit here because donkeys were not solitary creatures. In the distance, somewhere beyond her view, it had a herd within reach of a creek or a waterhole. Unexpectedly she began to laugh, but even as the muscles of her mouth stretched into a smile the tears came.

The donkey's ears, ludicrously large for its head, were upright and tuned to her every move. The animal was a vaudeville showpiece in the sunburnt savannah, its back almost black, belly and nose white and each dark eye looking out from a wide band of white circling it. The absurdity, the improbability of the encounter was too much. She slumped to the ground and gave in to ugly sobbing.

The shadows began lengthening, though the heat remained intense. She staggered to her feet and wiped the back of her hand across her forehead. The donkey had disappeared and good riddance to it. She returned to the rear of the van and found the screws in the dirt, which was a comfort of sorts.

She remembered to slip the screwdriver into the notch above the top pulley to lock it off before tackling the pulley nut with the wrench. Working the two tools at once was harder than the mechanic had made it look. Her mind emptied itself of any further instructions, instead flooding with the string of warnings he had given. 'If it's slipping and you keep driving, you'll flatten the battery. If the belt's broken and you don't stop, you'll cook your engine in a few miles. If you make the belt too tight, the pulleys are gonna wobble and destroy themselves, and maybe the generator or alternator too.'

She only had the one spare so if she failed it would be a long wait for help. Trucks regularly travelled the arduous route from Perth through the Kimberley to Alice Springs or Darwin, but they all took the sealed highway south of her. She would be relying on an adventurous traveller and who knew when such a person might come through.

The difficult choice was no choice at all. She already knew that. She would have a go, hope for the best. She needed to get on with it immediately. She had just passed her first anniversary in Western Australia but she would never get used to the way the night dropped, dead weight, out of the blue sky. Not gentle like the softening twilight she had known over east, dimming the world slowly as all went quiet, making way for the closing soundtrack of birds. Nightfall was a literal thing here and it would be happening soon.

She struggled with the wrench for what seemed an eternity, then lifted it off the nut to change the angle. This time the nut had some give and she stood to push down on it with her full weight until it let go and she could undo it. She removed the pressure washer but forgot to take her hand off the screwdriver to catch the spare spacer shims and they fell into the dirt. She retrieved them and wiped each one on her shorts before stacking them on the bumper bar. The front half of the pulley didn't come away easily like she expected. She would get this wrong, it would be her fault, like everything else.

When she tugged a second time it released. She counted the four working shims as she slid them off. The belt wasn't broken but the side was shiny where it had been slipping. She hooked it off the bottom pulley and tossed it at her feet.

Without the drivebelt the van was useless. She could taste the panic, oily in her mouth like she had leaned over and licked the engine. Her back ached with the longing to lie down on the bed platform in the van.

'Come on, Bec. You can do it.' Her voice hung in the air and was gone.

She took a deep breath, ripped the cardboard cover off the new belt and slipped it around the bottom pulley then the groove in the top pulley. Extra shims or fewer for a new belt? She couldn't recall how to manage the number to make the belt looser or tighter. She guessed and added five instead of the previous four. She replaced the outer half of the pulley and tightened the nut then looked down to see the spare shims still on the bumper bar. It was late, it would have to do.

Using the belt, she turned the pulleys a couple of times. The belt was travelling in the upper groove just fine, but when she pressed it there was no give. Bugger. Too tight. She turned it a few more times, studying the shape of the upper pulley halves. She could see that if she removed shims the pulley sections would leave a wider gap and the belt would ride lower.

Fifteen minutes later, after several test attempts, two shims seemed to provide the best tension. She put the spares back under the pressure washer this time and replaced the nut. Her hands were black and soon the sky would be too. She screwed in the grid and slammed down the hatch door. She needed to eat but first she needed to find a place where she could pull over for the night, well off the road.

She had just climbed into the driver's seat when it came to her that the mechanic had given one last warning. She had missed an important step in finishing up. It set off open warfare in her head, one voice arguing for rest and replenishment and another demanding she finish the job properly. Fighting herself was something she had turned into an Olympic sport, building the self-negation muscle before she had even started school. Always a show-down between what she wanted and what was expected, till any sense of what might truly matter to her had been whittled away. She had been terribly clever, marrying a man who could help the process along, chipping away any sense of who she was other than what she might give to keep the peace, to keep him happy. Though he never was.

Bec rolled out of the van, banging her knee on the door and landing awkwardly. The exhaustion went in so deep that even her teeth hurt. Retrieving the tools, she removed the grille again and paused momentarily to steady herself. This time, recalling the mechanic's final instruction, she locked off the top pulley with the screw-driver before busting the last of her strength on tightening the nut for the final time.

When she turned the ignition key, it was a relief to see that the generator light was off. She thought she could detect a squeal in the engine noise, she wasn't sure, but switched on the headlights regardless and drove into the night, straining to see where the edges of the road merged with spindly mulga. After half an hour, odd shapes made by the headlights seemed to form on the road and outside the windscreen. What seemed like familiar landmarks floated up at first, out of place in the dull edges where the lights faded out, then the shadowy forms morphed into figures, hovering closer. As they did they took on faces of those left behind. She shuddered and kept driving, arms stiff, jaw rigid.

She slowed when she saw the next break in the thin

scrub and nudged the van off the road. It was hardly hidden, but she was past caring. After guzzling warm water and eating a handful of nuts, she fell onto the bed platform and slept in her dirty shorts and T-shirt, sandals on and the doors locked.

At daylight Bec stirred and rolled out of the airless van to stretch her limbs. Her eyes were drawn to a low tree nearby, grey leaves turning pale green as the sun rose. Perhaps with reliable rain it would have soared upwards, but that was only a fleeting thought because something stranger drew her over to its crooked trunk. Much of the rough bark was sandy brown, but on one side it gaped in an open wound and haemorrhaged a thick red trail of sap almost to the ground. She touched the bleeding tree, pushed one finger into the place where the sap had darkened to a deep maroon and begun to congeal. The tree resisted, though only for a moment, and when she pulled back her hand a blood red circle of sap stained her fingertip.

She dipped it in what water she could spare, scraping at it with a thumbnail, but it had set in a sticky blob and refused to budge. It was in her line of sight as her hands moved the steering wheel, swinging the van back onto the road. A point of blood to mark where the tree had transferred some of its pain.

She shoved a cassette into the dashboard player. The tape had been a treat, a celebration of the award she had won for a series of human interest articles, scratching the surface of tough subjects like palliative care, disability, recovery after tragedy. The interviews and writing had made her feel useful, like she was making a difference. It was, in reality, a joke and one that was on her.

People had read the pieces, tut-tutted or had a moment of sadness then moved on. She had produced work that fed idle curiosity and nothing more.

The Eagles, Hotel California. The music had been a revelation when she first heard it, cryptic storytelling buoyed by upbeat electric guitars and orchestral spin. It never failed to raise her spirits. She turned up the volume. The opening bars were barely recognisable in the growl that came from the speakers. She punched the eject button and gripped the cassette to pull it free. The tape unspooled from the reels, a piece of it caught in the player. When she yanked it the tape broke. She swore and threw it onto the passenger seat.

As she glanced back up, a large road sign was disappearing on her left. She stopped and reversed up. In two hundred metres, she must choose. South to Kununurra, less than an hour away, and wend her way east then maybe up towards Darwin or head down to Brisbane. Or go north to nearby Wyndham and the coast. She sat for a long time while the engine idled, then released the clutch and eased the van forward.

At the intersection, her inner compass swung north at the last minute and the van followed, the rattle of metal easing as it met the bitumen for the final leg of the Great Northern Highway she had abandoned near Derby. After days of flat country the red fortress of the Bastion Range was a shock. The road itself was intimidated by the sandstone escarpments and crawled along at their feet. The sun spared nothing, throwing a harsh brightness on all it reached and leaving what remained in the blackest of shadows.

She drove through more tussock grass into the

scattered town, where the road kept going. Away from the last houses a long straight section of raised asphalt crossed spreading saltflats, which gave way on the left to dull grey mudflats bordered with mangroves. A large weathered roadside board declared 'Current Cyclone Status' across the top half with the rest of it empty.

Past a sign for Old Port the van thundered onto gravel again as the road led beyond a gaol, past a row of bloated boab trees, a string of houses on stilts, faded shops stacked up the street one after the other like wooden boxes, then a pub. Not a soul in sight except for a lonely figure seated under a verandah on the shady side of the street. Desolation row.

Bec rounded a bend and saw there was no further north to go.

The port was squeezed onto a strip of land stranded between the harbour on one side and a high rocky ridge on the other. Ahead was a long, curving jetty and the murky waters of the Cambridge Gulf, while to the right tall letters announced the Wyndham Meatworks. The cool stores and bays for unloading cattle were a dead giveaway.

She switched off the engine.

The lack of motion was unnerving and instinctively she slumped forward over the steering wheel and looked up to the sky, scanning for a streak of cloud, a quarter moon in its daytime white, a hint of the familiar, any place to rest her thoughts for a moment. Instead the blinding glare of mid-afternoon made her eyes well up.

Her water had almost run out and it had been two days or more since eating the last of the fresh food. She would stock up, rest for a night, maybe two. When she got out of the van to stretch her legs the onslaught of air was hotter than it had been in the red dirt. It came blasting at her from the sandstone hogbacks of the range behind, a wall of heat that must have been at least forty degrees Celsius, whipping her face as though she'd opened an oven door.

It was no cooler in the van. The mountain escarpments loomed above and she couldn't put a finger on why, but suddenly it was urgent that she get to higher ground. Turning the van, she remembered the sign to the lookout on the Bastion and drove back to the main town, the Three Mile. With nothing remarkable about the place, they had apparently not bothered finding a decent name for it.

She headed uphill and within minutes was parked high above the two-storey meatworks at the Five Rivers viewing area, where at last there was a breeze, even if the movement of the air had no cooling benefit.

———·———

Resting on the veranda, Lily had observed the van head towards the harbour. She had been sitting in her usual spot, which provided minimal relief from the heat but gave her a sense of being out in the world. She was an old woman now and there was little for her to do besides thinking her thoughts in the long hours of the hot afternoon.

The van was a blur, like much of what her fading eyes could see, but its green was the same colour as wings of the beautiful finches that once had visited, now long gone yet still fluttering in her heart.

She sensed the woman driving was not a tourist. The

driver did not slow her vehicle on its approach, like the gawking visitors who treated her as an object of curiosity, necessitating retreat into the depths of the shop.

Lily watched the van grow smaller in a whirl of dust. She stood slowly and shuffled inside, distracted from her painful joints by a certainty that she would see the driver again.

At the lookout, Bec studied a sun-bleached tourist sign and tried to make sense of the vast sprawl of landscape spreading in dull grey before her.

The King, Pentecost and Durack rivers were to the south, Forrest to the west and the Ord River to the north. Over the distance they moved sluggishly through mudflats before petering out in the Cambridge Gulf. She studied the map on the sign, seeing how the first gulf opened out to be swallowed by the vast jaws of the Joseph Bonaparte Gulf, then the Timor Sea.

The scale of the estuary dwarfed the spreading plains she had experienced in previous days; made the capital city left behind seem such a puny thing.

The mudflats were the same metallic grey as the water and in places the mud seemed to flow while the water did not. The illusion made her queasy, that what was solid could shift like that. She wanted to look away, but it was some minutes before she could. She went back to the van and moved it to the side of the large car park, positioning it side on to block the view of the tent she would wait to set up just before dark. She would hear any car straining up the steep road well before it arrived.

It was a long wait till dark. Eating a can of tuna and a

handful of almonds was a small act of resistance against the urge to pack up and drive back down the road to buy fresh food. Eventually exhaustion won and she stayed put.

As the night went on, the temperature barely dropped. Her body stretched tight till she thought it would snap if she dared roll over one more time. She desperately needed a shower and a chance to wash her stringy hair. It had been pointless in recent days to contemplate a detour to any waterhole, where without local knowledge there was always the risk of an encounter with freshwater crocodiles.

She needed to bring her mind to heel when night let it slip off the leash. It was worse now there was no more north to aim for, no point to rising in the morning for a start to the day.

First light was a long time coming. When it did she crawled out of the tent and sat on the low stone wall at the front of the lookout. There was no sign of life below, not even at the meatworks. She checked her watch, barely five o'clock. Adrenalin had powered her for days but it was fast fading, leaving her drained and uneasy.

She had reached the farthest edge of the continent with no clue about what came next. Whatever ideas she once had about the person she was had been stripped away in Perth. She deserved the blame for what had gone down in those final two weeks. There had been no point in staying around for forgiveness because she needed to forgive herself and that wasn't going to happen. It had begun as a glorious sunny day, benign, beckoning, then all it had taken was a sudden, sharp tempest that shook her centre, and a night turned sour and deadly. In the carnage of her life, all that remained was the van and it wasn't even her name on the rego papers.

She wheeled away from thoughts of the past to get the box of utensils from the van, setting up the gas stove to boil water for tea. The morning was already too warm for steam to rise from the mug, but from habit Bec cradled it in both hands as she sipped, ignoring the sweat rising on her palms.

After a slow breakfast of muesli sloshed with the last of the apple juice, she pulled the boxes and bags out of the van, emptied them and shook the dust from everything, including her clothes, before repacking the van. There was no hurry. Time was no longer a friend. It had become a parasite, a tick on the belly of a dog, of no concern on the surface yet burrowing down for blood. Well, if she was the unwilling host for memories, she would ignore their barbs, refuse to dig them out. Who knew what poison might get left behind.

By half past eight she had the van ready, but for what she still didn't know. She sat on the wall again and watched for activity at the meatworks. Its car park had filled while she had been drinking tea and occasional trucks rumbled back and forth between the tall buildings below and the road out of town.

A low whump-whump came from the west in the direction of a dark speck in the corner of the view, high above the gulf. The dot grew bigger, the sound building until the rotors of a helicopter became visible. Soon it roared overhead and continued out of sight with no evident destination, leaving the ground shuddering and her heart pounding.

She was at a loss up here in this part of the country.

The searing quality of light, the never-ending rocks and the big sky danced together through the day but she didn't feel the rhythm or know where to place her feet. She lacked the skills to read the geography, where a steep gorge could drop suddenly through a hole in the middle of a wide plain and high mountain ranges had no peaks but were flat as tabletops.

She didn't understand strange plants like saltbush, flourishing in drought, or swollen boab trees, trunks wrinkled like giant elephant legs, scattered where she least expected across the plains on the drive towards Wyndham then unexpectedly disappearing, only to re-emerge along the main street at the Old Port. Whatever she thought she had known was of little use to her now.

As for the helicopter, in the city she would have assumed it meant a hospital transfer for a medical emergency, in the bush maybe a National Parks resupply mission. Once, when she'd been walking on the Overland Track in Tasmania, a chopper had flown overhead towing what a cheerful ranger informed her was a sputnik, the name he had given the fibreglass pod ferrying out human waste from a nearby camping hut. Today's chopper had arrived from nowhere and left no explanation, only an echo in its wash.

In the van minutes later, she sat with the motor running in neutral, unable to find the impetus to push in the clutch or reach for the gear shift. At some point she must have done so, for she was pressing the accelerator lightly and the van was rolling off. It was a strange sensation, to be travelling yet no longer have a direction in which to point her nose. She started down the road just the same because the only thing worse than not knowing what to do was to stay frozen in the fear of it.

Bec turned right when she reached the main street, driving back towards the harbour to pass the time until the supermarket opened. Approaching the motel she pulled in near its fading front wall, the van rolling to a halt. She had not meant to stop. Perhaps it was a sign she needed an air-conditioned room and a better bed tonight.

She was easing herself out of the seat when the thought occurred that she could ask about any work that might be going. She could buy herself some time while she figured out where to next. Maybe bring order in an air-conditioned reception foyer. She could look efficient, command a desk, wear a black pencil skirt and white blouse, not that she had either.

The motel was modest, the entrance not evident. It took her a minute to spot the door on the left facing away from the road. She had worn a fresh top and shorts that morning and hoped they made up for the state of her hair. Inside, the lights were off and a lone ceiling fan battled bravely against the heat. No cool air. The disappointment was acute.

A man came through the bar door, bringing a trail of light as it opened. 'Sorry, we're not open till ten. You'll have to come back.' The sound of a human voice, the first for almost a week, nearly brought her undone, even as she took in the fellow in front of her. He didn't wait for a reply but reached down to adjust the folded top of one of his long socks, worn inside sandals. When he straightened up, his face had flushed red and she saw how his knee-length shorts struggled upwards in the vain effort of finding a waist. She suppressed a smile.

'Hello, I was wondering if the manager's in.'

'That's me, Kerry Blenham. How can I help?'

'I'm going to be in town for a while. Thought I'd drop in to see if you have any work.'

She waited but he didn't ask if she had any skills. 'I'm a fast typist, I can work a fax machine, handle money, have a good phone manner …'

He gave no acknowledgement of what she had said but seemed to size her up.

'We need a yardie. You can start tomorrow if you like. The last one left town days ago and I've been doing the work myself.'

She had no idea what the job was but it solved the immediate problem of what to do.

'Get here at nine tomorrow and I'll show you the ropes but after that you'll want to start at six to avoid the worst of the heat. Don't know if anyone's told you but this is Australia's hottest town.'

Though they were the only two in the building, he lowered his voice.

'Marble Bar might have the country's highest temperature if you're just thinking of a day here and there, but Wyndham's got it tougher. Highest average, year in, year out.'

She grinned as she shook his hand. The motel's name, splashed across the wall out the front in tall strokes of green, was the Four Seasons. It seemed the epitome of aspiration for a place with only two seasons—the wet and the dry.

She reeled back out into the sun, an employee again.

2

THE JOB INTERVIEW, IF THAT was what you would call the one-sided chat with the motel manager, was at odds with the forensic examination she had been subjected to a year earlier by *The Daily West* editor, barricaded behind his oversized desk. She had only been in the narrow chair for a few minutes when the heavily lined face of Gerry Mavers fixed on her, and in his take-no-prisoners voice demanded to know when she planned to have children.

It might have been 1979, with the United Nations Decade for Women in full swing, but she still carried the sting of being the first female cadet at the regional paper where she had started out, the butt of practical jokes, having to push twice as hard and fast as the boys. Not even a female loo on the editorial floor. Her face reddening with the humiliation of going to the night editor, who dared to grouch as she asked for the key to ground floor advertising offices, where apparently it was accepted that women needed to pee.

She had forgiven old Gerry for being her father's generation and pandered to him, feeling the shame of it.

'No plans for children. I'm focused on continuing to

develop and improve as a reporter. There's still a lot still to learn.'

The answer seemed to please him and he rewarded her with the job. God help a woman who knew her real place to understand the risk of demanding it. She had put the interview behind her and gone on with proving herself to the men she worked alongside each day.

Andy was older and had already made a name for himself as a reporter with an extraordinary range of contacts and the persistence to follow a lead to the answers, whatever the question. After three months on police rounds and a further three in the Parliamentary press gallery, she was asked to help him out on a big investigation. It was a badge of honour, not that her husband had seen it that way. Any small success of hers seemed to set him on edge.

None of it mattered now as she sweated along the row of motel units at the side of the pub, gathering large metal rubbish bins one at a time to take to the loading bay at the back of the bar. The housemaids had already emptied wastepaper baskets and bathroom rubbish from the rooms and the bins overflowed. The first one clinked and clanged as she lifted it, empty stubbies and beer cans shifting suddenly so she had to tighten her grip. She pulled the bin up, arms stretched wide to a handle on either side, lifting to steady it against her waist. The manoeuvre brought the stink of stale beer and the halo of flies close to her nose and she nearly gagged. She dumped the bin and almost upended it on the concrete. She tried again, pulling it to one side and securing it against her hip. It was no further from her nose but at least she didn't have to look at it as she carried it off.

The manager had been right about the early heat. She thought she would pass out as she lifted the final bin into the trailer and it was only half past ten.

The shower at the caravan park had been glorious and she had slept well the night before, at last, to the humming of air con in rows of caravans nearby. Any renewed energy, however, had evaporated faster than the moisture in her washing when she had pegged it out. By the time she had hung the last shirt, the underwear was stiff as a board.

In the shower block, a blonde who looked a similar age to her had introduced herself as Linney and set her straight about the other campers.

'Most of us are just here for the six-month meat season. My fella's working in the boning room and I got a job packing so we're hoping to get a deposit on a place in Perth and be gone before the wet season closes the roads. That's if I can keep him out of the pub.'

Bec had smiled and said nothing. She figured, one way or another, she would be seeing Linney again and wondered, as she worked, if it would be later today.

The manager had reversed the trailer into position, a small concession to the fact that although she was the pub yardie she was still learning the ropes. With the bins all emptied, returned either to the rear of the kitchen or the long verandah outside the motel rooms, she got in the ute and was given directions to the tip.

As her boss disappeared towards the office, she bunny hopped out of the bay, hoping no one had heard the trailer's high metal sides clanging when she accidentally slipped the clutch.

The early drinkers ignored her reversing antics the

first two mornings, warned off by Jack, but it was open season after that. They made little attempt to disguise their fun, jostling near the rear door of the bar as they bet on how many attempts she would need to aim the trailer into the bay. She never got to find out if she'd set a new record because within the week a couple of the men could not bear it beyond three attempts, after which they would lift the trailer into place.

This was her first day as roustabout, though, and she left the pub cushioned by a false sense of invisibility, unaware that the men in the bar had so little entertainment they'd bet on how far a beer coaster could be flipped.

At the rubbish tip a council truck was parked in the only patch of shade. Two workers in blue singlets sweated onto sticky vinyl seats and contemplated the ice-cold beers they would crack when they got home. The ute was the first thing that had moved for a good half an hour and their heads turned as she drove towards the tip face.

It was a big space and there were no other vehicles around so she swung in a wide circle then shoved the gearstick into reverse. The trailer jack-knifed to the left. She straightened up and tried again. Same outcome. She could see the men laughing and pointing, waiting for the next try. Let them wait.

She drove forward and circled back around till the ute and trailer were side-on to the area signposted for off-loading. She dropped the tailgate and unclipped the shovel from the mudguard then climbed up and began shoving out the rubbish. It landed at least three meters from the dump edge but tidying it up would give them something to do with the backhoe shimmering nearby in the sun.

Despite the small stab of rebellion she drove off with a flaming face.

Back at the pub, the manager called her over and introduced her to Sheryl, on the day shift behind the bar. The barmaid was maybe in her mid-thirties and didn't seem to fit the picture. Instead of large, hooped earrings or a tight-fitting shirt with exposed cleavage she wore a simple sleeveless shift dress, a plain gold locket at her throat, and her dark brown hair pulled back in a low ponytail, the colour matching a pair of shining eyes. The journo in Bec would have called her classically elegant.

The manager had disappeared back to his office. It had been a while since Bec had practised small talk so she wasn't sure where to start.

'Um, what's it like here?'

Sheryl had a generous smile and a voice much bigger than her slim frame. 'You mean you haven't heard? There's a saying if you're alright with a bit of strong language.'

Bec nodded.

'If the Joseph Bonaparte Gulf is the arse end of Australia, then Wyndham's sixty kilometres up it!' They both laughed.

'So, if it's not a rude question, how'd you come to be here?'

Sheryl's grin was replaced with a frown. 'Don't mind telling you, but it's not the sort of question to be asking in this town. Most people like to keep their past private.' She looked pointedly at Bec's left hand, where the pale circle on her ring finger stood out against tanned skin.

She wiped the bar down and shook out a narrow yellow towel, straightening it along the counter to reveal the brewery logo with the black swan. Swan Lager, swan lapel pins and stamps, the outline even on police badges. The whole of Western Australia was crazy about a bird that was a bottom-feeder and would attack if you got too close.

'There's no big story. Came here with my partner for the meat season a year ago. When it was done he went back to Perth but I didn't see any reason to.'

'Sorry to hear it, Sheryl.' Bec didn't know what else to say.

'Don't be. I'm not. Wyndham's a hole but it's honest about what it is. More than I can say about him.'

Sheryl lowered her voice. 'You better get moving or Jack'll be on your case.'

'Jack? I thought he was Kerry.'

'We call him Jack—not to his face of course—because he doesn't give jack shit about anyone, only the balance sheet.'

By two o'clock, the heat was hammering Bec's head and shoulders. She had not thought to wear a hat and sunburn was stinging her nose as she skimmed the surface of the pool then attached a hose to the outlet so she could vacuum the base.

Maybe it sounded good on the brochure but the structure wilting in the sun was the ugly cousin of swimming pools. It was an afterthought, stranded on exposed stony ground up some stairs at the back of the dining room. It might have been welcome in a shady suburban yard but was next to useless here. The metal surround circled above ground like a child's paddling pool on steroids, pumped up to eight or so metres across, conveniently allowing the sun access to both the walls and the water surface.

A few plastic chairs tumbled in an untidy heap on the gravel though no one had bothered to provide an umbrella, table or anything that might make the space useful. She tested the water with her hand. It clung like glue. A cold shower would be more refreshing.

Jack—the name suited him better than Kerry, she decided—turned up as she was packing away the hose and he showed her how to mix the chemicals and where to add them.

'It get used much?'

'Yeah, when the oil rig workers come in, they sometimes like to party up here. When it's quiet, the staff do too.' The demo finished, he walked off.

The beer garden was an equal exaggeration of promise. A slab of concrete off the entrance to the main bar and lounge bar, it sat about a metre above the car park and road. The obligatory palm tree was doing it tough, a few straggly fronds throwing little shade. Opposite, two planter boxes marked the edge of the path to the motel units. No amount of watering would save at least half the tired plants.

Flimsy glass top tables and nylon wicker chairs were strewn about in no particular order. A string of coloured outdoor lights looped along the bar verandah, bulbs missing in random places, about as festive as Christmas decorations in July.

The lounge bar and its dining area were the only public areas with air-conditioning, though each of the motel units had a wheezing air con box set in the wall.

The bar made do with a pair of ceiling fans. When she was not outside most of the work was in the storeroom behind the bar, where a lack of ventilation or insulation meant radiant heat was unstoppable as it fired through the roofing iron. It was a relief to get a hit of cool air every time she opened one of the doors at the back of the fridges, pushing the cold beer forward to pack warm cans and bottles in behind.

At the motel units the two housemaids flitted from room to room with the hem of their uniforms tucked into the elastic of their knickers. 'Gets a bit of air through so your thighs don't stick together,' Hazel, the older one, told her. Bec shadowed them for thirty minutes or so, on Jack's instructions, in case there was an occasion when she had to fill in for one of them.

'We haul out all their empties and other muck and make it tidy for the next round, just so we can do it all over again. A real frickin' privilege. Bet those oil rig workers don't get away with making this mess at home'. Hazel flung her arm up by way of an exclamation mark.

The wind had picked up and whirled dirt from the side of the road up high into the air. It was impossible to see how any surface could be kept clean.

By four o'clock, the armpits of her T-shirt were so wet the overflow was dripping down her sides and she was limp with exhaustion.

The meatworks paid well, by all accounts, with up to two thousand extras in town during the cattle season. Plenty of the blokes were single and that afternoon she saw them in action as she worked in the stifling beer store, stacking the second round of stubbies from the rear of the fridges. Through the glass doors facing the bar, a group of them were slamming whiskey shots like Scotland might go out of business.

Soon after, Jack came across her packing cans of pre-mixed spirits onto shelves in the lounge bar fridge. 'That'll do for today. Like I said, starting at six will be easier.'

He walked away, then at the door turned back. 'By the way, you get Mondays off.'

She was desperate to get back to the caravan park, where at least there was a row of trees, but the van steering wheel was too hot to grip. Six days a week. What fresh hell was this? She fumbled in the glovebox and found a pack of tissues, pulling out a couple of handfuls to pad her hands while she drove the long straight from the Old Port through the mudflats to the Three Mile, which the locals, she'd discovered, called the New Town.

What was it about the far north and the overblown descriptors? The motel pool, the beer garden and now the town without a single feature that warranted the use of 'new', unless they meant the freshly installed security shutters over the windows of the supermarket and bottle shop.

She sweated it out for another night in the tent at the caravan park, the air swollen in her lungs. She must have dozed off around three in the morning because she dreamed it had turned to concrete and was filling up her windpipe. Panicked, she sat up and pulled on her shorts and shirt.

Outside, brilliant white stars were pinned to a purple sky, but she ignored all of it and looked down at her bare feet, willing herself to feel the ground beneath them. Toes and heels rested on the dense crust of the Earth, dependable and constant, rising into mountains and falling to the sea. Yet it was only silica, aluminium, iron and calcium, mostly bound by oxygen, such an insubstantial element. All of it combined in the jigsaw puzzle of tectonic plates, moving and shifting and no one really knowing why, and at the centre of the planet, a furnace of liquid metal, endlessly churning around a dense ball of iron. The thought of the planet seething deep below made her feel sick.

It was far better to focus above, where other worlds beckoned among pinpoints of brilliance. She stared upwards in wonder. The splendour of it caught her off-guard, opening a raw place in her chest. She thumped her fist hard on the bone below her throat. The sound was hollow and the pressure stopped the lump that was rising. She had fled across an entire continent yet had not outrun herself and maybe that was the point, to go as far as you could and then do a three hundred and fifty degree turn and face who you were. If that was the case, she wasn't ready for it.

It seemed to Bec that under starlight the world was softer, freer without the acid wash of sun, harsh in the judgement of everything it touched. In the dark, with the town sleeping, it was possible to lean a little into the places that hurt and the harm you had done, to admit your failures but see that you'd been failed too.

It had started with being assigned to Andy.

There had been nothing of the crusader about him. He was far too methodical and steady for that. By the time she had begun working with him he was deep into the investigation, painstaking in working his contacts, conducting his research, finding his way out of the dead-ends. He had started with a tip-off from a trusted source about a huge tax evasion scheme and for weeks had been navigating the labyrinth connecting Perth's establishment figures.

It was not the individuals he pursued but an understanding of the scheme, how it worked, who was pulling the strings. He sought to expose the corruption of systemic greed and hoped to find the puppet master.

Neither she nor Andy had considered who might ultimately pay the price. Now it was the one thought that consumed her.

———— • ————

Three hundred kilometres to the south, the headlights of a truck cut the night in two. On either side of its speeding outline all was still, the land drawing in energy to last through another searing day. In the cabin, the driver talked to himself and occasionally hummed a few lines of a tune.

'Come on, Trev. Just another half an hour and you can pull over,' he muttered, though his vision was starting to blur. He drove on, riding smoothly on his seat while the engine shuddered, devouring the white line. There had been a delay at the warehouse in Perth the day before. One of the forklifts had been out of action and it was mid-afternoon before the truck was loaded. It had given him time to make a call to the boys, catching them just as they got home from school. They were glad to hear his voice but had little to say. Far more interested in the snacks Jan no doubt had put out on the kitchen bench.

'Bottomless pits.' Over the sound of her laughter he heard Lachie ordering Max around with all the confidence of a ten year old accustomed to bossing the brother three years behind.

'Might need an extra night if I'm late off-loading the last delivery.'

They had been married long enough for conversation to err on the economical side. 'Travel safe. We'll see you soon, love.' She hung up.

The pills were wearing off and he calculated he had another three hours of highway between him and Kununurra, where he would empty the smaller load in the trailer before going on to finish the beer run an hour or so later in Wyndham.

The long haul trips took some getting used to but the money was better than doing day deliveries out of the city. Besides, the freedom had appeal. Being on the road kept him away from gutters that needed cleaning, grass to be mowed, a wife who sent him to the supermarket when he would rather be on his back in the hammock with a cold ale. Twenty-nine and already hiding out in the shed like his old man.

He would call time at Wyndham tonight and kick back at the pub to sink a few drinks, then point the rig back to Perth first thing in the morning. The plan pleased him and meant he could afford to snatch a few hours' rest. He slowed the truck, shifting down the gears, and came to a halt off the side of the highway. He crawled into the sleeper at the rear of the cab, leaving the windows down, and passed out on the mattress.

———— • ————

Bec had just finished hosing down the beer garden when Jack came over to tell her she would be needed in the storeroom at one o'clock, when the beer truck was expected.

'It'll be a big load, what with Easter next week.'

She nodded, handing over a leather wallet flushed out earlier from under one of the outdoor tables. She had already checked its contents and seen the two hundred dollars in cash—more than she cleared in a week.

'Someone'll be glad you're honest.' He smirked. Either he thought she was a principled woman or a damn fool, but it wasn't worth hurting her head trying to decide.

She entered the male toilet off the bar, fumbling with a broom, mop, bucket and a large bottle of disinfectant, then paused to brace herself for the urinal stink.

'You've got to be kidding me.' Her voice bounced off stainless steel and the concrete floor.

Splattered across the urinal base was a mass of partially digested stomach contents. Worse, it was still identifiable as the remains of a steak sandwich cooked by the chef last night. Just as well she hadn't eaten breakfast. She rushed out to get an old newspaper, then scooped up the mess and dumped it in an outside bin before hastily mopping with a disinfectant mix so strong the fumes stung her sinuses.

In the lounge bar, the women's toilet did not need much cleaning. A bit of long hair to be fished from the handbasins, the bin emptied and a quick sweep. Jack was down on the hygiene of the Aboriginal women who used the bar but they were cleaner than the white single blokes by far.

The main bar was in full swing by early afternoon when she heard the truck come in. She had expected there would be a forklift and she'd need to do a bit of stacking but she was wrong. When she went to the rear of the beer store Jack introduced her to Trev and the three of them formed a line of sorts, her in the middle.

The truckie had already released the loading straps and begun lifting and dragging cartons and boxes, lining them up on the side of the truck facing a roller door Jack had opened.

First came the smaller boxes packed with bottles of spirits, each box handed to Bec, who took four or five steps and gave one after the other to Jack. He had given himself the task of stacking them in the storeroom, a move that kept him in full shade and failed to improve her opinion of him. Next came bigger, heavier cartons of beer cans and finally, stubbies. By the time she had handed over ten or more boxes, her arms were turning to jelly.

With each pass from the driver her head and shoulders copped a hit of sun, with only brief respite in shade as she passed her load to Jack. The angle of the truck meant every time she took a carton it was necessary to twist in handing it over to Jack. The torsion was punishing for her lower back. She needed distraction.

'You from Perth?'

Trev reached for the next slab of stubbies. 'Yeah, lived there all my life. I'm a sandgroper through and through.'

He saw the vacant look on her face, from a brain where heat had knocked a relay out of service. 'You're not from around here, are you?'

'No, grew up in Victoria's wheatbelt, on a farm near Horsham. Sandgroper?'

'Glad my boys haven't heard you ask.' He slapped a

palm on one thigh and laughed. 'Not a footie follower, either?'

What an idiot. Sandgropers were insects that burrowed in sand, and for obscure reasons, also the nickname for folks who lived in the west, as well as their Aussie rules team. Crow-eaters in South Australia, banana-benders from Queensland, no end to Australian inventiveness for bonding language.

To cover the embarrassment she went straight to her fail-safe strategy for shifting attention away. Twenty questions, she called it. She didn't even have to think, it kicked in so fast these days.

He straightened a little as she asked him about his family. There was pride in his face.

'Never thought I'd be one to settle down, but I wouldn't be without 'em now.'

Jack showed no interest in talking, so she pressed on. After a while the effort of talking seemed too great. She threw out one last question to wrap it up.

'Must be exhausting, driving that distance?'

'Yeah but a cold beer and a hot feed will fix that.'

She took a good look at his tightly creased face as he handed down the next carton. This was a man wound tight. He would burst like a tube of toothpaste if he couldn't cut loose soon.

By the time the truck was empty she had built a profile in her mind on the man with thinning hair, pegging him as a person with a diminishing sense of possibilities. Jack told her to finish for the day, and as she walked away she chided herself. It wasn't fair to be judging Trev when he was clearly a man trying to do right by his family.

She was in the car park when she heard her name and

looked up to see Sheryl leaning over the beer garden rail and waving.

'Do you want to come back for a drink tonight? Had a word with Jo before she went home. She says there might be a room available in the house she and her brother rent. They'll be here around seven if you're interested.' She waved again and disappeared towards the bar without waiting for a response.

At the town swimming pool, near the caravan park, it was unexpectedly quiet for a Saturday. She knew why as soon as she launched herself off the ladder. The water had seemed inviting, glinting against blue tiles under the sunshade sprawling along its length. Instead, it was thick with heat. She struggled to part it as she swam a lap and at the end gave up any chance of a refreshing dip and hauled herself out, flopping onto wilting grass in the shade.

She had to face facts. If she planned to stay for a while, the van and tent would be impossible. Maybe she should do as Sheryl suggested and at least check out Jo and her brother. She could drop by the pub later but not commit to anything. Solitude was her friend and the loss of it, even temporarily, seemed a steep sacrifice for easy access to a shower and a cool place to sleep.

Back at the van she went through her clothes, mostly shorts and the grubby T-shirts she had been wearing to work, all she had needed for the long drive from Perth. Most of her clothes had been left behind, except for the dark green pantsuit worn that last day at work.

She watched, somehow separate from the hands that stuffed clothes back into the bag. The fingers and the back of each hand looked like hers, she could see the childhood scar running vertically on the right one, near the main tendon. They moved, but not at her volition it seemed, as though the locus of control did not to lie with her.

She needed something to do. She would go to the old general store near the pub and see if she could get something fresh to wear tonight. Driving across the dry, cracked mudflats she glanced up at the Bastion, shimmering in the hot sun, its outline shifting as though it was sliding down towards the road. This was strange country, where mountains melted, soil could take flight and rivers seemed to flow back to their source.

She parked out the front of the shop and as she stepped onto the verandah, her attention was drawn to a still figure sitting upright on a wooden chair in the shade. One slanting strip of light from a missing piece of corrugated iron above shone across her shoulder. Bec gave a soft hello but the elderly Chinese woman neither looked in Bec's direction nor acknowledged the greeting. Shadows were deeper either side of the light, blurring the woman's silhouette, dissolving the opposite shoulder, the arms and legs, and were darker still behind the chair.

An uneasy feeling rose in Bec, that she was intruding on a private place. It was probably a trick of the light but the space around the woman seemed to pulse as though she was her own sun, radiating heat and energy. It had an oddly soothing effect and Bec paused without intending to.

The woman's frame was slight, bowed a little. The insignificance of her size didn't match the strength she exuded, which puzzled Bec, keeping her stalled near the open door, caught in the force field of her own curiosity.

It was rude to stand there any longer. The interior of the shop looked cooler than the street, its softer light inviting, and she took a step towards the entry.

Listen to your ancestors. Not a suggestion. More like a command.

She swung around. The only presence was the old woman, motionless, staring across the street with no sign she had uttered a single word.

Bec opened her mouth to say something but in the moment of confusion her feet took over and she entered the store. A middle-aged man with a face similar to the woman outside was packing shelves behind the counter.

The room relied on natural light illuminating displays of mismatched goods forming a giant cabinet of curiosities. Nooks displayed painkillers, cooking utensils, spark plugs and spanners with equal fanfare. She was drawn to a couple of harmonicas still in their boxes, Hohner Marine Band, the same soulful instruments Bob Dylan and Neil Young played. Food, candles and household goods featured in corners and on more shelves, while several racks of clothes were lined up to one side.

So much to explore, she could forget the moment on the verandah.

'An amazing shop. You've been here for a while?'

The man seemed pleased with the question.

'It was my father's from the early 1900s, then my mother Lily ran it till it got too much for her.'

The untreated wooden floor had a silver sheen from more than a century of drover's boots and the feet of the Afghan camel drivers now buried in their own cemetery. She had seen it coming into town, tombstones facing west towards Mecca.

His mother had been a tailor originally, he offered, working out the back of the shop. 'She's a bit hard of hearing these days but happy enough.' He smiled and tipped his head with pride in the direction of the verandah.

'Burns a candle all night to honour my dad, buried back in the fifties, and all the ones who've gone before.'

Bec stayed near the counter, encouraging the son's chat. The journalist in her was fascinated by the woman, at least that's what she preferred to think.

'Seen the place through boom and bust. Only time we lived elsewhere was when we were evacuated during the war. The Japanese bombed the meatworks, you know, and the aerodrome. Broome and Derby too.'

He shook his head a little, as if to say that was enough talking, and turned back to the job of stacking shampoo bottles. She was glad because as he had spoken, it was as though she had been there. She could hear the whine of a formation of Zeros overhead, warplanes far from cities expected to be the target. Feel the panic as people realised their remoteness had not been a protection, that the bombs had found their way here.

She pushed the images away and moved off to browse. The smell of spices and dust mixed with the stale odour of old paper and motor oil. The overall effect was dizzying and she turned around, steadying herself by narrowing her gaze to a row of lightweight sundresses. They were the kind in fashion five or more years earlier, with spaghetti straps and bright floral patterns that made it hard to blend into the background, unlike the work clothes she had once chosen so carefully. She bought one anyway, a yellow dress with tiny white flowers. At least it reached to her knees and would be cooler than the stretchy T-shirts clinging to her back as she worked.

On the way out Bec purposely avoided glancing along the verandah, ignoring the woman seated there as she turned the van and drove off.

She thought about the words as she drove, the way they seemed real. What did it mean, listen to your ancestors? What did anyone need with ancestors? Her mind was playing tricks. It would do her good to go out tonight.

3

I T WAS ALMOST DARK WHEN she arrived at the beer garden to meet Jo Kemp and her brother, Dave. The pub looked different at night, the string of lights throwing a soft glow, women's voices joining with the men. She was tempted to say it had atmosphere but remembered the beer swill sucking at the bottom of her sandals in the bar that morning. The smell had gone down the back of her throat and onto her tongue. It had been so bad she'd helped herself to a packet of salt and vinegar chips and scoffed them in the storeroom to clear the taste.

The brother and sister were from Wainui Beach on New Zealand's North Island. 'Left one of the country's best surf breaks for this.' Dave's dark, short hair and ironed shirt were not suggesting he was a surfer. 'Clearly us Kiwis are stark raving mad.'

Bec laughed with them but said nothing about her own origins. 'I'm starving. Shall we order and get a drink?'

The brother and sister were easy in their conversation, undemanding, and over a beer and burger she decided she liked them. For the first time in weeks her muscles were willing to let go a little and she stretched back in the chair.

Dave had seen her van the first morning. He was a chopper pilot ferrying workers back from an oil rig out in the gulf to Wyndham, where they overnighted before a road transfer to Kununurra airport and a flight south for days off.

'Came for an adventure and got a bus route instead.'

She managed a smile but all she could think of was the chopper flying overhead and Dave looking down at her like an insect pinned to a display board.

'And how about you, Jo?'

'Bailed out of uni and was working in a shop in Auckland but the boredom got to me. Thought I'd join Dave for a few months and get my head straight about what I wanted to do. Nearly a year later, still here!'

'More like a broken heart,' Dave grinned. 'Boyfriend ditched her. But I'm glad she came.'

A breeze had kicked in and was stirring the half-dead palm fronds. Bec saw Linney nearby, eating with a tall, thick-bellied man she presumed was her husband. A group of men spilled out of the bar and gathered around a couple of tables, stubbies in hand, to wait for their food. Linney's husband went over to say hello and Bec noticed Trev join the throng.

Jo's voice called her back to the conversation in front of her. The New Zealander was keen to share the house.

'Could do with someone who knows the right end of a dishcloth.' She mock-slapped her brother on the arm.

The house was close by, as it happened, opposite the Chinese shop and only a few doors along from the pub.

They lingered over another round of drinks while they settled on the terms. Bec agreed to move in on Monday.

Though Jo was the youngest, the siblings had clearly spent many years perfecting their style of affectionate one-upmanship. It was easy to sit back without needing to say much. About halfway through her second beer, Bec realised she was enjoying herself and in no hurry to return to the tent.

She was walking through the foyer after a trip to the toilet when Sheryl caught her eye and gestured her into the bar.

'So, what did you decide?' The question was shouted over raucous laughter from a bunch of twenty-some-things clustered under one of the ceiling fans, swilling schooners of ale. The men wore shorts that skimmed the top of their thighs, exposing hairy legs Bec would have been just as happy not to see.

'Yeah, it'll work really well. Thanks for setting it up.'

'No problem. I'd like to see you stick around for a while.' Sheryl barely made it to the end of the sentence when the men banged their beer glasses on the counter and called for one of their mates to buy a round of rum.

'Didn't realise it would be this lively.' Bec raised her voice over several decibels of background noise.

'This isn't the half of it. Better get the kids their lollipops.' With that, Sheryl was gone.

Back at the table, the nearby group of men had also settled into serious drinking and razzing each other to save the effort of conversation. They were spending more on shots of tequila and bourbon in one night than Bec would earn in a week.

One man was bellicose, could be heard above the

others. 'I'll give you a hundred bucks if you jump off the end of the jetty'. The force of the dare pushed the truckie back a little from his table. Some of the others began goading, grinning. 'Yeah, easy money mate. Take it'. Trev waved an arm in the air, swatting them away.

'Bloody idiots.' Dave lowered his voice. 'Dunno who is worse, the meatworkers or the guys off the rig.'

Soon after, the men went inside the bar to order food, taking their racket with them.

Encouraged by the relaxed manner of her companions and the effect of the alcohol, Bec thought it was time to volunteer a scrap of information about herself and fessed up that she had a background in journalism.

'Exciting.' Jo was impressed. 'So, what are you doing here?'

She had anticipated the question. Despite Sheryl's warning, it seemed to be the way out-of-towners sized up each other, dogs sniffing at tails. 'Thought it'd be good to see another side to life.'

Before they could ask anything further, she directed the conversation into neutral territory, gesturing towards the bar. 'And what do you for fun, other than this superb celebration of humanity?' She hadn't intended the sarcastic tone but it was too late.

'Let's show you.' Dave downed the last of his beer and stood up. Jo laughed in a conspiratorial way and the two women followed him out to the footpath.

'Back in a minute,' he said.

'This is all very mysterious.' At Bec's comment Jo rolled her eyes and smiled, venturing no response.

The rowdy group emerged from the bar, some of them ramping up the volume to maximum. Trev could be heard in the thick of it, showing he could mix it with the single blokes. It was a relief when Dave returned with a couple of torches.

The three of them walked away from the harsh flare of the fluorescent lights in the pub car park, towards the meatworks, under a web of glittering stars. At a Buddhist retreat in the experimental period of adolescence, Bec had listened with closed eyes as the meditation master spoke of Indra's net, an intricate gossamer flung across the vast expanse of outer space, and at every intersection of thread a jewel hanging in its glory, one for every person in existence. Sitting cross-legged in the gompa, she had received it only as a laboured metaphor on interdependence and connection. But now, head thrown back, she saw it was real, stretching effortlessly from one horizon to the next in the inky foreverness of night sky.

The road curved away and red dirt thrown up by trucks in gritty clouds during the day lay undisturbed, the trio's footsteps leaving barely a trace. The other two seemed to know the way without needing to use the torches, Bec following close behind. As they reached the jetty, Dave flicked on a light and pushed it into her hand. The air was soft as they walked out above the water, invisible beyond the torch beam, though she could hear a gentle slap-slap against the pylons a long way below.

'Giant tides push through here,' Dave called back over his shoulder. 'They can get to six metres, sometimes more.'

At the end of the jetty, Jo suggested she lower the torch. 'Stand here.' She guided Bec to the handrail. The fans in the cooling system at the meatworks spun endlessly in their cages.

Dave turned on the second torch.

'Over there.' She trained her beam down in the same direction as his. When she saw what was below the jetty, she instinctively recoiled.

Three pairs of bright red eyes stared up at her. In the shadow cast by torchlight, the primitive form of their bodies was in sharp relief, bulky, with long snouts and tell-tale ridges along their backs. Large saltwater crocs. And she was in their territory.

'Bloody hell.'

The crocodiles watched, so still not even a ripple broke the water.

'That's only a few. There's maybe fifteen of them and a couple are as long as a half-ton truck.' Dave whispered, as though suddenly unsure that the steel and concrete structure beneath their feet would hold.

'All the blood from the slaughter room runs out of a drain near here. This is a supermarket for the big salties and sometimes even a shark.'

She flicked off the torch. Dave and Jo were still focused on the crocs and in their shadowy faces was awe, respect, while she was frozen, an image stuck behind her eyeballs of one of the primitive beasts leaping at her from the water, jaws wide open. The terror of it made her shake even though she knew the creatures hadn't moved. She gripped the rail.

It was midnight by the time she said her goodbyes and returned to the caravan park. She'd once loved to be awake at the point where the hands reached the top of the clock, at the magical interlude between one tick marking the end of the old day and the next heralding a new one.

Now it signalled a head-sore wait for daylight and any excuse to rise off the mattress and be busy.

Tonight, though, the face of the old woman at the store kept intruding. *Listen to your ancestors.* She strained to remember if she had heard it in a woman's or a man's tone. Had she even heard it at all? She was no closer to understanding, but every time she thought of the words they were vibrations from a tuning fork resonating under her skin.

Best to forget it. She was not the superstitious kind. It meant nothing, other than providing a new reason for insomnia.

Daybreak showed up eventually and she was soon in her work clothes, heading back to the pub a bit early for her shift because it was somewhere to go when all around were campers sleeping late on a Sunday. Near the motel, it was odd to see cars already out the front, at least four hours before opening time. As she got closer, it was evident they all had blue lights. Her first thought was that they were looking for the van, which set off a spasm in her empty stomach.

She stopped where she was on the side of the street. She could go back to the house, stay out of sight. But what was the point when so many at the pub knew where she lived. She walked on.

The dining room was open and some of the men from the previous night were lined up along the wall outside, chairs spaced apart. One of them leaned forward, his head heavy in his hands. Through the door she saw Jack putting out water jugs and glasses while speaking to a policeman in a brown cap and khaki uniform. Jack looked over and gestured her to one side but not before she had seen two other officers in separate corners, each interviewing a man.

'What a bloody night,' Jack hissed as he went towards the bar, indicating she should follow. 'Been up since four, when the local cop rang, but we've had to wait for the two sergeants to come from Kununurra.'

Bec looked around the bar. 'Was it a break-in? Have they smashed things up?'

Jack's face twisted but before he could get out the words, she knew.

'It's the truckie, isn't it?'

'Yeah, stupid bastard. Those blokes waved a few lousy dollars in front of his nose and it was enough for him to jump off the end of the jetty. The constable's out there with a bunch of locals trying to find the body. Fat chance of that.'

Jack went back to his rant about the broken night's sleep and didn't notice she had reached for a bar stool and fallen onto it. Every muscle tensed with the urge to get in the van and go but her body was also flooded with the need to get on with her work and act normal.

She slid off the stool and went towards the cupboard where the cleaning supplies were kept, pausing to steady herself on the bar counter. Jack didn't notice.

'Don't worry about the dining room. I'll keep it closed today.'

In the men's toilet, she took the lid off a bottle of bleach and sniffed deeply. It was a weird thing to do but she hoped it might cauterise the part of her brain that had begun a slow spiral, down, down, down, where there might never be a bottom. She washed the floor, driving the mop head so hard from one side to another that a splintering pain shot through her wrists. Down, still going down. She moved on to the women's toilet and when that was done, the main bar, sweeping, mopping, wiping, dusting. Turning, turning. Sweat dripped from her forehead but she let it run down her face.

In the storeroom she ripped open cartons of potato chips and peanuts and scooped up armfuls of the packets, taking them into the bar to fill baskets under the shelves of gin, rum, vodka and tequila. Bending down made her head spin. The heat in the building was mounting as the sun rose higher but instead of adjusting to a slower pace she worked on furiously, replenishing the near empty bar fridges then hurrying outside to start the rubbish collection.

Sheryl was preparing to open the bar, rattling coins into the cash register a bit before ten, when she saw Bec striding up the walkway in front of the motel units, clutching a rubbish bin. She heard glass breaking in the trailer then saw Bec rushing along the walkway to replace the empty bin and collect another full one. She was damn near running.

Life in the dry season was brittle. It could snap at any moment. She went out to the trailer and tapped Bec on the shoulder.

'What's wrong, hun?'

'Nothing. Just behind a bit with everything going on.'

Sheryl wasn't buying it. 'You're overheating. Go into the storeroom, I'll bring you a cold lemonade.' Bec protested.

'Hey, that's an order. You should know better than to cross a barmaid.' She laughed and went inside, returning almost immediately with a frosted drink.

They sat opposite each other on a couple of upturned milk crates, the storeroom door pushed open before the sun made it to that side of the building. The sounds of the pub seemed to pause in the silence that surrounded the women.

'You saw the truckie last night at the pub and those goons egging him on, didn't you?' Sheryl stated the facts simply, keen not to probe.

She reached over and touched Bec lightly on the arm then withdrew her hand. The other woman nodded, ice trembling in the lemonade as she placed the glass at her feet.

'He had two boys, a wife. What were those guys thinking?'

Sheryl heard a deep well of desperation and said nothing, keeping her eyes fixed on the other woman's face while she waited for the right time to respond.

'I guess they didn't consider how it would end.' She spoke softly.

When the tears came, Bec tried to hold them back, looking away to study cracks in the concrete floor.

'You're holding on to quite a load there. I don't know what this is all about, honey, but I can see you're suffering.'

The kindness in Sheryl's voice was too much. Bec threw both hands over her face and wept.

4

I T WAS DIFFICULT FOR BEC to know how much
to tell Sheryl, but as her spluttering subsided a string
of words loosened from their locked box and started
rolling out of her mouth.

'Someone died, back in Perth, and I was responsible
without meaning to be.'

There, it was out.

'It was supposed to be my lucky break. I was asked
to work with a senior journo on a big story. There was a
lot at stake.'

Sheryl nodded. 'How did it happen?'

Bec cast her mind back to the beginning, when Andy
first cracked the biggest scandal the state had known for
decades, a global tax evasion scheme run from an office a
few blocks down from the newspaper.

'I was excited to work with him. Andy was all that I
wanted to be. He had grit, intellect, persistence.'

She had followed in his slipstream, the sorcerer's apprentice eager to learn all he had to share, not because
the man had a nose for a story, though he had that gift
too, but because he understood human nature. He sensed
which direction greed might run, when a lie was hiding

in plain sight, and was not fooled by titles or status and their capacity to mask a hole in the soul.

If he wanted to make money for himself, journalism was the last place to be. No, money wasn't personal for Andy but a force that buckled power and influence, bending it ugly.

She still remembered what he'd told her.

'It's the big bucks every time, Bec. We've all got a shadow somewhere in our hearts but it's the dollars that turn it into darkness.'

By the time she was assigned to assist, Andy had already followed the money to Calder Saul, a man dressed more like a Cold War spy than flamboyant fraudster.

Bec looked over at Sheryl. 'It was a massive tax fraud scheme, you see, and the guy who set it up was a clever con man. He fooled the establishment.'

She could still see the photo pinned to the office wall. In the black and white image, Saul was seated on a park bench, leaning back nonchalantly, legs crossed, looking straight at the camera with a wry smile, one corner of his mouth curled up and the other frozen, thick silver hair swept to one side. He wore large spectacles with thick black frames, unfashionably at odds with his Italian wool overcoat. His hands were pushed deep into the pockets.

By the time she'd started working with Andy, Saul was already gone, skipping the country before the federal police had a chance to charge him.

"I had to door-knock one afternoon, talk to the guy's Dalkeith neighbours, try to build a picture of who he was, how he came across to others.'

She had been renting in West Leederville, a weatherboard cottage with a rusting bullnose verandah, dead grass for a backyard and a soundtrack from the Mitchell Freeway. The green enamel cooker threatened to burn off eyebrows whenever a match lit the gas, while the furniture came from charity shops. His soaring house sat in a prestige suburb of avenues and parades, nothing as common as a street, with sweeping views over the Swan River and the distinction of the highest per capita concentrations of doctors, mining magnates and self-made entrepreneurs in the entire country.

She couldn't shake the grubbiness of the task, nearly as bad as a previous job where she'd been an ambulance-chaser on police rounds. This side of the work made her question what senior staff really meant when they talked about the public interest.

She'd tried to get out of it, making a desperate plea to Andy to avoid the job.

'Wouldn't I be more use if I helped follow up where the federal police are at?'

Andy had taken off his glasses and rubbed his temples. 'He was a person, Bec. If we can't relate to him as a man, then this all feels like a fantasy.' He had swung his arm at the map on the wall. There were connecting lines tracking the money trail and handwritten notes pinned on several countries, one of which might already be harbouring the fraudster.

She had challenged Andy. 'Why should that matter, though?'

'Because this is the truth of what one man can do. We need to see it, touch it. He was enabled. All this corruption didn't happen in isolation, it happened because people were willing to look away.'

The conversation with her colleague was still vivid, had not faded in the weeks that had passed.

'I was totally drawn into working on this story, Sheryl. I was proving myself.'

She had not been sure why door-knocking made her uncomfortable. She was not averse to delving into private lives when it might generate compassion or political action. There'd been a nun who shared the deep humanity it took to companion the dying. Siblings opening up about family strain when a brother or sister had a serious disability. The lawyer who came home from work to find his wife and two children murdered, yet went on to start a support service for the homeless. Aboriginal women in prison greens, aching to feel their feet on the land of their kin, the country where they belonged.

She parked in Saul's leafy street, hoping to see a passerby, maybe a paid dog-walker, but it was empty. She loomed at each door, feeling for all the world like a crow flipping a cane toad onto its back, feeding on the belly to avoid poisonous glands.

Yet Saul had been no media victim, far from it.

'This guy was like a magician with a black top hat but instead of a white rabbit, he dropped big sums of money in there so they'd disappear. They'd show up in far-flung places, tax-free.'

Bec was calmer now. The telling had taken over.

'Saul's scheme meant big rewards in terms of tax cuts. It was irresistible to many of the city's highly paid medical specialists.'

Some of them would doubtless end up bankrupt once the Australian Federal Police had finished their work and handed them over to the tax office. It was not as if Saul deserved respect, but it had still felt tawdry to be poking around the entrails of his life.

'It was strange, but he was actually so ordinary.' Though Bec spoke to Sheryl, she was staring off into space.

If she had expected to find intriguing quirks during the hour in his suburb, she was sorely disappointed.

He had washed the car on Sundays, taken his children to sports matches, lived a quiet life. Nothing unremarkable, the neighbours said. Nothing to reconcile with the man who donned a suit and went to his St Georges Terrace office, wedged between leading legal firms, immigration advisers and big insurance companies, to feed a creature of deception with pincers in eight countries.

It was jarring when, her head full of an ordinary man, she walked back to her desk mid-afternoon to the sound of Andy exploding in exasperation.

'God almighty.' He had gotten wind of another Swiss finance company, plus a business address had emerged in Hong Kong with incorporation in Liberia. The map was already too small to pin up six years' worth of ways to fake the loss of large sums through a tax dodge dressed up as commodity trading.

The story had been running for a week or so and the rival newspaper was now on the case, too. She picked up their edition and began parroting that morning's editorial in a theatrical voice: 'The story reads more like a plot for a novel by Ian Fleming or Wilbur Smith …,' she paused for mock effect. '… But there is no fiction in just how disastrous this has been for Western Australia.'

She had tossed the paper down and laughed, but

Andy had been unimpressed. 'Let's stick to the facts and leave the hyperbole to others.'

It had been tricky to keep the facts straight, so she'd offered to create a spreadsheet as a reference for the editorial team. Diamonds had been bought and sold, along with silver and works of art. Money had gone through an antiques dealer in Holland, a company in London, others in Singapore and Israel. It had taken a whole morning to document the confirmed information provided officially and through trusted sources.

'Even now, Sheryl, it's hard to believe the scale of the operation. Ex-elite soldiers couriered huge sums out of the country, maybe a hundred trips altogether. As much as half a million dollars in one flight alone.' The barmaid's eyebrows shot up.

It had been such an efficient system that other money smugglers sometimes hired Saul's couriers.

And then there was Saul, the untouchable. She imagined him in Europe but Andy had inside knowledge he intended to hide in South Africa.

When he disappeared, twelve million dollars vanished with him. Doctors and other professionals participating in the scheme, some ignorant of how it worked or the corruption at its centre, were left to carry the can.

The *Daily West* had paid a freelancer to track down the fugitive in Switzerland two days earlier and it was a measure of Saul's arrogance that he had agreed to a brief interview. The team stood around the day editor's desk when the story came in, unable to contain their disgust. The newspaper published the interview in full. Saul had gloated like an old-school gangster. 'They'll never get me back to Perth alive.'

At the end of the week, Bec and Andy were in the morning briefing with chief of staff, Leo Grant.

'We need to start putting some local faces on this now,' he said. 'We've got to get insight into why well-educated, reputable men would join this scheme. Were they fooled? How much did they actually know? What kind of money did they invest? Find someone and get an interview.'

Andy agreed. 'Bec, you should get onto that.'

She was pleased that Andy showed Leo how much he trusted her. This was much better than sniffing around Saul's house. She began making phone calls to police contacts. She spent a morning in the archives, trawling the photo records for pictures of Saul at social events, noting the names of any doctors photographed with him then ringing their surgeries. She rang the State branch of the Australian Medical Association, not expecting to get any information but putting the word out that she wanted to give medicos the chance to give their side of the story, on the record or off.

By the end of the second day, she was stuck in a dead end. The day shift was over, the night editor updated, and her handbag was over her shoulder when the phone rang.

'You left a message with my receptionist. I hear you're doing a story that might involve me.' It was a voice that belonged to a man who was confident, accustomed to being in charge.

'I'm willing to give my side of this. I'm an anaesthetist but I'd prefer not to give you my name at this stage. And I want to meet you at my home, not at work.'

The conditions seemed reasonable. When they were

face to face she would broach the matter of the interview being on the record. 'Where?'

He gave her the address and she jotted it in her notebook then read it back to him to confirm the details. She had barely hung up before she crossed the office to announce the breakthrough to Andy.

'This could be the leak we need. See if you can get some other names.'

'My thoughts exactly, Andy.'

She had booked a pool car for noon next day and hurried out the door, much later than usual. She'd have to hurry to get home before Glen, who'd likely finished his day shift as sergeant at Wanneroo Police Station in the city's north.

———•———

Bec glanced over at Sheryl and got a grip on herself. Her husband, she didn't want to go there. Picking at one layer of shame was all she could bear.

———•———

The anaesthetist's address had been only a few streets away from Saul's. The spreading house was a swathe of cream-coloured Mediterranean stucco and terracotta tiled roof. A walkway ran along the front, with arches cut in to let light into the full-length windows. It was reminiscent of the worst of 1960s tourist resorts. Two tall palms grew to one side and a low hedge curved around a path that surrounded a three-tiered fountain and led to the front door.

It was one o'clock and the sun was high overhead,

heat softening the asphalt as Bec got out of the car and went to the side gate, as instructed. His wife was at work and his children at school. 'That way I can talk without interruptions.'

If she could freeze that frame in time and not go any further, it would be so much easier. Her hand on the gate latch, a touch of nervousness and the blood rushing in the excitement of a possible big break. There had been no thought of pausing or turning back.

'All I could think was that I might get a front page byline in the afternoon edition if I could wrap up the interview quickly.'

'It was your job, Bec. It was what you'd been trained to do.'

She ignored Sheryl's remark, stalled as she was in the image of that hot afternoon, unfolding in slow motion as she had gone through the gate.

Did she remember the way the sun slanted against the texture on the wall render and cast patterns like the join-the-dots puzzles she had loved as a child? Or was that something she added later, an embellishment to keep her at the side of the house a little longer. And the way the latch dragged in its groove, the weight of the wooden gate bearing down. Had she imagined that too?

The rear garden sprawled around a peanut-shaped swimming pool with a pair of cane sun lounges and an eight-seater glass-top table to one side. She counted only seven chairs around the table or was the counting something that also came later? The lawn was manicured and the lush kind of green only achieved by a qualified gardener paid to mow, rake and fertilise in accordance with a weekly schedule.

Reflections shifted on the water surface, a play of light and shadow and colours that rippled and swayed. The breeze dropped suddenly and the patterns gave way to a reverse image of a tall plane tree near the fence, with sunlight and leaves and sparkle in the centre, and on the right, the dark outline of a limb that had almost fallen from the tree and was hanging by a thread.

The light hurt her eyes and she lifted them from the pool, squinting as she searched out the gentle sway of the branch, the only movement in the shade of the canopy and so insubstantial for a limb. Below it, on the ground, was a fallen chair and she turned away immediately to the garden setting where there was a gap, right where the eighth chair should have been.

She looked back under the tree to the semi-circle where the sun was barred from entry and the lawn failed to grow. The colour had leached from the shadow thrown by the canopy; the sun has sucked it all out, had drawn every bit of green and yellow and blue into the brightness of the day. The colour was also gone from the face of the man hanging there.

He was heavier, much heavier than a man should be, as she struggled to free the rope from his neck. She seemed to scream but no one heard and it was not his blank grey face or the strangled quiver of her voice that disturbed her most but the way she had to leave him swinging while she ran next door for help.

She had tried so hard to get him down, to ease him into her arms and onto the patch of dirt below the tree, where at least he might find some rest and perhaps her, too. She had tried and been defeated. She knew this was the case because she had carried him across an entire continent and still could not lay him down.

'It wasn't your fault, Bec.'

She knew Sheryl meant well. 'Try telling that to his wife and kids.'

'He set you up right from the start. He wanted you to find him to spare his family.'

'But I was the one who drove him to it. I was pressuring him to speak out.' The certainty of it was indigestible, worse than tough mutton fermenting in the gut. She did not want to look into the eyes of the men from the pub last night because all she'd see would be their failure too.

Sheryl was deliberately slow to respond. 'That's quite the responsibility you're owning there. Some might say you're crossing a line to a place you don't need to go.'

She reached over and squeezed her friend's shoulder. A chunk of the story was missing, she couldn't quite tally what had been shared with the strength of the reaction.

Bec heard the barmaid's sentiment, knew it came from genuine intent, but it landed a distance from where she sat and she felt nothing, only saw where Sheryl's offering fell, empty and alien.

'Thanks for listening, I appreciate it, I really do. If you wouldn't mind, I'd prefer you didn't tell any of the others.'

Sheryl spent her working days around men who reached out to connect but the minute they did, needed to brick up a wall. She knew not to push it.

'Hear you're moving in with Jo on Monday. Give me a shout if you need a hand.'

Bec reached for the lemonade and stood up a bit too

fast, tipping awkwardly to one side before recovering her balance. 'Will do, ta. Better get back to it.'

Jack could be heard bellowing to Sheryl about why she wasn't in the bar.

5

I T WAS HABIT REALLY THAT led Bec to flick on the bar radio each morning, catching the first news broadcast of the day. After two weeks the rank odour of stale, slopped beer was still overpowering when she unlocked the door, but by seven o'clock it was pleasant to inhale the smell of the freshly disinfected floor as she propped on the end of the counter to catch the headlines.

The metal stools scraped on the floor as she lined them up along the bar. Jo or Sheryl, whoever was on the morning shift, would enjoy the temporary order before the room began its slow descent to chaos at closing time.

The announcer droned on while Bec wiped greasy fingerprints from the door. It was a woman's oddly monotone voice that made her pause—the woman whose two-month-old baby girl had disappeared from the family tent at Uluru, near the base of the soaring rock form. The mother had seen the shadow of a dingo leaving the tent but despite reporting it to police, an undercurrent of suspicion about the woman's role regarding the missing baby had persisted.

Bec knew how it would go with the media and maybe even the cops. Lindy Chamberlain's lack of emotion made her a target. They wanted the hysterical woman collapsing into her husband's arms, weeping messily for the television cameras. Only a mother who was evil would behave the way she did, no keening, screaming fits or breaking down to sob in front of the microphones.

It didn't matter that others had seen a dingo nearby or that campers had observed her behaving in a loving way with the baby and two older boys. The facts were irrelevant. She was not grieving according to their expectations and was being punished for it, as though the lack of what they considered normal for a mother made her a monster.

'Leave her alone. Don't you know she can't afford to feel.' Bec stamped her foot in the empty bar. With no television reception she had only seen one image of the woman, on the front page of *The Daily West*, which took three days to arrive from Perth. It was a frozen face, trapped in the moment where shock had wiped it clean of sensation. Bec longed to stand beside her, to brush her shoulder and say: 'Don't let them steal you like that wild dog stole your little girl'.

She switched off the radio and pushed the mother's face from her mind but the deadness in the woman's voice remained in her head as she talked to the house-maids and got organised for the tip run.

The truckie's death, on the other hand, had only warranted a couple of page three mentions in the Perth papers and a filler or two by way of coverage over in the east. It was barely a footnote to his death and that was a sadness all of its own.

The bins were just as full as they had ever been, with the volume of drinking continuing unabated in the two weeks since the poor guy's death. The only change had been that Jack now showed up for the last hour before closing time on Friday and Saturday to make sure the rowdiness did not get out of hand.

When a sergeant and constable turned up to give Jack an update they had nothing new to report. 'There'll be an inquest, of course,' he told Bec later, when she went to his office to confirm what she needed on the order for cleaning supplies. Bec had covered coronial inquiries as a court reporter and had seen first-hand the ordeal it was for families and witnesses, their lives siphoned into months of waiting while the mothers, fathers, wives, husbands, siblings were clinging on for answers that never came. The questions always ran ahead.

At least in Perth she had been spared that. The police had interviewed her for more than four hours the first day to get a thorough statement, then followed up with a further two hours later in the week. Their investigation concluded it was suicide and the coroner had apparently been satisfied with detailed evidence in the police report, including a note found in the family home, and did not deem it necessary to examine matters further.

When the lead detective showed up at work the chief of staff had let them borrow his office, so the visitor could bring Bec up to speed with the coroner's findings. She was distracted by the detective's sandy hair, the tips bleached in the way that salt spray stripped surfers' locks. She could barely recall what he said yet, strangely, remembered every detail of the way his hair fell in a cow lick on one side.

Leo had been the one to set her straight. 'Good that you won't have to front up to give evidence.'

Jo was pulling a beer as Bec opened the bar door mid-afternoon, putting her head in to say she was heading off.

She beckoned Bec over. 'I've just found out it's the cook's birthday and there's going to be a bit of a party up near the pool tonight when he finishes his shift. You'll come?' Bec felt obliged, given she was new in the job.

Sweat made her feet squeak on the soles of her leather sandals as she trudged the few doors up the street to her new home. Sun was reddening pale skin on her arms and legs. She had burned and peeled several times and although the freckles on her face had spread it was clear she would never achieve a tan.

On the opposite side of the road, the elderly woman was seated again in the slanting shade of the shop verandah. A shapeless green dress skimmed her ankles though it was her solitary being she wore with most obvious ease.

Bec raised a hand in greeting but there was no evident response. She was in a generous mood and supposed there could have been a nod or the lifting of a few fingers in return. It was almost forty degrees Celsius and the heat beat down with a force that would hammer a body to its knees if shade could not be found. It was a relief to get to the driveway, where a sparse sticky kurrajong, already shedding its leaves, threw up a few cupped red flowers in a desperate attempt to hold back the sun.

The ancestors know the truth.

Bec spun around. The street was empty, save for the woman, hands on her lap, body still as a stone angel. A truck droned past on its way to the meatworks, gusting thick clouds of dust in its wake. When the dust cleared, the verandah was empty.

The words swarmed before her eyes, drawn by a friction whose source she could not see, buzzing like static electricity in her hair. They had been hollow the first time, barely heard, the air snapping shut behind them so fast she could believe they hadn't happened at all. This time it felt personal.

She was a rational person, she reminded herself. She could march over the street, stride into the shop and ask the woman if she had spoken, or if she knew what such a statement meant. But she did not, and it wasn't because of the heat. Hidden in her heart was a sliver of hope holding out for the unknown, for if there could be mystery then she might chance upon a doorway through which she could disappear and emerge into the life she might have grown.

The unknown invited possibility, for the sealed container of her days might open into a greater world that could be travelled from a new place. Sometimes she could almost catch that shimmering potential out the corner of her eye.

But then, a container could also shatter under pressure, and afterwards hold nothing and be nothing.

The messy thoughts made her nauseous. She went inside, straight to the bathroom for a cool shower, and was dozing on the couch when Jo got home.

———— • ————

Lily watched the young woman walk up the street and turn into her driveway. She could not see the face, the limbs, the way she once might have. She could know, though, what was before her in other ways, like the way the woman's body swung a little as she walked, not quite anchored in the space it occupied.

It reminded her of the striped spinning top her children had loved to twirl, how it lost its centre of gravity as it slowed, wobbling in the moment before it tumbled.

There had been a time when, like the woman before her, she had been that spinning top, swaying, falling.

So much had come to pass since those days. Lily was an old woman now and had grown into many versions of herself then slipped each off as naturally as shedding a light cotton robe. These days she thought of many things from the past but no longer thought of the future. Sometimes she even caught herself speaking aloud, though her ears only heard a dull, distant sound.

She wanted badly to tell her new companion how to make it right, to find equilibrium. Yet she understood each person must walk their own path to its source. All she could offer was the connection she had found, in the hope it would help her friend recognise that what was needed was already close at hand.

———•———

The screen door banged open and Bec woke with a start.

Jo appeared, tugging at her green polo shirt with the brewery logo. 'Let's make an effort and dress up tonight. I'm over this old thing.'

"Sure, let's.' It would have to be the yellow sundress but maybe she could wear some makeup.

Dave arrived as they were heading for the door. Jo was quick to pounce. 'We're getting a bite at the pub.

Thought you could join us later.' He had been gone since five thirty that morning and it showed on his face but his sibling wasn't giving him the chance to protest. 'See you there.' She did a whirl in her halter neck dress, a kaleidoscope of blue tie dye sweeping around her calves.

Though it was mid-week someone had turned up the music in the bar and Elton John blasted out into the beer garden.

'Hope that's a mix tape. Not an Elton fan myself.' Jo was shouting to be heard, which suited Bec because it put limits on conversation. The younger woman managed to get the music turned down before Dave showed up about nine, shaved and in a change of clothes.

'Is the kitchen closed?'

'I'm sure I can call in a favour.' Jo winked. 'What do you want?'

She left with his order for steak, chips and mushroom sauce. It was the first time Bec had been alone with Dave and in the long pause she tried to reel in some small talk, though nothing came. She figured her brain wasn't built to rove wide. She was happiest when she found a fascinating subject and dug deep, for those were the conversations that made her light up.

Dave bailed her out. 'So, how's it going? Hope the house is working out.'

'Really good. I've never lived in a place on stilts or one where the walls open and shut, so that's been a new experience.'

'Well, you're lucky your bedroom's at the back. I get the dust from the trucks over everything.'

The house had a simple layout with a separate kitchen and combined dining and sitting room at one end, opening to a long hallway with two bedrooms on either side. Every room had a creaking timber floor.

The exterior walls were the usual kind from the roofline down to the halfway mark, where they suddenly stopped and gave way to wide metal louvres Bec had only ever seen in garden sheds. It was easy to believe a sun-addled builder had held the house plans upside down.

They mostly left the vents open. They provided virtually no movement of air but held the promise of capturing a rogue breeze. Each bedroom had a ceiling fan, though Bec had quickly discovered it was useless unless she lay underneath it covered in a damp towel.

'Our grocery order goes to Perth in the morning. If you want, you can put your list with ours and we can figure out the cost when it gets delivered.' The order went south once a week then the groceries were trucked up over three days.

'Thanks Dave. Must say, I miss fresh fruit and veg. Never been one for what's frozen or canned.'

Minutes later Jo was back and didn't skip a beat. 'Leonie's secretly baked a cake. Chef's going to go off when he sees it.'

The staff all knew the waitress made her evenings bearable by taking every opportunity she could to stir up the chef, a bearded fellow called Pete who demanded a level of cleanliness in the kitchen that did not extend to his ramshackle personal hygiene.

'You know we call him Pete Pong?' Jo dug Bec in the ribs with her elbow.

'Can't wait to see the look on his face when she brings out the cake. She's iced it like a durian, but I think it's actually vanilla sponge.' She roared with laughter. There were only five years between their ages yet in moments like this Bec was a different generation.

Dave spoke as if he'd read her mind. 'It's a bit cruel isn't it, sis?'

A couple of hours later Bec slipped her handbag off the back of the chair and prepared to leave when Jo grabbed her arm.

'You can't go, Bec. We're all heading up to the pool soon. Sheryl's going to be disappointed if you're not around when she finishes up.'

Bec saw her through the window, smiling behind the bar, handing out change and taking orders all at once.

'Okay, I'll stay for a bit.'

It was quieter as they climbed the stairs at the rear of the pub. Sheryl had lowered the volume of the sound system to signal fifteen minutes to closing time.

Up the top Hazel was already settled in with the other housemaid, who was explaining her name was Kieran. 'And not kiwi for Karen.' She slapped her knee with glee, enjoying her own joke at the New Zealanders' expense.

The two women were part-way through cans of vodka and orange. Three men from the oil rig sat opposite, ice melting around the contents of a slab of beer in a coolbox at their feet, several empty cans underneath their chairs. Dave knew them and did the introductions—an electrician called Al and derrick hands Paul and Sy.

It was hard to tell if Al was less inclined to be talkative than the other two or if his companions confused the need to breathe with the act of speaking. Either way they had a lot to say and Al very little.

Bec sat to one side, with Dave nearby. Jo was enthusiastically selling the wonders of New Zealand to the electrician, who had made the mistake of mentioning he was due for a holiday. As Paul and Sy's conversation wound itself on, tight like a spring, Dave leaned over and half-whispered to Bec.

'The rig's dry. They've been alcohol-free for two weeks. Making up for lost time.' He winked and went over to the pair, joining in a toast 'to freedom, at least for as long as it lasts'.

Sheryl was not far behind the others and when she arrived the rig workers gave her a round of applause. 'Good to see you got legs. Only get the top half when you're behind the bar,' Sy drawled.

Dave shot him a withering look.

'Jack not coming?' Bec asked her quietly when the fuss had died down.

'Nah, he prefers to stay away. Kind of suits us as well.'

Pete and Leonie had finished in the kitchen. Bec saw the dining room windows go dark then the pair come up the stairs, following the silver trail thrown onto the concrete by security lights.

Bec nudged Sheryl and lowered her voice. 'Where's the cake?'

'Leonie got me to hide it near the stairs.' She did a half grimace, confirming she wasn't the only one to wonder how it would go down.

As it turned out there was no problem. By the time they got to singing happy birthday Pete's quota of beer had disconnected the part of his brain that could recognise a durian. He grinned from ear to ear as Leonie cut the cake and everyone shouted hooray, though not for the reasons Pete thought.

Bec noticed Dave had stopped drinking soon after they had come up the stairs and with the cake cut, he made his farewells.

'Got to get some shut eye guys, or I might end up driving you to Katherine in the morning instead of Kununurra airport.'

The coolbox was emptying out and Paul and Sy had begun slurring their words, not that they had said anything worth listening to all night. Bec could feel the tension grabbing her gut. She wasn't much of a drinker and it set her teeth on edge to see the boozing still going full-bore. Hazel and Kieran continued to work their way through six-packs of vodka mixer, flirting with the married men, and even Al was getting worse for wear.

'Hey, how about I slip down to the bar and get us some chips and nuts? Anyone want to throw in a couple of dollars?' Bec's suggestion was met with noisy enthusiasm.

She collected the money and was glad to slip away. Once she'd delivered the snacks to soak up the excess grog she was going home. She used her key to slip inside the main bar. Sheryl had told her where to find the canvas banking bag for the cash on a shelf below the cash register. She was counting the money into it when she heard keening sobs.

Jo came in the door, her arm around a crumpled Sheryl, dripping water onto the floor, crying so hard it could have come from her tears.

'I'll get something to dry her.' Bec returned with an armful of white towels from the housekeeping store and a wicker chair, then eased the sobbing woman into it. She raised her eyebrows at Jo.

'Silly buggers decided it'd be funny to dunk her in the pool. You help Sheryl. I'm going back to break this party up before Paul and Sy get more out of hand.' She was maybe a hundred and fifty centimetres tall but working in the bar had made her tough with drunks.

Bec wrapped a towel around Sheryl's shoulders and used a second one to rub her hair, trying to fathom why her friend was so distressed.

'My locket, my locket.' Sheryl repeated the two words on a closed loop.

Bec gently lifted it from Sheryl's throat and held it in front of her eyes. 'It's here, you're still wearing it.' The attempt at reassurance produced a wail.

'Did they scare you? Maybe you can't swim?' She was flailing around for the source of her friend's anguish. Sheryl shook her head, eyes swollen, looking sore. Bec didn't need to be a mind reader to know the wretchedness was about more than a piece of jewellery.

She knelt in front of Sheryl. 'What is it? I can see this is really hard for you.' She stayed close to the barmaid, careful not to touch her till she had a sense it would by okay.

Sheryl fumbled with the locket, pressing a fingernail into the join then flipping the heart-shaped chamber open. One side was empty but on the other section were the pulpy remains of a photo so water-damaged it was impossible to see who it was.

'It's my girl.' Sheryl moaned. 'And I am never getting her back.' She fell forward and collapsed into Bec's arms.

'I didn't know you had a daughter.' Bec's voice was gentle as she kept one arm around the barmaid while dragging over the nearest stool in reach to sit beside her.

They stayed where they were, folded together, like figures in a painting Bec had seen years earlier while backpacking through Europe. In one corner of the vast Oath of Horatii painting at the Louvre two women were collapsed against each other, bearing pain, except those figures had elegance and grace. Not a wonky chair or torn tissue in sight.

Eventually the crying subsided. Sheryl straightened up.

'She came up here with me. It was all an adventure for a twelve year old. Her dad was okay with it, with her having a year then going back to Perth, to her old school.' Sheryl managed a wan smile at the memory.

'I was so glad I wouldn't have to be without her. It had been mainly the two of us since her dad and I split a few years back. She got on well with my new fella Bram and he didn't mind her coming here to live with us.'

The bar was warm and Sheryl was almost dry but she was shivering just the same.

'You never get to wind it back, Bec. Something tips over an edge and it's done and there's no way to fix it.'

It had all gone well for four months or so, Bram at the meatworks, Sheryl with her job in the bar, Saffie making new friends at school.

'She'd always been a good kid, sensible. We'd talk things through. She knew she could always come to me. But then she started behaving strangely. The teachers called me in a couple of times.

'When I asked her what was going on, she'd storm

off to her room. She was spending a lot of time in that room.'

Sheryl had stopped crying, though Bec thought the tears had been easier than the weight of hurt in her voice. They sat for a moment in silence. Jo carefully cracked open the door and sized up the situation. She mouthed 'you okay?' to Bec. When she got a nod in reply she flashed a grim semblance of a smile and gently retreated.

'Sometimes she would scream at me. She'd never done that before. And a couple of times, to my eternal shame, I screamed back.'

When Saffie had begun refusing meals it had become more serious. Then a week later, just before school holidays began, Saffie announced she had rung her father and was flying back to Perth to live with him.

'I couldn't fathom what was going on. I had no idea. Bram was so supportive, telling me he'd been the same at that age, that it was just teenage hormones kicking in. I wanted to believe it.'

Sheryl looked over at Bec, a pleading in her eyes. 'You see, Bec, I was blind. Stone cold blind.'

She drove her daughter to the airport at Kununurra and hugged her. 'I didn't know it might be for one last time.'

Saffie was gone two days when the phone call came.

'It was her dad. He was livid, his voice burning down the phone line like a lightning strike. Even now it's hard to get my head around. He had to tell me three times before I could let it sink in.'

She straightened up and took a deep breath. What she had to say stuck fast in her throat until she coughed, just the once.

'He'd been preying on her, Bec. All that time Bram was acting sympathetic with me about her moods he had been touching her, doing worse things when I wasn't around. I can never forgive myself.' She looked Bec straight in the eye, staring down any possibility of sympathy.

'She's not coming back. She won't live with me again. She feels I betrayed her by not seeing what was going on.'

'Maybe she just needs some time.'

'No, it's been eight months and she hasn't budged an inch. She won't talk to me on the phone and when I write letters she doesn't reply. She's lost to me and it's what I deserve.' Sheryl spat out the last few words.

Bec had nothing to say. Grief could grow dense, first a few thorns then before you knew it, an entire thicket and no way to find a path home. She reached over, wrapped her arms around Sheryl and held her for the longest time.

6

FIFTY-THREE STEPS, THAT'S HOW FAR the walk was from work to home. Bec had counted them, sixty-five if you included the distance from the foyer door, where she let herself in each morning, to the car park out the front.

The ground radiated out from beneath her feet, spreading to salt pans, mudflats, sluggish rivers, chiselled mountains and desert beyond, spiralling out across the continent on a scale so extraordinary that people preferred to cling to the edges of the country like the animals they were, gathering together so they did not have to contend with the threat of the endless unknown.

It made her breathless when she thought about it. Not the spreading, empty landscape, for that was country that had cared for her in its own harsh way, but the fact that she too had turned her back on it, ring-fencing herself without meaning to, her days defined by sleep, work and heat-whacked twilight time on the couch. She didn't know who this woman was any more or maybe she never had, it was impossible to tell.

Dave was home for dinner after a week down south, so Jo defied the thirty-two degree evening by cooking a roast chicken. They sat out the back near the clothesline, marvelling that they could eat a hot meal when salads, the cooler the better, were the usual fare. The ridge of the Bastion threw a sharp outline against the final glow of the sky. Soon the gathering dusk stole it away but not the hot air trapped by the rocky slope.

'Nearly as good as mum's.' Dave raised a glass of white wine, something he didn't drink at the pub. 'Here's to you, sis.'

Despite the way he teased Jo, his face shone with brotherly love. It caught Bec in the throat and she took a couple of swift sips from her glass to disguise the tremble at the corners of her mouth. Dave was away a lot for work, it was true, but when she moved in, she'd been focused on getting somewhere to sleep with a proper bed and now, she realised with a jolt, she had not thought it through.

Dave seemed to sense the shift in her.

'You got any brothers or sisters, Bec?'

She was answering before her mind had even processed the question. 'No, there's just me.'

Jo pounced. 'Ooh, an only child. Lucky you.'

She didn't bother to set her housemate straight.

They had barely eaten when Jo rushed off to ring a friend in Auckland. 'Four hours ahead of us. If I don't do it now, she'll be in bed.'

Dave was picking over the chicken bones. He wiped greasy fingers on kitchen paper they were using as serviettes. 'She's a bitzer, you know. Part Labrador with a dash of Rottweiler if anyone tries to push her around.' He chuckled to himself.

'So, just the one sibling then?' He glanced up briefly then back towards the table, still busy with his food.

Bec stiffened. 'Why do you ask?'

'Look, Jo's a good person but her cheerfulness can get in the way sometimes. Besides, you answered in the present tense which made me wonder if there had been someone once.'

He pushed away the plate and was looking towards her now. Tealights in the centre of the table flickered then brightened, illuminating genuine interest on his face.

She hesitated, though not long enough to protect the seal that stopped the past from bubbling up.

'A brother. I had a brother.'

He did not try to press her to share any more, but she had gone too far to stop. She set her glass down on the table.

'It happened years ago, a lifetime ago.'

'That doesn't make it any less significant.'

'No, it doesn't. I guess I mean that sometimes it seems like I never had a brother at all.'

They could hear Jo laughing in the house, then her conversation took a more subdued turn.

'What was his name?'

'He was called Daniel, never Dan. A couple of years younger than me. A bit sporty but he had a sensitive side. Went to school one day and didn't come home.'

Dave took a deep breath but remained silent.

She halted at that point. It was all the story she could bring herself to tell these days. The years had taken to it with a threshing machine, beating it down to the bones. Maybe it was selfish but she needed to keep some things back, to keep alive the shimmering boy he'd once been, to keep him for herself.

'Do you ever wonder who he'd be now?'

She shook her head. It was difficult enough to cradle baby Daniel, helpless in her lap, or to hold out her arms for the toddler staggering as he learned to balance and walk in the back yard. She could still smell the hair of the seven year old who had climbed into her bed one night, thunder rattling the windows, lightning darting outside. If she ticked off the years, the closer she got to him at fourteen the more her memory blurred. Now he no longer had a face.

Jo bounced back to the table, full of news from New Zealand. Bec ignored the concern on Dave's face, excused herself and left them to it.

She flicked the bedroom fan onto high and lay under it wearing only knickers, her torso covered in a wet towel, and surrendered to the blur circling on the ceiling.

———•———

He had been thirteen when the bullying began, just because a bunch of older boys needed a punching bag.

The brother she loved fell apart in slow motion as she watched on, helpless. His voice disappeared first, then muscles refused to function. He gave up sport. Other than school hours he stayed in his bedroom with the curtains closed, his beloved guitar left on its stand. Within six months his spirit had abandoned him. They all knew it.

Their parents did what they could but mental health services were non-existent in rural areas like theirs. Their mother resorted to sleeping on the floor of his room, eyes open for hours as she lay on the mattress. Their father wrapped the sharp kitchen knives in calico and hid them in the farm ute. They cleaned out every medication from the bathroom cupboard, even the headache tablets.

Bec tiptoed through the house for weeks, afraid one wrong move might upset the delicate balance, until she thought she might blow her top. She rose early one morning as darkness was fraying on the edge of nearby hills and walked to the furthest paddock on the farm. Standing on a rise, cattle stirring to graze below, she opened her mouth and released the pent-up energy in a scream. The echo that returned seemed the first thing to meet the mess inside her.

She trudged home, nursing the relief.

It was short-lived. The tension in the house was constant, a tripwire that snagged her when least expected.

'For heaven's sake, Bec. What were you thinking?'

'I'm sorry, mum.' She held out her hand to help her mother up from the floor where she had fallen after catching her foot in a strap on the backpack left in the hall.

'So bloody inconsiderate.' Her mother was shouting, face contorted. She slapped Bec's hand away.

She could still feel the sting of it more than a decade later.

There were worse things in a family home than tension, though. Silence, uninvited, showed up weeks later and sucked the oxygen out of every room, leaving only dullness and a slow desperation.

The facts were straightforward enough. Daniel had bought a handful of prescription pills from a kid at school, the mate too caught in puberty to grasp the ramifications—then calmly exited the main gate in his lunch break. A woman walking her dog found him late afternoon under a spreading macrocarpa pine in the reserve behind the town's Scout Hall.

Their mother had been wrapping the present for his fourteenth birthday when the cops turned up, so Bec answered the door. The local constable, young, nervous, removed his hat but it was the older sergeant who spoke.

She could picture his mouth moving but had no recall of what was said. Unlike the guttural cry from her mother as she'd collapsed on the floor, a sound that could never be erased, despite her best efforts.

The ceiling fan was making her dizzy. She rolled onto her side and repositioned the damp towel.

Listen to the ancestors. The words tumbled down from the spinning blades.

She was struck, again, by their emphatic energy. The words were a riddle, seemingly carrying meaning, yet a puzzle she could not make out.

What good would it do even if she could listen? She no longer heard the voice of a brown-eyed boy she had loved so dearly, who had grown up under the same roof. Her mother and father had wrapped themselves in guilt and bottomless pain and she rarely spoke to them these days. They seemed to find it easier to sever themselves from the fact that they'd ever had a family at all.

At the funeral, seated in the front pew, all she had seen was the vision from the previous day of her brother's pale face under the sickly light in the viewing room at the funeral home. The man he intended to become had already begun signalling itself in his cheekbones and firming jaw, the promise harshly negated by an outrage of white satin.

'Where there is death there is life, for God has given us eternal life.' The Minister intoned at the lectern, a few metres from Bec. He could have been on Mars for all she knew because she was seized by panic at seeing the lid screwed tightly to the coffin. It took all her willpower to maintain the effort of keeping her seat while her hands trembled with the desire to wrench off the lid, get the trapped boy out of there and hug him again.

Outside the church her parents had clung to each other, shipwrecked on their private island of grief, while she had stood awkwardly off to one side, bearing the stunned, sad looks of Daniel's entire school class.

No, these days, she had no elders. She liked to imagine she'd arrived on Earth, fully formed, functional, programmed for survival. When pandas had twins, one was nurtured and the other abandoned to the wild. Daniel had been the chosen one and her parents had done everything in their power to keep him alive. When they failed there was no thrashing through the undergrowth to search for the one they'd cast aside. She had been left to provide her own protection, to find her own way.

She did not hear any ancestors at all. She almost laughed aloud at the thought. So why did she expect the past to knock at her door?

———•———

As she settled into her daily routine the heat was no easier to bear, but she adjusted to its constant presence by changing the way she moved and when. It was faithful, if not a friend, waiting like a loyal dog at the foot of the bed, ready to pounce when she woke.

Thirty-five steps, thirty-six, she was nearer the house than the pub on her way home. Gliding at a slow but steady pace, sparing what little remained of her energy reserves. Forty-seven, forty-eight, forty-nine.

The Chinese woman was back in position, a frocked-up ninja who materialised each day on the chair, or so Bec imagined. She had never once seen her walk to get there.

Fifty, fifty-one. Bec stopped counting and with no consideration for why, crossed the street and sat on the edge of pavers running the length of the building, settling half-way between the woman and the shop entrance. She sat there for a while, hugging her knees, before turning her head and giving the woman a smile. The woman looked in her direction, giving a half-smile back. The heat was at its peak and no customers were foolish enough to be venturing about so Bec stayed put and as she sat, had a curious sense of emptying out.

She wasn't sure how long she stayed but eventually the need for a shower surfaced and she slowly stood.

'Thank you.'

A small tilt of the woman's head came in reply.

Bec braced for the hit of sun as she left the shade and strode the rest of the way home, hoping the shopkeeper, clearly protective of his mother, wouldn't ask about her motive for the visit. For she had none.

The next afternoon, Bec diverted again after work to rest underneath the verandah, a little closer to the chair.

She leaned back, arms outstretched behind, palms flat on the warm pavers to support herself in the field of stillness that surrounded the woman. A flock of masked finches gave up the quest for food in a scrubby patch of grassland by the road and with a flash of yellow beaks lined up on a nearby eucalypt branch. They made a few listless chirps, then took to the air and were gone.

Bec lifted a hand as though expecting something solid to meet it, then let it fall back behind her. The circle of quiet was full of meaning yet lacking words and the ceasing of motion it brought was strangely pulsing with life.

The elderly woman seemed neither happy nor sad and when Bec stole a sideways glance, she expected it would be resignation on the wrinkled face, but it was not. Grey-streaked hair was parted in the centre and tied back in a low bun. The face that it framed was round and engaged the world with a look that was whole, complete.

In more than a decade as a journalist Bec had talked with people who were barely getting by, with others at their best and some at their worst. She had never seen a face so composed. Water could turn to a similar calm when the wind had finished stirring a river or lake and moved on. Air too, when a stormfront had blown through and left the atmosphere clean, clear, at rest.

The woman continued to sit, unperturbed, and Bec stayed in position, with no desire to move. As she sat, the chemistry of the moment set off strange reactions in the scaffolding of her life and it began to fall away. A prop seemed to loosen here, a guardrail there, then a cascade of corner braces tumbled down. Ambition crumbled then was gone. Wanting to make the world a better place faltered and faded. Yearning for possessions, maybe a house of her own one day, scattered like a handful of seeds tossed onto rocky ground.

None of it held weight. She was overcome with the insubstantiality of all she had longed for as it floated off, a string of white balloons into the sky. If anything remained perhaps it was her humanity and if so, that seemed on shaky ground. She rose suddenly from where she sat so there could be no chance the dissolution would follow its course and leave her with no identity at all.

'Well, it's been good spending time with you again.'

Bec flipped her sunglasses from her head to cover her eyes, inhaled deeply, and propelled herself through heat that radiated off the road and pulled at her feet with such force she could swear the gravel had been spread with a thick coating of molasses.

Minutes later, collapsed on the couch, she tried to understand what the elderly woman possessed but it was like trying to understand the taste of honey with a stick instead of a tongue.

———•———

Without intending to, it became a ritual each day, crossing the street to rest for a while in the shade, the only words spoken a greeting and goodbye. Her companion was a living being with roots deep in the ground and Bec sensed she had been invited to sit, to be touched by the woman's well of peace, perhaps consoled.

Jo had noticed Bec sitting there a couple of times.

'She's a bit old to be a mate, don't you think?'

She laughed at her own joke but let it go after that. She was too busy being giddy about one of the square-jawed regulars who frequented the bar. He was taller than the barmaid and Bec had seen him flirting, towering over the girl, just as he did with other women when Jo was not there. She had seen his type before.

Sheryl mentioned it when she went into the storeroom for some extra bottles of dry ginger ale. 'I tried to tell her but she didn't want to know. He's going to eat her alive.' Bec heard the grating of worry in her voice and she had to agree. It was like throwing a goldfish into a pool with a piranha and expecting its golden innocence to keep it safe.

'Maybe I can have a word with Dave, get him to warn her off.'

'Good idea. But make sure he doesn't let on that we're behind it.'

Bec had to wait three days till Dave was home on an evening when Jo was on the late shift. They shared potato and egg salad Bec had made and the last few slices of ham from Dave's shelf in the fridge. Bec had been paid that day and had treated herself to a bottle of gin. She dropped ice cubes into two glasses, poured a generous nip, topped it with tonic water and lamented the lack of sliced lime as she handed a glass to Dave.

'Ever notice that really tall fellow who's often in the bar?

'Can't say that I have.'

Bec pushed a large forkful of food into her mouth to buy time before she spoke again. She knew better than this. She had started the story in the middle to conceal her discomfort and lost the momentum of it instead.

'Good looking, a bit arrogant. Think it's his second season here.' She clocked Dave's face to see if he was travelling with her as she spoke. He seemed to be listening, waiting to see where this might go.

'What about him?'

'Seems he's interested in Jo.'

'Oh, might do her good. She's been pining a bit for the fellow she left back home.'

Bec was flummoxed. This was supposed to be a

warning and it had flipped into a show of support. She debated letting it drop.

'You don't seem the gossiping type, Bec. Is there a reason you're telling me this?'

She was momentarily blindsided and ran a few replies through her head but in her confusion opted for the truth, at least as she saw it.

'He's a bit of a player, Sheryl and I have both seen him at it. I guess I'm a bit concerned Jo could get hurt.'

'You think she needs protecting?'

This was trickier than expected. She'd been an expert at thinking on her feet, a reporter who amped up a solid interview to a remarkable one with an unexpected line or two. Now she was on the receiving end and Dave had asked what they called in the trade the leading question.

'You obviously know her much better than me.'

'Ah, but you haven't answered my question.'

'Well, it's not my place to say what you should or shouldn't do.' Dinner was rumbling unpleasantly in her belly.

'True, true. And yet you feel strongly enough about it to raise it with me.'

The tone of his voice was neutral. She was anxious about where this might go when he was a housemate and his sister, too. It was just the pair of them at the table and her mind was a camera panning back to see them alone in the house and no one else around. The muscles in her arms and chest contracted.

He shifted in his seat and smiled broadly, holding out his hands, palms up.

'Just kidding. I can hear you're worried about her.

I'll suss it out. And you're being far too cautious about what you say to me.'

She didn't know whether to thank him or slap him so she did neither. They were part-way through their second gin and tonic when she returned the challenge.

'Why were you teasing me before, implying I was an interfering cow?'

He laughed and leaned his head to one side. 'You strike me as someone who's learned to carry your cards close to your chest. Guess I was trying to draw you out.'

She slugged the rest of her gin and jumped up to wash the dishes. He was too bloody cocky by far. She left him drying plates and disappeared to her room.

———— • ————

In the kitchen, Dave mulled over the evening as he clattered cutlery into the drawer. About nine hundred hours a year on average in the chopper, that's what he flew. You didn't get to do that accident-free without knowing exactly where your eggbeater was in relation to objects in your air space or on the ground. Their new housemate, on the other hand, flapped one way, bumped another, and still didn't know how to land.

It reminded him of the paramedic after that awful day on the mountainside back home. Dave had flown a rescue crew out to pick up a bushwalker badly injured in a fall. It was a tight location, with only one small winch area surrounded by thick forest. The paramedic went down and secured the injured walker around the chest in a rescue strop, instructing him to keep his arms by his side. The pair were winched up but as they neared the chopper skid, the patient became unconscious and began slipping from the harness. Despite the efforts of the paramedic and the winch operator, he fell to the ground, sustaining fatal injuries.

Afterwards, they had all been affected. For weeks, Dave had run the incident through his mind on repeat, searching for any tiny window where he could have done things differently. Yet at the first opportunity he got in his bird and flew, knew he had to.

The paramedic had resigned, no longer able to deal with situations requiring a decisive response. His personal guidance system had broken. Bec had evidently gone the same way.

He waited up for Jo to finish her shift. He needed to talk to her tonight because tomorrow he was away again.

7

KIERAN WAS OFF SICK SO after Bec did the bar, the beer garden and toilets, she helped Hazel finish cleaning the units. It took longer than expected to make beds, pamper towels, fold the end of the toilet paper roll, and vacuum. By two o'clock she still had not done the tip run and was starving, so dashed into the bar for a packet of peanuts. Five or six men were already lined up on the stools and she saw that one of them was Jo's pursuer.

Her housemate was starting her next run of morning shifts and followed Bec into the beer garden while she hastily ate her snack.

'He's just asked me for a swim and a barbie tonight at the lake at Kununurra. What food do you think I should take to impress?'

'I dunno, Jo. Maybe ask Dave, he's more likely to know what a bloke would find special.' Bec remembered then. Dave was out of town. 'Does he know you're seeing this bloke?' She was fishing to see if Dave had tried to warn her off.

'No. I only got asked out then.' Jo was looking at Bec as though she'd lost her mind.

'How about asking Sheryl? She'll be here in a

minute and she's better than me at this stuff.' If Dave had cautioned her to be careful then Jo wasn't taking it on board. Perhaps Sheryl would have a better chance.

She gave it one last shot. 'Maybe the lake's not a good spot. I'm told wildlife officers had to shoot a big saltie that found its way into the water last year.'

Jo squinted, looking right through her. 'No, there's a few small, harmless freshies, that's all.'

Bec rushed off to the ute before she dug a bigger hole for herself.

A couple of hours later she was on the couch with a well-thumbed thriller, not something she would normally read but given there was no television reception it was marginally better than staring at the wall. Jo swept in, apologising for the rush. She dropped a bag of ice into a coolbox, along with a couple of steaks she'd been lucky enough to score from the supermarket's narrow range of supplies.

'This place!' She kicked the coolbox lid shut with her foot. 'A meatworks at the end of the street and all of it exported so we have to wait for steak to come from down south.'

Jo was out of the shower and in bathers, with an embroidered dress thrown hastily over the top, when a vehicle horn blasted outside. 'Don't wait up,' she squealed as she hurried out the door.

Bec smiled. The girlish joy was endearing even if it made her feel a hundred years old. It was a different sensation in the brief pause each day on the verandah over the way. Time and age, neither seemed to matter. When she sat with her companion in the shade, all that had been, or could ever be, coalesced and stalled.

The simplicity of it, the cushion of a reality that never swerved unpredictably or teetered ready for a fall drew her back despite herself. She perched on the verandah, a frail baby bird, and the certainty of the silence around the other woman fed her again and again.

On the radio at work that morning, she'd heard a shift in Lindy Chamberlain's voice. Bec felt it come through in the broadcast, a voice that had given up, the imperceptible flutter of a woman who knew she was prey. She hadn't waited to hear the rest of the news report; she had snapped off the power button with such force she was surprised it hadn't broken off.

What did it take to be a woman in this world? It was none of what she'd been told or thought she knew. She'd been careful to read the cues, to sit and stand and walk the highwire when she should, to copy what other women did, to be strong but not too strong. No doubt that poor woman had risked the tightrope, too.

Bec had done her best to be enough but not too much. Wasn't that what was required of a woman after all? Always off-balance because the invisible rules never stayed the same. But it wasn't what was needed. She knew it to her core. Because you never got it right, no matter how much you flailed, and right in the centre of your heart the trying clawed out an empty hole.

She dozed on the couch till well after dark then dragged herself off to bed.

———— • ————

'So, you from Perth?' Jo asked, wishing he would switch on the air con instead of driving with all the windows open. She could hear the coolbox sliding about in the back of his four-wheel drive.

'Yeah, Manning.'

She stole a sideways glance. He was just as good-looking in profile as face on. Different to the man she had left behind in Auckland; black hair instead of brown, bulkier from the weights he'd told her he lifted in his makeshift home gym.

He didn't seem to welcome conversation but she gave it another shot. 'What did you do for work before coming up here?'

'This 'n that. Did a couple of years on a forklift at the oil refinery at Kwinana, down south.'

She chirped away with a few desultory comments about the remoteness and coping with the heat but when he gave little in the way of response she let it drop. He'd been chattier in the bar but maybe he wasn't in the mood for conversation while he was driving.

Less than an hour later they were at the lake on the edge of town, seated on a couple of fold-out chairs at one of the barbecue shelters. The locals weren't stupid, Jo thought. They were all at home with fridge doors open or the air con going full bore. The sun still had sting so a swim would have to wait for now.

Her date snapped the ring pull off a stubbie and glugged about half the ale down.

'Ever been in the boning room at the meatworks, Jo?' She shook her head. It was enough of a bloodbath sometimes in the bar.

He pointed to a sticking plaster on his forehead. 'Bloody lucky not to lose my eye.'

'You did that with your knife?'

'Yeah, we gotta work fast on the production line. It's good money but not if you lose any body parts.' He roared with laughter at his own joke.

He drank another stubbie, maybe two more after that. She tried to keep pace and by the time she was turning the steak the tongs were steady in her hand but her body was swaying to the pop and sizzle from the barbecue grill.

They faced the lake as they ate off paper plates. The breeze had given up and the sun was slipping away, clinging on momentarily with fingers of fiery orange on the glassy surface of the water, mirroring grasses and woodland fringing the shore.

'Not bad for a man-made lake, eh?' He spoke quietly, resting a hand on her arm.

She leaned towards his touch. 'Not bad at all.'

By the time they had finished eating the light had faded and the lake was dark. She left him working his way through another beer and jumped up to scrape the barbecue and pack up the food. She was almost finished when he bowled up behind and wrapped his arms around her then nuzzled her neck. She smiled to herself. It felt good but it was like being hugged by a boab tree.

She watched him drink some more. At this rate she would be driving his vehicle back to Wyndham.

'How about that swim?' She pointed to a gap in the dark row of rushes growing along the waterline.

'Great idea.' He leapt up and began pulling off his T-shirt while she tugged her dress up over her head. He saw her one-piece bathers as he was kicking off his shorts.

'This is the north.' The way he chortled made her feel

stupid. 'You won't need those bathers. We skinny dip up here.' The white moon of his bottom disappeared into the gloom.

She slid off a strap then paused, unsure. She was sobering up so why was she still off-centre? It was silly because she had skinny dipped with girlfriends plenty of times before. 'Come on, girl. You're not a prude,' she muttered to herself, then left the bathing suit behind.

The water was deeper than expected, probably because the lake was managed by a dam down at Bandicoot Bar. She swam towards her new friend, who splashed her playfully then began doing the Australian crawl in wide circles around her, strong strokes pulling him along. She treaded water, watching his rhythm of white flashes as each underarm, untouched by the sun, swung up then plunged down so smoothly he barely broke the surface. He swam in close then away until she couldn't see him anymore.

The softness of the water and the silence settled around her. She flipped onto her back and let the lake hold her while she watched star upon star blink into life and take its place in the sky. She searched for the scorpion, its curving tail, the giant red Antares at its heart, but the Earth had another hour or so to turn before the pattern would slide into view. She opened her arms wide and rested on the water. The sky deepened, seeming to dip closer, and she wondered how many stars she could gather in her peaceful, outstretched body.

From nowhere a pressure gripped each shoulder and pulled her under. When she surfaced an arm held her waist even though she was batting it away.

'Haha, got you a beauty.' He began splashing with the other hand.

She wasn't amused but pretended to laugh and let him spin her around. He kissed her and she reached an arm out and wrapped it around his neck.

When he pulled her in tighter, she pushed against his chest and struggled away. He took it as a game and came towards her while she swam as fast as she could to the shore.

'You got a head start but I'll still beat you out.' He drew ahead, pulling through the water with long strokes, reaching the grassy lake edge ahead of her.

Her feet were slipping in silt near the bank when he shot out a hand and grasped hers firmly, as if to help her steady. She'd hoped he would be back at his vehicle towelling himself down, getting dressed, but the street-light at the car park entrance outlined his naked form.

She thanked him and pulled back her hand then headed across the grass, looking for her discarded dress. Her body had already forgotten the weightlessness of the water and it was stone bearing down as she moved her legs over the ground, his footsteps close behind.

———— · ————

The dreams never stopped, faces known and unknown and always one in particular. The sounds were acute and many times Bec tried to answer a phone that rang and rang but she could never get there. Her mind made other worlds as she lay paralysed by sleep in her room. A huge wave might rear up on a mysterious sea and she in a flimsy boat waiting for it to crush all that lay in its path. Cars refused to start or if they did the brakes failed. Once a baby fell from her grasp down a bottomless cliff and she woke with a pillow soaked in tears.

Bec slipped in and out of dreams through the night, never sure what was sleep or wakefulness unless she hauled her consciousness through the fog and pinched herself to return to her body.

The sounds were worse somehow. The knock on a door she couldn't see, a siren wailing in her ears for an emergency that never arrived, the groaning of a dark, dark woman who held her head in her hands and cried. The moaning was quieter now but pitiful just the same and it went on and on. She dragged herself out of the dream, fixing her eyes on the soft glimmer that shone from the moon around the border of the curtains.

She sat up. The sound was still there. A muffled, low keening that came from inside the house. It was dark outside her bedroom and she ran her hand along the wall to find her way. She tapped at Jo's door and the crying stopped.

'You okay?' She waited. No reply.

Bec headed back towards her room. It was not her business. She hardly knew the girl after all. She focused on the grit sticking to her bare feet as she padded along the empty hall. 'Oh heck,' she muttered and turned around.

Opening the door a few inches, she leaned in. Jo had her face pressed into the pillow. Illuminated numbers on the bedside clock clicked over to two in the morning.

'Hey there,' she ventured in a low voice. 'Don't mean to be intrusive but I'm a bit concerned.'

No answer. Bec stepped lightly over and sat on the side of the bed. When she placed her hand on the girl's leg she could feel her shaking with the attempt at holding in sobs.

'You don't have to tell me about it but please, come here.' She held out her arms and Jo folded herself into them, collapsing into hiccupping sobs. Bec stroked her hair and held her tight. The embroidered dress was twisted around her but the bathers were not in sight.

'Oh sweetheart, whatever's gone on, it's obviously been really upsetting.'

'You were right. I shouldn't have gone.' The crying cut off anything more she might have said.

'Are you hurt, Jo?' Bec was scrambling to think. The hospital was small and she didn't know if it would be open overnight. The police station was unmanned but what good would it do even if someone was on duty.

'No … yes. I don't know.'

Jo pulled away and sat up in the bed.

'I'm so embarrassed, Bec. Thanks for the hug but I just need some time to myself.'

'Well, I'm just down the hall if you change your mind.' Bec closed the bedroom door behind her and left. The wretchedness on the girl's face lingered on her retinas when she closed her eyes.

She was surprised next day when Sheryl turned up in the bar mid-morning.

'Thought you were on afternoon shift today?'

'Jo's off sick. Jack will cover my shift this arvo. I thought you'd know.' Sheryl searched Bec's face then gave her hip a playful bump. 'You really shouldn't take up poker, my girl. What's up?'

'I don't know what to do. Something happened

last night with that bloke and Jo was distressed but she wouldn't tell me anything. Plus, Dave's away.'

'That's no good. What if he's hurt her? She's too young to deal with this on her own.'

'I know. I'll try to talk to her again later.'

She trudged up the road a bit after three o'clock, walked past the woman on the verandah and went straight home.

Jo was in bed, motionless, the curtains still closed.

'Can I get you anything?'

'No thanks.'

It was like speaking to an injured kitten picked up from the side of the road.

'Dave's away till tomorrow, Jo, so I'm not leaving your room till I'm satisfied that you really are okay.'

Bec waited. She coaxed. She waited some more. Eventually Jo consented to being led to the kitchen for a sandwich.

'He was stronger than me.' She turned her head away.

The sandwich lay uneaten on the plate.

'I'm so ashamed. If I hadn't gone with him, it never would have happened.'

'Jo, whatever he did, it wasn't your fault.' It sounded lame. For heaven's sake, the Federal Government had been appointing men as Ministers responsible for Women's Affairs. She was trying to show the girl her rights mattered when at the highest level it was plain that women were of little account.

'He had me on the ground. I was screaming, fighting, but he was too strong. I couldn't stop him.'

'Oh Jo, that's just terrible. Then you had to sit beside him while he drove you home?'

'No, I couldn't stand being near him. When he'd finished I grabbed my dress and ran off into town.'

A woman had been closing her café and had seen him following Jo, trying to get her into his vehicle.

'She took me to the police station at Kununurra and the duty constable drove me back. It was pretty clear he thought I was just an hysterical girl.'

She pushed up her sleeve and held out her narrow wrist. A purple bruise spread in a band around the flesh.

'The worst part is I'll have to face him in the bar.'

'Jo, what he's done, it's a crime. You're not the one who needs to feel bad.'

Bec believed it yet she couldn't stop her mind flashing to the interview she'd done with a female police prosecutor a few years earlier. She'd asked the sergeant, off the record, if a sister or friend had been raped would she encourage them to report it. 'No, I wouldn't. The process hurts more than helps.'

Jo sucked in her breath. 'I can't go scurrying back to Auckland. I just have to let it go and move on.'

'Will you tell Dave?'

'He doesn't need to know.'

'Have you thought about the fact that you're not the only one? He's likely done this before and will do it again.'

'You think I haven't?' The raw anger flattened Bec against the wall.

'He was rough. I saw his face,' she screamed. 'He got off on holding me down.'

All the air drained out of the girl. 'You know how this works. We swam naked in the lake. If I report the rape, they'll just say I was leading him on.'

Bec had the urge to stand up right then and march across the road to her shady spot on the worn pavers, to the cushion of peaceful nothingness that waited there. It took all her resolve to remain in the chair beside Jo.

'At least tell Sheryl. We can't do anything to make it go away but we can keep an eye out for you around the pub.'

Bec was expecting her to say no.

'Okay, but I don't want to see her face when she finds out. I'd rather you tell her for me.'

Bec sealed the pact with a squeeze on the girl's shoulder.

'I'll do it tonight so she can warn any others off that bastard.'

Sheryl was still incandescent with rage when Bec left the Three Mile hours later. 'As soon as I get the chance, I'm going to spit in his beer.'

Jo had retreated to her room. Bec turned off the lights in the kitchen and trailed down the hall. She slumped onto the bed; her body exhausted despite jagged energy rushing in her veins. Her eyes rested on a couple of cardboard boxes, dumped in the corner when she had unloaded the van weeks ago. They were a sign of another lifetime, on the other side of a chasm that had opened up behind her as she fled.

She'd only had fifteen minutes or so to pack essentials from the West Leederville house, her ears scanning for sound. She had heard a car go by. Then a pause, before a flock of rainbow lorikeets started squealing as their sharp beaks ripped into the red flowering gum on the street verge. Every nerve had strained to hear. There'd been no attention left for checking what she grabbed in her hands and had shoved into the boxes.

She opened the top one and began aimlessly drawing out the contents. An old notepad fell out, scribbled words combined with random shorthand, her secret language to record what she encountered at work and to hide personal thoughts when they couldn't be contained.

She flipped through it then froze. She thought she had torn out the page. She usually did when she wrote something out properly. It was a poem.

> *I am not writing about fear*
> *because as soon as I do*
> *it gets an invitation*
> *to dine on me.*
>
> *Fear makes a meal from*
> *the softness. Soon I will be*
> *all holes like Swiss cheese*
> *without even a curd.*
>
> *It steals through the grey.*
> *Yet I hear a voice say:*
> *'Put out the best china, girl,*
> *and open the door'.*

The notepad landed back in the box with a thud. She didn't need to look any more.

7

AH, THE SPECIAL FINCHES, HOW Lily had loved them. She was an old woman now, stiff as she sat on the chair, her companion Bec quiet nearby, others now gone. In the beginning, the bright birds had been her only friends.

Her thoughts often looped back through the past and sometimes, when Bec settled on the pavers she thought she might share a memory or two with the young woman, but then stopped herself. The ancestors pulled in a different direction for now. They would let Lily know when they needed her help. The time would come, it was surely the reason they had drawn Bec to her.

As the two women sat in the pleasure of nowhere else to be, Lily half-dozed. The spool of memories rolled forward, absorbing her in a way that often felt more real than her days limited by her old body. The memories grew stronger somehow in the young woman's presence. She leaned back and gave herself over to them once more, seeing her new home that first night in Wyndham.

———•———

She had arrived in 1921, the Year of the Rooster with its busy, demanding energies. Downpours rattled the tin roof as the monsoon rolled in, while she explored the living quarters at the back of the shop.

The space was more spacious than the shanty she had shared with Mother. She now had the good fortune of two small bedrooms, as well as a kitchen and living space boasting a table, four straight-backed wooden chairs, a bench next to the oven providing space for preparing food, and two padded chairs with worn arms.

Yet she lay awake for hours beside her new husband, three decades older, questioning why she had agreed to the arrangement.

In the orange first light of morning, she opened the back door while waiting for the pot to boil for tea. Steam was rising from the sodden ground and a light breeze shook the last of the raindrops from leaves on a small cabbage gum that had defied conditions to reach a little higher than the roof. A sudden motion to the left drew her attention. There, behind the neighbouring shop, on the sun-bleached limb of a straggling dead tree, a row of bright birds greeted her. Their impossible colours spoke of promise after so much grief.

In the following months she discovered that the trappers were drawn to them, too, and it pained her, looking back across the decades to that rain-fresh morning, that thousands had been caught in cages and shipped to faraway lands, pets for display in wealthy homes. Baubles for the rich and nothing more.

Her sweethearts were the zebra finches with their blunt red beaks and black and white striped tails. Her true love, though, she saved for the ones most desired by the traders—the Gouldian finches, messengers of joy in their rainbow plumage and the first finches to welcome her as she began her new life. Their faces were black and wings bright green. On each chest was a vivid purple patch and below it, molten gold.

In those early days the Gouldians had come for the seed she spread on the ground near the back door, bobbing greedily to snatch what they could, heads twitching back and forth as they kept a lookout. Occasionally one with a scarlet face would arrive and it made her happy to see it was treated no differently by others in the flock.

Memories of those stolen moments with the colourful throng were still strong but despite the government clamping down on the trappers her favourite birds were mostly gone. Back then it was hope that was endangered. Now it was the birds themselves.

They were on a list that sometimes rolled through her mind, the many faces that had come into her life then fallen into the arms of time. Her personal name was there, too. Hee, lotus flower, though everyone had called her Lily.

An image of a lotus flower bloomed in her mind.

It was gone when she stirred, disturbed from her reverie by the scrape of Bec's sandals as she stood to leave. She watched her cross the road, then slipped back into the twilight world of the past, where beginnings merged with endings.

Her own life had been marked with an ending before she had even drawn her first breath. She had come in one door in Darwin, late in 1900, soon after Father, See Hoo Teung, left this world by another.

Her first memory was of Mother, Que Gnit, taking her to Guangzhou when she was two. They had stayed for four years, helping care for Grandmother until she died. It was the only time her Chinese name had been used in public and the same could be said for the city, which the westerners preferred to call Canton.

Her father had not been wealthy enough to keep a wife and family in China and a second in Australia, as some did, so there was no son. It was left to her and Mother to light the incense and pray at his altar.

When the ritual was over, Mother would share stories of his life so that Lily could draw closer to her father.

'That way, when your time is over, you will know him in the afterlife.'

He had been a miner at the Pine Creek goldfields and when the gold ran out had slaved on the railway from Port Darwin, though they called the town Palmerston then. After that, he had dug wells and irrigation ditches for market gardens on the fringe of the city.

'Those fine men from the Pearl River Delta, they feel the pulse of earth and water,' Mother would say. She also said, though he died with a fever, it was exhaustion that crept in at the stroke of midnight to steal him away.

Lily was six when they returned to Darwin and a one-room home with the back wall fashioned from flattened kerosene tins. The companies and bureaucrats had been happy to use the sweating men to dig, do the dirty work, carry loads under a hot sun and to die before their time, but what was delivered at such a price only went one way.

They returned from Guangzhou to a country that did not want them. The newspapers called them celestials and said they were dishonest, treacherous, degraded, while the government praised the laws it made to pretend it was a White Australia.

What was a widowed Chinese woman with a young child to do? Mother abided by the customs she had grown up with in her home country, where widows were discouraged from remarrying. She had no choice but to flow with circumstances, as she explained to her daughter.

'We are still here, we go on until we meet our own time, beloved child. This is the destiny I have been given.'

She leased four hectares of land and began planting. Soon rows of mango trees, guava, star fruit and custard apple had been laid out and ginger, chillies and garlic grew in neat garden beds. Chickens enriched the soil and produced eggs.

Though she was small, Lily was expected to help. As Mother worked her way between the rows with the hoe, the girl followed, gathering weeds into a bucket. She was strong enough to cart buckets of water from the well and, after compost was shovelled from the pit into a barrow, helped spread it around the fruit trees with a rake that had a handle cut down to her size.

The chickens were kept in a wire netting enclosure with a roosting shed at the end. As Lily walked from town to the garden in the pale first light of morning, her hands could already feel the smooth, warm eggs she would collect when she and Mother arrived. Each egg, waiting where there had been nothing but clean hay spread in the roosting boxes each evening, was a thing of magic, a wonder conjured from vegetable scraps, caterpillars and shell grit.

During the day the chickens were allowed to forage in sections of the garden where beds were fallow or crops newly harvested. Occasionally an unexpected egg was left on a mound of soil or leaves. Once a crow swooped down while the chickens squawked, but by the time Lily reached it, the black raider had eaten its bounty, a golden yolk, and was flapping skyward. She watched over the chickens more carefully after that.

The pair worked till mid-morning then ate and dozed till mid-afternoon before picking up their tools and working till the light faded.

In summer when the custard apples ripened Mother would pick one warm from the tree when they ate their lunch. Buddha's head, Mother called them, and would scoop out the velvet flesh and spoon all its sweetness into her daughter's open mouth. Twice a week they picked fruit, harvested vegetables, and loaded the bounty into two woven baskets along with the eggs.

Mother balanced the baskets on a bamboo pole, carrying on her shoulders all that kept them from destitution. When the gods were kind and the garden flush she sold fresh produce to businesses in Chinatown and a few restaurants who served the wealthy. Such a tiny frame bearing the weight as she walked down the road, wearing a cone-shaped straw hat, traditional black trousers flapping with each step, her long white shirt always clean.

She did it all for Lily, who even then thanked Mother every day, the child understanding she would not survive without such patient labour. In return Mother gave the special smile, reserved only for Lily, as they straightened their backs or leaned for a moment on the tool shed wall in a patch of shade.

Mother would have been only thirty years at best but toil had scoured the soft contours of her face and hot air dried her skin, leading the child to form the view that she was an old woman. Not that it mattered to Lily, who was proud of the dignity and honesty in Mother's productivity.

It came as a surprise, when Lily approached adulthood, that Mother was determined to spare her the rough work of a market garden.

'Though you will be a wife and mother you must have a skill to help support your family.'

'But Mother I would rather keep working with you.'

'That is not the way of things. Your father and my parents came to this country so the children could do better. It honours your father to work with clean hands.'

Mother found her a job as a seamstress in a tailor shop, working the first two hours each day in the steamy laundry out the back. For two years she learned the feel of scissors against cloth and the rhythm that propelled the needle along the seams until she could sew a man's suit in less than a day.

During that time the girl was shed like a discarded snakeskin and she came of marriageable age. With the shortage of Chinese women in Darwin there would be no delay.

She had just turned seventeen when she arrived home from work one afternoon to find Mother back from the garden before Lily had even begun preparing their evening meal. They sat in the doorway, Mother's face captured by a serious conversation needing to be set free.

'I gave your name and birthdate to the matchmaker and he has selected a suitable husband. He has studied the year, month and day of birth for each of you with great care. It is a favourable match.'

Tears sprang up in Lily's eyes as she swallowed a protest.

'Last week I asked the fortune teller to consult the tung shing to consider the most favourable wedding day. I am pleased to say it will be in three weeks.'

It was too soon, Lily wanted to say. She was not ready, had not expected the matter of marriage to be broached for one or possibly two more years.

She looked at Mother, who was clearly relieved that her efforts had come to fruition despite the absence of a father to assist in decision-making. It would be a great offence to resist.

With much work to do at the tailor shop there was barely time to make a new skirt before the ceremony. Chin Wah Shoue was six years older and although the correct steps had been taken to ensure it was a good match the marriage carried no guarantee of affection or consideration.

The betrothed had two brief meetings and little conversation in the following weeks. The night before the wedding, Mother took Lily aside.

'I know this is not what you hoped for.'

Her heart quickened. Mother had recognised the mistake, had changed her mind about insisting on marriage when her daughter was not ready.

'Trust me, child, all will be well. Marry first, then love.'

Lily had misunderstood. 'It is too soon.' She broke down, sobbing.

———•———

During the ceremony, all Lily had seen was a stranger,

the otherness of a man, not something she had experienced, given the absence of a father.

Yet as the weeks passed, she was relieved to find that a natural warmth began to arise with the man who would be, from now on, the central force in her world.

Gradually she discovered that her husband had many fine qualities, including patience with his wife. Known as the Fat Cook, he was respected insofar as a Chinaman could be. As a younger man he had worked at the popular Hotel Victoria, then for the Northern Territory Administrator at Government House, preparing English delicacies in the kitchen of an imposing stone residence, built by Chinese masons labouring alongside prison gangs.

He had ambition, a good thing in a man, and soon after they were married left his job to start the Australia Café with a friend in Cavenagh Street, at the centre of China Town.

Her husband's long hours in the new venture left her lonely much of the time so it was a comfort when she knew a baby was on the way. Their daughter arrived with the first rain of the wet season, sliding into Mother's hands as water rushed from the roof onto parched ground.

Such a precious one, the girl was sweet-natured, soft as finest Canton crêpe. They called her Goot Song. In the early mornings Lily loved to lean down with the baby on her lap and breathe in the magnolia smell of her hair.

The joy was a new experience, rising unbidden despite the exhaustion and the little one waking often in the night to feed. Some days she walked with the baby early, greeting Mother at the market garden then staying to rest in the shade of the tallest mango tree at the height of the sun. It allowed her husband to catch up on sleep in their two-room tenement house after finishing late in the restaurant kitchen.

When Mother lifted the girl to see all the green growth in the orchard, love stretched Lily's heart, pumping it so full she found it hard to tell if it was pleasure or pain.

Goot Song had changed the marriage, too, brought new closeness that Lily had not expected to find between husband and wife. They were truly blessed and every morning she gave thanks for her good fortune at the corner shrine in their living space, lighting the incense and watching the smoke waft up to the celestial heavens, drawing the ancestors close.

It was the matchmaker who had led her to her husband, yet Lily reserved the deepest gratitude for Mother and her instinct in understanding that it was the right time, after all, for her daughter to flourish as a woman.

———— • ————

The child was not quite once around the sun when on a Wednesday, just before dawn, Lily was dragged from deep sleep by a burst of thumping at the door.

'It's the police. Let us in, we have news for you.' One voice, then a second.

She bundled the baby in great haste but confused and not fully awake, failed to grasp what the officers were saying. She accompanied them regardless, compelled by the urgency of their words.

The policemen delivered her and the baby to the hospital and it was only then, hemmed in by white walls in the foyer, that she began to grasp a mighty severance had sliced through her life as she slept.

A doctor came through double doors and gave a hurried report on the situation then led her down a long corridor, while Goot Song slept, curled inside her mother's embrace.

On the ward Wah Shoue lay quite still on his back, arms resting on top of a neatly turned down white sheet. The sheet covered a hospital gown and underneath that, a wide dressing over the soft tissue of her husband's abdomen, silently bleeding along the trail of a revolver bullet lodged against his spine.

'He has slipped into a coma.'

The doctor looked away and signalled to a woman in a stiff white uniform, seated at a desk where the sole lamp threw shadows into the room even as daylight began to brighten the windows. The nurse came over and pulled a chair across for Lily. Around them other male patients slept or sat up in silence against their pillows, eyes dull. The nurse pulled a screen around the couple then she and the doctor hurried off.

Lily continued to stand motionless in the dim light, one arm holding her daughter against her shoulder.

'Husband, I'm here.' She spoke in a whisper. When he failed to respond she stroked his face, leaning close as he took small sips of air, each with a long gap between. She willed him to breathe more deeply.

She sat beside him and held one of his hands, alert for the tiniest movement that might be a sign he knew she had come. His hand was warm though without the slightest twitch or flutter.

The nurse returned in swift strides to take his temperature, lifting aside his arm to secure a thermometer against his armpit. The disturbance failed to rouse him. Lily pictured the shrine at home, summoned all the imagination she could, took herself there to fall on her knees and pray for deliverance of her husband.

She prayed and rocked the girl even though the child continued to sleep. The face of the man beside her was growing dull, losing the distinctiveness she had come to love. As the birds woke and flew from their trees, he lifted away with them like a kite. Though Lily held on with all her might, the string slipped from her grasp. Goot Song stirred and whimpered as her father's spirit passed by.

Lily left the hospital a widow, not yet twenty years old.

In the hours and days that followed it was a difficult thing to fathom, why an upright man such as her husband should die young, why she deserved such brutal punishment. She had been a dutiful wife and a good daughter. She had honoured the ancestors as Mother had taught her, yet evil spirits still sought her out, through the disordered mind of a man who held a gun.

She was numb as she read the newspaper report two days' later while Mother tended to the child. Her husband and his co-proprietor had farewelled final customers for the evening, cleaned the kitchen, locked the restaurant door and, on a whim, gone to the local movie hall. It was an innocent act. He could not have known that the urge came from dark spirits that had seen fit to guide him there, leading him to the wrong seat.

As she read, Lily understood now that he had been a good man to the end. He had recognised almost immediately that he was at the mercy of evil forces and tried to avoid what was coming, for the newspaper reported he was crouching on the floor when the bullet struck him.

'Why, Mother? He has done no harm to anybody.' She wept anew.

The police visited two weeks later to say they had arrested a man for the murder. They had pieced together the facts, which they laid out for her as though they placed vegetables in a row, ready for chopping.

A noisy scuffle had broken out as the feature movie began, caused by the accused's attempt to exact payback for money stolen by a well-known thief from a nearby gambling den. A shot was fired and missed its target, instead propelled across two rows of tiered seats.

She imagined the bullet in flight, seeking out her husband, fulfilling the destiny it aimed to deliver.

———•———

The trial began the following month. Lily did not wish to attend, a Chinese woman in a courtroom full of white men, but she could not abandon Wah Shoue in the closing moments of his story.

The medical officer was direct at first in describing the injury. 'The bullet pierced the left arm.'

Then, standing in the witness box, he shifted his weight deliberately from one foot to the other, clearing his throat. His next words rose over the stiff wigs and collars to fill the room with a poetry of death.

'The bullet went on till it caused a groove in the surface of the third lumbar vertebra and reached the ascending abdominal aorta. The end was predictable with so much blood pooling internally from the wound.'

The power of it shook Lily loose from her stupor.

All the days that followed cast themselves off from the calendar while time became one moment only and that moment swelled with grief and fear. She was rice paper, her tears fraying the edges and weakening the fibres binding her together.

She did not go back to the courtroom when the jury returned its verdict. The twelve pale-skinned men acquitted the accused. It was as though her husband had been murdered a second time.

Soon after, Mother insisted that the proper movement of qi energy should be restored through action to help her mend.

'You must get up from your bed and take the girl across the sea to his family. He was their son and they should know the part of him that will go on.'

'I don't know that I can. It's not in me to be strong like the tiger you are.'

Mother was kind, as always, and firm. 'That is not the way of things, daughter. We are a sapling bending to the weight of snow or the force of the wind and it is in the bending we grow a strong trunk.'

In the absence of any purpose of her own, Lily acquiesced.

She paid to have identity photographs taken of her with the baby. A reference for her good character was obtained from the senior sergeant at the police station and another from the former Mayor, a long-time customer of the market garden.

She attached it all to the application for exemption from the dictation test. The forms were completed with great care, using a fresh nib to sign in her best copperplate. Without an exemption she would not dare travel because she would be barred from re-entry to the country.

Everyone knew the test was simply an excuse to turn the Chinese away from Australian shores, and if there was any doubt, a drunken customer had set her straight years earlier while collecting his new suit. It seemed to amuse him as he told her the dictation test was sometimes delivered in Portuguese or French. Not that she needed any proof of its true purpose. Hundreds had been forced to undertake the test in the previous decade and not a single person had passed.

To her relief the exemption papers were duly signed and she was free to make the journey.

Over the decades since she had kept a copy of each of the two photographs in an envelope at the bottom of the carved camphor box in her wardrobe. In the images her daughter's bright eyes were forever glancing to the left while she would always be the shy nineteen-year-old mother, dark hair pulled back in a bun, head dipped slightly to avoid the photographer's stare.

The back of one of the official documents carried her thumbprints in ink with Goot Song's thumb smudges nestled alongside. She could still conjure up the sensation in her hand as she took one delicate thumb at a time and placed it on the ink pad then pressed it to the paper to make each mark beside hers.

Their documents were in order for a fifteen-month absence when they embarked in the middle of July on the *Mataram*. The steamer, like her, had suffered a catastrophe. The previous year it had been returning from its usual run to Singapore when fifty passengers and crew fell ill with the Spanish flu. The vessel attracted attention as the first infected ship to enter Australian waters. By the time it reached its final destination of Sydney, many more on board were ill and the captain was ordered to drop anchor at the Quarantine Station so passengers could be isolated and the ship fumigated.

It was an inconvenience to be sure for Chinese families booked on the next sailing, but hardly a disaster until the first whisps of smoke were detected from cargo hold number two, filled with rubber, spirits, copra and other flammable materials.

The blaze that followed soon overwhelmed the crew, who had almost given up when reinforcements arrived on a firefighting boat. Jets of water pumped into the cargo hold caused the steamer to list and the crew feared she would now sink. Against the odds, the *Mataram* remained upright.

Reports of the drama had been closely followed by Darwin's Chinese population, many of whom had travelled on the ship for annual pilgrimages home. When the repaired steamer sailed back to Darwin earlier in the year, it had been welcomed with great fanfare.

Now, Lily stood on the deck for her departure, Goot Song close in her arms, trying not to think about the ship's past. She focussed on the vibration of its engines and the shudder as it pulled away from the dock.

The horn gave one long blast that slowly faded and above the hum that lingered she heard the vessel singing to her from the waterline, up through the hull, a song of its distress and the mending that had followed. She began to pray as the ship continued its lament, pleading for whatever it would take to shore up the weakened places in her character.

When they reached China, she had been afraid her husband's parents might want to keep Goot Song. Fortunately they did not wish for the burden of a girl. The trick of it still astonished her, the way she had held onto fears that were of no consequence while the real threat was hiding in dirty water in the fields where her husband's father worked.

Day after day Baba, as he insisted she call him, returned at dusk from the fields carrying corn or wombok, maybe a few yams, in damp hands crusted with soil. Day after day he handed the vegetables to his wife then took his granddaughter onto his lap to look through her eyes into those of his son. Not even he could see, however, the germs hiding underneath his nails and in the folds of his skin.

Lily remembered drifting, dreamlike, for most of her time away and on the return voyage. It was the customs official who struck her awake, not with his bare hand but with the pencil he held, though it did not leave the page of her papers as he processed her re-entry to Darwin. The force of his action left a trail of letters across the first page. It sucked the breath from her. *The child did not return with mother.* Then two pages later—*child reported died in China.*

The toddler had fallen ill within weeks of their arrival. At first Lily had thought her little one would pull through because many with dysentery did, but Goot Song was still young and the journey to China had sapped her energy.

Perhaps, too, the girl's father had been unable to find

peace until he called her to his side. It would have been better if the girl had been saved and the flame of her own life extinguished to keep him company, but the choice was never hers to make.

So it was that Lily had returned to an empty home. A ghost mother, ghost wife.

DISSOLUTION

Lightning strikes expected, accompanied by thunder.
Stay inside, away from windows and doors.

9

J O WAS ON A DAY off and Bec had just trudged in the door. Dave was at a loose end. 'Come on, we'll go for a swim at The Grotto. The water's always cool there.'

It was the first Bec had heard of the place but Dave knew where to go. They climbed into the chopper company's 4WD Troopie, big enough to transport rig workers to Kununurra Airport.

About thirty kilometres out of town he swung off the highway to the right and followed a dusty road that stopped in the middle of nowhere. All she could see was a rusting forty-four-gallon drum secured as a rubbish bin by a leaning frame. Not obvious enough, she gathered, from the empty wine casks, food wrappers and toilet paper scattered across the baked ground.

Dave led the way to a few stone steps that hung off a cliff edge, seemingly in mid-air. A dark gash spread out below, with overhangs and rock shelves plummeting over each other to the ravine floor. At the bottom, more than a hundred metres down the sheer cliff face, a waterhole waited, most of it hidden from the sun.

Jo leaned over and saw the stairs snake steeply back

and forth then disappear. 'There's no handrail. I'm not going down there.'

'You'll be fine. I'll go first. Just lean into the rock face and watch your feet instead of the water.' Dave took her towel and she followed, Bec at the rear.

The stairs had been sliced from the cubic rock of the chasm wall, in places shrinking to barely the width of one person's feet. They descended slowly, Bec not daring to check the view. The switchbacks were tight and on one she paused momentarily, glancing up to see a bottle tree flaunting itself, a lone rebel on a high rock ledge.

Near the bottom they skirted boulders and emerged onto a small patch of level ground. A water monitor on a rock near the line of shade flattened its scales and pointed its head towards the sun. Bec slipped off her sandals and dipped toes into the edge of the pool, expecting the temperature to be yet another local exaggeration, except it was cool. The other two laughed at her disbelief.

'A couple more weeks into the dry season and it'll get stagnant. The waterfall hasn't flowed for a while,' Dave said.

'A regular tour guide, you are,' Bec teased to fill the silence that surrounded Jo.

She peeled off her shirt and shorts and launched in at a shady spot, treading water while looking up at tree roots and vines swinging against fractured rocks.

'What, no togs?' Dave was quizzical as Jo splashed in wearing shorts and a camisole top.

Bec had lingered on the shop verandah going home from work and the peacefulness was still with her, a raft on which she floated with little effort. She skimmed across the waterhole, the bottom dropping from sight as she breast-stroked further out.

A few spindly trees grew out horizontally from the cliff-face, ignoring the laws of gravity, their long, thin limbs outstretched. The leaves cast lacy patterns onto the water and they parted as she swam into the light on the far side of the pool, drawn to the trees by the impossibility of nature's green existence where no soil could be seen. She had fallen into a dream.

She floated and turned her face up to the sun, heat from above and coolness below pricking in equal measure on her skin. A rush of aliveness began at her feet and fingertips then ambushed every cell as she closed her eyes and let the sweet relief of it sweep through. Heart, lungs, liver, she felt them release, refresh, and find equilibrium again.

She flipped over and swam back into the shade, disturbing the water as little as possible. The hush of the walled place had quieted the brother and sister, who floated nearby with only wet heads visible.

She rolled onto her back again, arms outstretched, eyes closed, surrendering to the deliciousness of buoyancy that came naturally to her body. It was minutes before she could bring herself to open her eyes again and when she did, they found their way above, towards the atrium of sky.

The edge of the ravine cut a jagged boundary, black against the bright light, and she traced it along the lip to the point where it dipped to meet the start of the stairs. There the contrast of rock and blue sky was broken by the outline of a man. With a jolt she registered the stance and profile.

The Grotto closed in around her. She struggled across the pool, arms and legs beating out of rhythm, and left the water quickly. Ignoring her towel, she pulled on clothes over wet bathers. When she looked up the figure was gone.

'Finished already?' The voice echoed from across the waterhole, where Jo was waving.

She and her brother had swum to the opposite side and were resting on a low rock ledge in the shade. Bec waved back before skirting the flat ground at the end of the pool to reach a section of overhang against the wall. She crouched beneath it, pressing her back against the rough stone so hard it hurt, waiting for discomfort to quell the trembling.

A murk filled her mind and obscured whatever was beyond it. Out of the muddy grey emerged a swirl of pixels, shifting and weaving till they formed a shape. She remembered how she had wanted to believe it wasn't real, yet the shape formed an object that had a name. The name gave it weight, made it solid.

It was a knife.

She had been making their bed in Perth when she'd found it under his pillow, inches from where she had laid her head. The form was beautifully crafted, elegant in its design, with a slim handle and narrow blade ending with a gentle upwards curve.

Staring at it, a stark intrusion in her life, she had sensed how balanced and light it would be to hold in her hand. Then she had flinched as she'd imagined swift strokes slicing strips of flesh from barramundi or trout, as only a filleting knife could.

The image was still sharp in her memory. It was Dave

who dislodged it, consigning it back to a cave in her mind as his big voice bounced through the air, a lifeline thrown from the base of the stairs where he stood.

'Hey lazy bones. Don't know about you but we're heading up.'

They spoke little as Dave drove, the three of them lined up in the front of the 4WD, Bec desperately wishing she'd insisted on taking a seat on one of the hard bench seats in the back.

'The swim's chilled us all out.'

The two women left him to his conclusion as he swung the shuddering vehicle from the dirt track onto the main road.

Bec was jittery. After they had climbed back up the stairs to the 4WD, she had scanned for any sign of the man she'd seen, hoping to find a stranger who was a similar height and build to her husband.

The area had been empty.

Her imagination was getting carried away, she told herself, yet every road bump was another voice tapping with the truth.

Jo had her own reason to be quiet, Bec surmised, doubtless minimising the risk of her tone giving anything away to her brother. It was hard to disguise a voice. Harder than you'd expect because it had a signature that flew out of your mouth the same way that ink flowed from a pen into the pattern of your name.

If Bec had needed proof, she got it when she did a favour for a friend before the move west, a media skills course for volunteers running local groups her friend co-ordinated as a community development officer. After lunch Bec had videotaped mock radio interviews. Every person who took part had been shocked to hear how distinctive they sounded.

So two years earlier, when she'd finally summoned the courage to make the anonymous phone call to police headquarters, it came as no surprise that even though she had strangled her voice a little, the sound that came out belonged to nobody else but her.

She had asked to be put through to the internal investigations unit, though she wasn't sure what was driving her action. Just as well it hadn't been hope.

'You really want to go ahead with a complaint against your husband? He's a serving police officer. You do understand he could lose his job.' Steely authority in the man's voice.

Bec's hand had slammed down the phone before she'd had the thought to hang up.

Another place, another time, another woman back then. She leaned her head against the seat and pretended to doze, her neck unable to carry the weight of her skull or the worry. She wasn't sure she had the energy to keep running. She certainly wasn't ready to leave the measure of comfort she had found in people who made no demands of her.

The fears rose up like shadows, each nothing of itself, merely a representation, yet carrying the form of something more threatening. They were impossible to hold back. There'd been a time when she had tried to engage with them, but no more. They had worn her down.

She would keep to her routine for now because she didn't know what else to do. She longed for tomorrow's work at the pub to be done, when she could steer out of turbulence and step into clear air on the shop verandah.

In the moment, eyes closed, it was her mother's voice that came to her.

'You've made your bed, now lie in it.'

She was tired of trying to figure out how to survive. It felt like, one way or another, it was all she'd done since Daniel died. Best not to think at all.

Back at the house they pooled the last of their food before the grocery delivery next day and shared a simple meal of tinned fish, mayonnaise and Mexican beans. Jo went to bed early while Bec tucked her legs underneath her on the couch and tried to focus on her book.

Dave had gone to do laundry in a shed out the back, tackling the top-loading washing machine that deserved a heritage listing rather than armfuls of sweaty clothes. When he reappeared his face was troubled as he leaned on the doorframe.

'Didn't pump out the water, again?'

'All done. Everything's on the clothesline.' He straightened up and turned to go then thought better of it and came over to sit on the arm of the couch.

'Do you know what's up with Jo?'

'What makes you think something's up?'

'C'mon Bec, I know you're a journalist but you don't need to turn the questions on me. She's way too quiet and isn't saying why.'

'The trip with her boyfriend the other night didn't go well.' She composed her face into features she hoped would look neutral.

'On a scale of one to ten, how badly did it go?'

'Dave, this is the last thing I'm going to say.' She glared at him. 'It was a minus ten.'

He disappeared down the hall and she heard the rumble of voices ramp up to shouting. She went to her room, jammed on headphones and turned up the volume of the cassette player to a deafening beat. Which meant she didn't catch the sound, minutes later, of Jo sobbing in Dave's arms when he finally made it to the other side of her flimsy attempt at a barricade.

Bec climbed into bed an hour later, the house now quiet save for the thrum of the ceiling fan above. Her ears were still hurting from the bass thump of the Rolling Stones.

At the pub next day, she steered clear of the open areas and was happy for once to restock the wall of bar fridges, taking her time unpacking cartons in the storeroom.

Every day she filled the fridges before opening time, only to see them empty again, needing a top-up before she left in the afternoons. She was Sisyphus endlessly rolling a boulder up the hill with none of the muscle and not even a damn stone, only empty stubbies and beer cans rolling back down. Once or twice she hadn't kept up the pace so the wrath of the drinkers had rained down on her head instead. They could survive the frenzy on tissue and muscle in the boning room at the meatworks but not the indignity of warm beer.

If the bar wasn't pumping, Sheryl or Jo might catch the clink of warm bottles as she thrust them across wire shelves behind the rows of cold ones and they would pull faces through the glass door.

Sometimes she enjoyed the cool draught so much

when she opened a fridge that she forgot herself, pausing for so long that condensation ran down the inside of the door opening into the bar. Jo was on her mind when she did it this time, how relieved the girl had been at breakfast now her brother knew her secret.

'He was great, Bec. I should have known he'd understand. Says for my sake he'll try not to kill him.' She had managed a wry smile.

A brother who was around and one who was supportive. A unicorn on either count.

She was still on pause with the last door open when through the condensation the outline of a man's upper body, head on a familiar tilt, took shape through the glass. She quickly shut the door and involuntarily took a step back, forgetting the half empty carton at her feet. With a flurry of arms and legs she fell back onto the concrete, the breath hammered from her by the impact with the floor, fortuitous because it prevented her from accidentally calling out.

She'd pushed away the memory from the Grotto of the figure hovering above the waterhole. Had managed to convince herself it had been a mix of mirage and imagination. Such fragile conviction could not withstand this sighting.

She limped down the loading ramp and into the kitchen via the back door. It was lunchtime and the kitchen hand was ferrying food orders to the men lined up on stools along the bar. Pete was mopping sweat from his brow with a tea towel he'd tucked into his belt. The kitchen hand was hurrying past, balancing a tray with three baskets of crumbed seafood thawed by the smoky oil in the deep fryer.

'Anyone interesting in the bar today?' She breathed slowly. 'Thought I saw a uniform. Cops hanging about?'

'Nah, just the usual. And a couple of out of towners.' The young bloke threw a mock glance of admiration in Pete's direction. 'No doubt lured here by the sterling reputation of the food.'

The cook flicked the tea towel at him and sent him on his way. 'He's lazy enough, Bec. Don't encourage him to stop and yack.'

Her shift was almost finished. She only had the pool to do, then she could get out of there, go home, shut herself in the bedroom. But the thought of the exposed gravel up the top of the stairs was almost as bad as the open street and the sixty-five steps it would take to get home.

A bubbling pot of potatoes gurgled on the row of gas burners near Pete. The water churning, busy, going nowhere just like her. The worst thing about a lie, if you'd told it to yourself, was that somehow you weren't worth the truth and no amount of convincing yourself could make it otherwise. There would be no walking away from a life she didn't want. Or the uncertainty of what she may or may not have done with a knife.

She did a quick mental audit. The van was parked out of sight behind her house. She had been careful not to register her new address or share it with anyone. She hadn't even resigned but had stopped at a phone box on the outskirts of the city to ring Andy and let him know she wouldn't be back.

She had thought he hadn't heard her, the pause on the line was so long, but in a cracked voice he had asked why and where she was headed. It had pained her not tell him anything, but she couldn't risk it.

Maybe her husband had lodged a missing person's report? She immediately dismissed the idea. His colleagues would have questions that even he, clever with the minefield of jargon, attuned to the tribal culture of the force, would struggle to answer. He wouldn't be stupid enough to leave himself open in that way.

If she stayed away from the vicinity of the bar she wouldn't be seen, plus it would avoid the chance of Sheryl calling out her name. And anyway, it could be a mistake and he wasn't there at all.

She went back through the storeroom and sidled into the foyer. It was empty, fortunately. She kept her back against the wall, tipping her head to peer through the glass panel on the bar door. Glen was unmistakeable. In civvies. The sight of him triggered a hit of bile to the back of her throat. She retreated to the stacks of cartons in the store.

Bec was still there, immobile, when Sheryl pushed through the door.

'Thought you were already gone. We've had a run on barbecue chips. Got any more?' Bec composed her face. It was too late to assume a friendly demeanour, so the best she could hope for was a look that might seem neutral. She retrieved a carton from a nearby pallet and handed it over.

'Busy day, Sheryl?'

'Has been but it's emptied out now.' She tucked a damp strand of hair behind one ear. 'No doubt when the next wave comes through at knock-off time, Jack will need to tap a new barrel.'

She took a few steps then turned. 'Fancy a bite and a drink at my place tonight? It's Saffie's birthday and to be honest I could do with a friendly face.'

What could she say. 'Sure. See you at eight?'

Less than an hour later, regardless of the temperature stalled at its daily peak, she strode up the street at full speed, focused only on the need to have the walls crowd around her in the share house. Despite the single-minded purpose she suddenly veered right, a mass of iron filings drawn to a magnet, though was careful to sit deeper in the shade than usual. For once the agitation remained.

'I could do with a word from the ancestors.' Her voice was quiet, with a mocking edge, as she scanned the street. Lily said nothing but after a few minutes reached down and brushed a hand across Bec's hair. At least it felt like she had, though Bec didn't see the woman's arm move.

———•———

The panic had reached Lily before the soft outline of her friend came into view. As Bec folded herself against the wall, Lily knew the woman was lost to herself, as women often were before they gained the strength to find themselves.

Lily sat in her own centre now and was glad to share with her companion the well of calmness that she had found. It had not always been that way. She had been lost, too, had been forced to start over with no guarantee of success. Worse, she had not understood the way she cut herself off from the very source that would nourish her spirit. For if the spirit was properly fed, all could be well.

While she wanted to share with Bec what she had learned in her lifetime, it was not the right way. The ancestors worked with their own timing, to their own plan. Her role was to listen and follow their promptings. They had drawn the woman to her. That was all Lily needed to know.

Her new friend had a destiny of her own and the voices of those who had lived before her would be her guides. She sensed them near her companion as the young woman rose to leave.

———•———

Bec took herself home. It felt too exposed in the street.

She was scrambled every which way and needed to think herself straight.

In the shower memories came as fast as spray from the nozzle on the wall. The time he blocked the doorway when she was trying to get out. Said if she left him he'd call his mates at the station, say he was concerned about her mental state and have her sectioned. Another time he'd warned her that if she tried to leave he would kill himself and she'd have to live with blood on her hands.

The week before leaving for Western Australia she had been in Horsham to cover a committal hearing for a man on a murder charge. Waiting for the court to go into session she had chatted with a friendly female constable, probably in her mid-twenties, dewy-faced like she'd grown up on a local farm.

When the magistrate broke for lunch and everyone filed outside she'd chanced a guarded conversation with the officer, running a carefully worded hypothetical past her. It might get a more helpful response than the anonymous phone call to internal investigations.

'Anyone in that situation needs to be careful.'

The constable lowered her voice and Bec leaned in. Despite feeling vulnerable she needed advice.

'He might get put on restricted duties and it would only inflame things.' The woman in blue had drawn a deep breath.

'You know, it might help if the person in question was more understanding of the stress we're under in this job.'

Driving home from Horsham that evening, wide-eyed and in dread after filing her story in a phone box, it had been plain she wasn't facing one policeman but an entire police force.

It seemed a lifetime ago. She towelled herself dry then dressed and hovered in her bedroom, filling in time before dinner with Sheryl. Maybe she could pretend the van had a problem and borrow a car, but Jo did not own one and she could hardly use Dave's monster 4WD.

The van was bulky and the colour of the bright green tree frog that had sneaked through the open bathroom window in Perth and flopped onto her bare back. It was just as unmistakeable in the faded town as the frog had been in the white bathroom. She waited as late as she dared before driving off.

Sheryl was renting a corrugated iron house in a street that marked the southern border of the Three Mile. The house was an oblong stranded on a bare block surrounded by a high chainmesh fence; the temporary kind found on construction sites. One section had been dragged open and Bec drove in, skirting the house and parking near the back door.

The house, like most others, was on stilts but the block sloped up and at the rear it almost touched the ground. Bec bounded up three narrow steps and knocked on the door.

'Welcome to *Vogue Living*.' Sheryl gestured her in with a sweep of the hand. 'The kitchen and living room, as you can see, feature walls providing the aesthetic of pea soup, a charming sentimental nod to the 1950s.' She grinned and continued the commentary.

'Complimenting this unusual palette we have floors with the restful hue of dog vomit, though even that description doesn't convey the full impact of this particular shade of dull brown lino.'

'And an orange couch. How very 1960s.' Bec got in on the fun. 'It's not a house, Sheryl, it's a time machine.'

'Good to see you outside work.' Sheryl gave her a quick hug and went to fetch the food.

'Tuna mornay was the best I could do but I managed to get a lettuce so at least we can have it with salad.'

'Anything that hasn't come out of Pete's deep fryer will be absolute bliss.'

They drank chilled chardonnay, batting conversation back and forth with a light touch until their plates were empty.

'I'm sorry it's been a rough day, Sheryl. You must miss Saffie terribly.'

'I'd like to say it's been okay. But it hasn't.'

Bec had made a living with words but not one was up to the task of consoling her friend. She let the silence linger as the only balm she could offer.

After a time, Sheryl drew breath and shifted in the chair.

'So, who were you hiding from this afternoon?'

The question, so quiet, so light, slipped under Bec's guard.

'My husband.'

Sheryl poured them both another glass of wine. 'It's not the first time he's had you cornered, is it?'

'Look, it's way too hard to explain.'

'There's no need, Bec my friend. The look on your face when I came into the storeroom said it all.'

She had no defence against the pincer grip of shame that caught in her gut. Sheryl had spoken so gently, with compassion, yet she felt naked and had to battle the urge to cover her eyes, curl up. For the second time that evening she failed at finding words.

The feeling evaded definition but its stickiness engulfed her. It was absolute. She was bad, bad to the bone. Every failure in her life told her so, the brother she had not saved, the man she had helped send to his death, the husband who could never be made happy.

'We have to fight it, Bec.' Sheryl was leaning back at first, a picture of nonchalance, then suddenly she lurched forward and turned fierce.

'Everything in us and out there screams that it's our fault. It's easier for everyone if we're the problem. Weak women, flawed women. That way, we don't count.'

Her friend's rage drained the energy from Bec's body. The wine had lost its appeal. She needed to get home.

Sheryl managed to get in one last question.

'What will you do, Bec. Get away?'

'I don't know. I don't know anything anymore.'

10

Bec was measuring chemicals for the swimming pool next morning, a task requiring precision and focus. She'd been awake much of the night, flip-flopping between the desire to stay in town and the urge to flee; the need to keep the sanity of her routine or to find her husband and confront him. It was a relief to work with a decision that merely required the application of a simple formula.

The brief respite from worry was encouraging. She quickly moved to her old mode, directing her mind away from her own life and into a story, the way she had done as a journalist. Because she had discovered that the existence of the town was based on a lie.

Kieran had waved her over to one of the units earlier, thrusting a local history society pamphlet at her.

'A tourist left it and I thought it was right up your alley 'cos you're someone who likes to know stuff.' She sounded apologetic, like she feared she had caused offence. Bec was quick to reassure her, though secretly she was astounded she'd only been in town a few months and even Kieran was getting her measure. It was sure hard to hide who you were in a place that circled on itself, a snake eating its own tail.

She skimmed the brochure during her break, sitting on an upturned milk crate at the back of the storeroom.

The brochure aimed to present the area's past in the best light but it was easy to read between the lines. There was no mistaking that the beef industry had grown from a deliberate fabrication.

The place suddenly made more sense. Water, cement and sand were stirred together to create mortar. Here, though, they had changed the mix, adding conflict and incongruence in its own kind of bind.

So much could be explained by how the town had begun, in the overblown reports recommending quality pastoral land, sent back east by early explorers. Doubtless they'd have hoped for personal recognition and maybe, too, the rush of interest that came in response.

Never mind the issues with native grasses, naturally low on nutrients, or the challenges of introduced beasts and station owners in adapting to extreme weather conditions.

Far worse was the dismembering of connection to country for local indigenous people. It wasn't in the brochure, but of course it wouldn't be, that generations of belonging and tradition were shattered, Aboriginal inhabitants decimated as their land was seized. She only had to look at the sepia photos in the pamphlet to see that surviving Aboriginal men and women became slave labour on the cattle stations, dispensable in their dark skin yet indispensable to the financial success of the burgeoning beef industry. She sensed how displacement, death and disease still ran in an undercurrent of distortions through the town.

But then, she could hardly judge those who'd come

before when her own presence in the town was founded on mistruths. She carried them every day, a blunt ache in her lower back. Her reckoning had come. What decision should she make? Hide, run, stay paralysed, it all ended the same, with her further than ever from knowing how to craft a life with little but her bare hands.

Shaken by her indecision as much as her fear, she had left the pamphlet on the crate and gone out the door, past the rear entrance to the kitchen and the dining room's humming air conditioner fan, going the long way up the back of the pub to the pool.

The chemicals were added, the skimming of the water surface and the vacuuming of the pool floor were done. As she went to replace the metal lid on the bucket of chemicals it slipped from her sweaty fingers and clattered to the ground. A hand came from nowhere, lifting it before she could bend to retrieve it from the gravel.

She knew who it was without turning to see.

'How are you, Bec?' The voice he used to charm.

'What are you doing here?'

'Just wanting to make sure you're okay. I've been really worried.'

She kept her volume reined in. 'So you've stalked me all the way from Perth to here?'

'I tracked you from Derby with the help of some colleagues but only because I was looking out for you. I was worried you weren't coping after everything that went down.'

She began backing away towards the stairs.

'I know I wasn't all that helpful after the doctor

fellow suicided and I'm sorry about that.' He was adopting a coaxing tone.

'Not helpful? You treated me like I was dirt.' She knew better than to antagonise him but she had lost her footing with his sudden appearance.

'Well, you did go out partying with your workmates a couple of nights later.'

She had almost forgotten. This was how it worked— he would take a solid truth, reduce it to slurry then pour it into whatever mould gave him the result he wanted.

'Come back to Perth with me, Bec. You know we can work this out. It's all a misunderstanding, you'll see.'

She recognised the pattern. Whatever he wanted he'd work on her like this for hours until she'd give in. She had lost contact with what she might want for herself because she had learned to surrender early and avoid friction from the grinding stone of his ever-shifting needs.

'No. I'm not going anywhere.'

'I'm not here to make trouble. I'm staying with a mate at the police house at Kununurra so I can come back, no problem. I'm sure you'll see sense in a day or two and be ready to leave.'

'Don't bother. I'm staying. We have nothing to discuss.'

He stiffened in response. 'We need to sort out the van at least. It's still in my name.'

'I don't care. Take it if you want.' It would be a small price to pay if she got rid of him, though she felt a familiar self, despite knowing better, drawn to wanting to believe he could be fair.

'Bec, I'm not mad you took the van. I know you were in a bit of a state.'

She was angry now. 'A bit of a state? Easy for you to write me off like that.'

He began to protest but she cut him off. 'Leave me alone. I've got work to do.'

'I'm being reasonable, unlike you. To be honest I haven't pushed for the van to be recovered and I'm not pressing charges for the injury you caused so you should be grateful.'

There it was. A line that to anyone listening would sound positively conciliatory, disguising the threat at its centre.

'I'll see you in a day or two.' To her astonishment, the minute he said it he walked away.

She pulled her hat low over her eyes and told herself it was the sun that hurt them so badly.

———·———

There had been no sympathy at home the night after she found the man swinging from a rope. In the face of her desperation for comfort he'd doubled down on needing understanding for his own tough day.

He was in one of his moods and had barely slept for weeks. Sometimes, in the bewitched hours of night, he would sit up and start punching the mattress. She was never sure if it was because he was angry at his wakefulness or enraged by the fact that she slept. She couldn't help wondering if she would be next.

She had travelled thousands of kilometres solo but if there had been a sense of isolation on the long journey up the continent's west coast it had been nothing compared to the loneliness growing ever more smothering each year that passed in her marriage. It had become harder to guard against the crack opening inside where life force leaked out.

In the beginning, when she had met the man she would marry, there had been compassion. He had shared that he was the eldest son of a war-time rifleman, part of the Australian fodder scattered before the Japanese in jungle-matted mountains on the Kokoda Track.

His father had endured, he told her. He had not died yet was filled with death. His best friend had been shot through the neck, dying on his lap. He had seen arms, legs and guts sliced by shrapnel, witnessed the mercy killing of a horribly wounded battalion comrade. It was more than any human mind could bear and if his hands trembled endlessly, well the Army had said it was to be expected.

There was much he did not say, too, for he seemed to prefer avoiding it.

Alcohol is a volatile substance and it gradually became clear to Bec that the war her father-in-law carried into their family home had vaporised into an ever-present threat. It had taken a long time to get her head around the full story, released in a slow drip of anecdotes.

By the time Glen had turned eight he had assumed the role of protecting his mother, sometimes taking a boot in the face or scoring a bruise from a wall as a result. It had made Bec cringe to think about the undefended boy.

His mother kept the shame shut in behind the front door, like a generation of wives of returned servicemen. Bec had been surprised, though, that her husband in confounding ways accepted it as normal that his father had a short fuse.

They had been together for more than two years

before she truly stumbled into the dark corners of his childhood. He kept it parcelled in small units, each carefully separated to avoid one striking sparks off another and the whole lot going up in a blazing explosion.

She had seen the pain early on and had married him because of it, or maybe regardless: she no longer knew which and perhaps it no longer mattered. His father's rage had been greater than one man could bear and it had fallen to the son to carry it. She had not understood it then and now it was too late for understanding to be of any use.

The marriage had operated in lockstep from the beginning, him leading with his right foot in a distorted waltz and her reaching back with the left in response, anticipating his every move until, that is, she found the man swinging under the tree.

———•———

The second night after the incident, as the evening shift had prepared to leave the editorial floor at eleven, Murray did the rounds inviting everyone to a birthday drink in his honour at a nearby nightclub.

'C'mon Bec. Come with us. It'll do you good.'

She hadn't meant to go but her husband was on evening shift, too, and the empty echo of the waiting cottage was already in her ears. She figured if she went for an hour she could still be home first.

She drank a glass of wine and joined the throng on the dance floor, feeling free for the first time in two days, spinning slowly, feet light, giving herself over to the siren call of the music, letting it move her. The beat pulsed steadily, offering a freedom she needed to start

147

gathering up some of the old self, to begin patching a new one together.

She bathed in the soft lights, letting her body do the guiding, feeling safe with colleagues nearby.

When she thought to check her watch it was already well past midnight. She was clammy even as she ran to the cab phone in the foyer to call for a lift home. The cab did not turn up for twenty minutes, so it was almost one in the morning when she got to the front gate of her house, where every light was on.

She steeled herself for the interrogation to come.

'I've been beside myself. Where've you been?'

He was shouting in her face before she had even stepped inside. She pushed past him and went to the bedroom, taking out her drop pearl earrings, deliberately slow, casually placing them on the bedside table.

'We went for a quick drink after work.' Instantly she knew she should have spoken more carefully.

'We? Who the hell is this 'we'?'

She didn't remember what he said after that because she was watching the heat in his face. The next thing she saw was his hand come up and with it, the glint of the blade. The knife had disappeared days earlier, after she had questioned him about it.

Time slowed. The corrugated iron roof cracked a few times as it released heat from the day. In the distance, a truck squealed down through gears on the highway. She jumped when the front door creaked, slamming shut in the draught drawn down the long hall and out the open back door.

The bed was neatly made, the same as she had left it

late the previous morning. She longed to collapse into it and sleep.

The bathroom was at the back of the house. She would go there, give him a minute or two to calm down. 'I need to clean my teeth.' She stepped to one side to go around him.

As she did, her brain slipped its gears and images began jumping out of sequence, jerking forward, rushing backwards; she couldn't make sense of them. Colours flashed, maybe the green of her dress or the blue of his shirt. Her eyes hurt, salty tears adding to the shifting shapes and swaying room.

The knife was moving. It was near him. It was coming at her. She had the thought that if she could get it in her own hand, it would part his ribs like putty.

Shadows rocked and circled when he bumped the thin paper shade on the hanging light. A grunt issued from her as she fought back. She was trying not to scream as spit flew from his gaping mouth.

'I'll be damned if I'll let you get away with this.'

She stumbled back and almost fell on the bed. She remembered that part in vivid detail, the moment of free fall, her body weightless in space for less than a second before her legs stiffened and she could spring-board forward, straining off to the side to avoid the knife, wondering what she was supposed to be getting away with.

She was off balance, lurching to the left. He caught her wrist before she had the chance to straighten up. The thought flashed through her mind that she was fighting his bullish father and not him.

'Who were you with? You're lying to me!'

She twisted her opposite shoulder back in a bid to shake free. The tip of the blade was menacing her face and instinctively she flung her right hand up, attempting to grab his arm and deflect the knife. Her sudden move made him flinch and pull back but her hand gripped below his wrist and they were locked together.

'Put the knife down. It's not going to help. We need to talk.' She didn't like the shrunken voice that came from her, betraying the panic.

If he heard he didn't let on because his fingers were still wrapped around the handle when she felt the tendons of his lower arm tense.

What followed was a skirmish, though she'd often wondered if it was the right description for the mess of blade and arms and hands that ensued until blood poured down his trouser leg. Whatever it was, in that moment one thing had been blindingly clear. She had been fighting for her life.

Far worse, though, was the memory of the rage that had coursed through her and the certainty, in every taut muscle, that she had it in her to plunge a knife into his chest. With so much chaos there was a very real chance she'd been holding the handle when it sliced his thigh.

He wouldn't let her call an ambulance. Instead, he schooled her in the story to tell as she drove him to the emergency department at the Royal Perth Hospital, him still wearing his uniform, with one of her scarves tied around the leg.

'It was an accident. You'd been drinking, you were being silly with the knife, pretending to re-enact something you'd seen on a movie, and got too close.'

It was the lamest thing she'd heard but she was in shock and had no reserve to dispute the excuse.

When they arrived he pulled himself out of the car and took his weight on the uninjured leg. 'You need to be more careful in future. Lucky you didn't get me in the abdomen.' It was said with utter conviction.

A wrecking ball of despair dropped inside her. He was already believing his fiction.

She offered him her shoulder as a crutch and by the time they had reached the sliding doors it was sharply evident, clear as the bright red emergency sign above, that she'd been walking through her marriage in a trance. It had taken a knife waved in her face to snap her out of it.

Afterwards it was a long week, waiting for him to be fit to return to work; suffering him monitoring her every move, counting each minute she was away from the house.

On the morning before his return to work she was standing in front of the bedroom mirror, freshly showered, applying makeup while he lounged in bed.

'What are you doing? You look like a cadaver.'

The remark had his desired effect. She had almost finished the walk to the office before realising she was slinking along, degraded like a beaten dog.

In the end, one of the pearl earrings had almost derailed her. It had been missing since the night of the fight and she had looked for it everywhere that final morning as he got ready for his shift. She had longed to feel its sweet shape in her hand, crying when she couldn't. It had been hard to walk away, abandon it to that house. It still gnawed at her that it was languishing somewhere, wedged in a gap or lost in the dust.

Now here she was, far from the city, still plagued by a nagging doubt that if she could get him some help for his demons he might be okay. She was glad to go down the stairs to the beer store and keep putting one foot in front of another, distracted by having a routine.

She plodded on through the morning, wary as she moved about the pub, watchful on the drive to the rubbish tip. The sight of council workers, hairy arms exposed in blue singlets as they shovelled soil over part of the tip face, was more welcome than they would ever know.

By three o'clock she longed for reprieve from him marauding in her mind. All she wanted was the peaceful companionship of her silent friend at the front of the shop. She went directly there and settled in the usual place, nodding briefly to a customer who was on the way out the door.

The intrusion of her husband into this new life had sharpened her senses and for the first time she scanned the profile of the woman beside her and considered how her life might have been. Lily must be well into her eighties. It wouldn't have been easy for the dignified elder, an outsider in an era of antipathy, living in a district that was a frontiersman's domain.

'Your son said you left the Chinese community in Darwin to come here many years ago.'

Silence.

'It must have been incredibly difficult, being a woman and working, raising a family in such a remote place.'

152

The sentiments seemed trivial but at least they distracted from the anxiety pressing in her chest.

'The challenges must have been extreme. It's a tribute to you that you made it through, kept the business going.'

The attempt at empathy had turned into a patronising hash and she scolded herself then apologised and shut up.

How could she possibly comprehend what her companion's life might have been. She was coming to see that Bec Fielding wasn't all that special—every woman bore at least a few scars, sealed in dark caves under the skin.

She turned to face Lily then spared her the scrutiny by looking away. She barely lived in her own story so how dare she speculate about what it might have been for this woman, making her way while fenced in on all sides. At least these days women were gifted with free choice, or so she wanted to believe.

Lily had been on Earth more than three of Bec's lifetimes. The affinity she felt with the older woman defied logic. The thread of connection was made of a substance she couldn't fathom and the longer she sat on the verandah the less it seemed to matter that she couldn't coral it into language.

———— • ————

Lily hardly heard a word Bec had said, but she didn't need to. She had seen the same troubled look on many women's faces over the years, including her own. It was the reason for her habit of staying away from mirrors.

Troubled, a word that contained far too much light and lilt for the dark state of her mind when she had returned to Darwin, where the green, growing orchard and garden taunted the parched soul she carried inside.

She'd refused to return to the tailor shop, needing the elemental touch and smell of soil, water and the rotting humus in the compost heap. Working beside Mother, she was aware that the girl who had once toiled in the garden, dreaming of a summer harvest, was gone forever.

During Lily's absence Mother had continued to explore her resourcefulness, starting a lucrative arrangement selling mangos for top prices to shopkeepers in Wyndham. She had developed a way to pack them. It was time-consuming but meant the mangos were shipped in first rate condition.

'The greengrocer near the wharf sells me empty cartons. I take the mangos there and he lets me use a bench out the back for a small fee. I wrap each one in wax paper then lay them in rows with straw packed between them.'

Lily was proud. The seeds of such enterprise would not have received favourable conditions to grow had her late father lived.

The wet season would begin any day and they worked together, digging channels to stop erosion from heavy overnight downpours, ensuring rainwater was directed to the orchard and to crops where it was most needed. Many of the garden plots also needed mulching with straw to stop seeds washing away.

It was hard physical work and Lily's hands were still toughening up. She was resting in the shade of the tool shed, examining blisters on her palms, when Mother sat beside her, pulling out a small square of paper from the band of her trousers.

'I have a photo to show you, Lily.'

The photo looked official, a face staring directly into the camera, head bent forward in the way of men accustomed to hard physical work.

'Take it.'

The picture meant nothing to her but she did as Mother asked, studying the image. It was a thin face, a little drawn, with sunken areas under the eyes and a smattering of fine pockmarked scars on each cheek.

'He has his own shop, which by good fortune he was running before the meatworks opened at Wyndham, so is doing well. I am told he is diligent and a hard worker, having spent many years as a cook for Victoria River drovers.'

Lily had not expected this. She had become reconciled to a life working in the market garden, perhaps taking over managing it in time.

'Mother, I know you are looking out for me but this man, I can see he has more years than you.'

The older woman looked across the orderly rows of cucumber and pumpkin plants, their first shoots visible.

'If we do not have any dreams for our life we may as well be a fish in the sea.'

Lily was hardly a prize, a widow who had already birthed a child, though she understood that with many Chinese deported or banned from the country since the politicians changed the rules there were fewer Chinese women available as wives.

'Times are changing, different to my day. You must remarry. He will give you more children, Lily, hopefully sons.'

Mother drew breath, steadying herself for the final

argument. 'Don't you see? Whatever happens you will always have the shop.'

Tears began falling fast and soon Lily's lap was wet. Mother waited patiently.

'However much you resist, Daughter, life will still come to claim you.'

They sat in silence. Eventually Mother pushed herself up to her feet. She still needed to weed rows of beans, water spinach plants and apply a sulphur treatment to ward off bud mites on two young mango trees.

'He will be here tomorrow. He seeks to meet you and make an offer. You must wear your blue embroidered robe.'

They met late afternoon in the shade of the frangipani overhanging the garden entrance. Given the circumstances and age of each, Mother had forsaken any formalities other than greeting the newcomer and performing introductions. She had then removed herself to a suitable distance to give the pair privacy.

At fifty-five, Eddie Yong was unusually late in life to be seeking a wife and his first impulse was to reassure Lily that there were legitimate reasons for the delay, the foremost one being the necessity to be a proper provider.

His work as a cook on Kimberley cattle stations and along the droving routes had kept him in temporary accommodation, unsuitable for a family. Though he had taken over the Wyndham shop more than ten years earlier, the income had only become reliable in more recent times.

He was taller than her, slightly built, economical with words.

'The years may have overtaken me more rapidly than

I would have wished but I have a stable situation, am a respected shopkeeper, and the business is my own.'

As he paused she studied the humble manner of his hands folded on his lap. When she dared look at his profile, it was surprising how little space her suitor seemed to occupy.

Undeterred by the situation, he was intent on building a bridge between them.

'I also once lived in Darwin and, like your esteemed father, was born in Canton. Although I speak English in the shop it would suit me very well to converse with a wife in Cantonese.'

He took her lack of response as an indication of agreement.

'I will make arrangements for the ceremony to be held on my return in a month.' When he was in Darwin, like most Cantonese he usually frequented the Woods Street Chinese temple. For the significant matter of their wedding, however, they would attend the stone-lined Anglican Church above the waterfront.

While Lily had only ever participated in rituals or prayers at the temple, she understood that Eddie was no different to many others with Chinese heritage, particularly those with business undertakings, in seeking to appear more western.

It was decided.

She was a sleepwalker, dazed as she moved through the days leading up to the ceremony. If Eddie Yong had any doubts about the marriage they were not shared with her, though perhaps he had not allowed for the notoriety that persisted. For when the time came, their union warranted a mention in *The Northern Standard*.

A one paragraph report proclaimed that Rev Light had conducted an interesting wedding, as though she were a shameful bauble, singling her out as the widow of the Chinese victim of the shooting affray at the Stadium Picture Theatre two years earlier.

The ceremony complete, next day she farewelled Mother with a heavy heart and boarded the *Bambra*. Her husband had been considerate of her status as a bride and had taken the unusual step of booking them a cabin in second class rather than steerage. The steamer, like her, was on its second metamorphosis. Originally the German Kaiser's private yacht, the *Prinz Sigismund* had the misfortune to berth in Brisbane under a German ensign when the Great War broke out, whereupon it had been seized by Australia for its own purposes.

She had heard seafarers declare it was unlucky to change the name of a ship and the *Bambra* had proven it to a fault. In its time on the Western Australian coastal run the ship had stuck fast on sandbanks, demolished the side of the jetty in Derby, been subject to failure of its steering gear and survived a bunker fire.

Despite her concern about its abysmal record, it carried them safely to her new home in Wyndham. She saw it as a propitious sign.

Her second husband had lived a full life before she entered into the union and was accustomed to his own company. Apart from asking for occasional help moving stock in the shop or dusting shelves, he left her to cook, clean and find her own way. Four weeks passed before she gathered up the courage to ask if he might buy her a sewing machine for the room out the back so that she might provide tailoring services to the town.

'The tailor shop near the Post Office has been here for many years.' Though the statement was matter of fact, it sounded like he meant it to end the discussion.

They were eating bowls of rice and spicy kung pao made with chicken raised in the Darwin garden. Lily's eyes were cast down at the food, but then the sight of it reminded her of Mother's perseverance. She drew herself up in the chair.

'Perhaps they are not always able to meet the demand, especially when the seasonal workers are here at the meatworks.' She liked the fact that she sounded as though she understood the workings of business.

'If I cannot repay the cost within one year, I would be happy for it to be sold.'

Eddie studied her carefully as she spoke. He knew some of her story and the sadness of the husband and girl who had died, though it was not enough to form a foundation for a steady attitude to each other. He needed the chance to see what character his wife might have.

'If you provide me with your specifications, I will see what I can do.'

She smiled into her bowl and it pleased him on two counts—that she was happy, though it was not a requirement, and that she was a woman who looked to the future.

———•———

Lily was now eighty years and more, still living at Wyndham. Everything had changed, except the fact of the town and the shop, both of which remained. She had come to see that troubles did not last but good people did. She desired to share the knowledge with her young

159

friend beside her on the verandah. Of course, it would be no more useful than pulling up a bucket of water from the inlet and expecting the tide to drop.

It was necessary for a person to approach such learning the right way, holding it in their own heart and hands.

Bec, for her part, was directing what effort the heat spared to avoidance of thinking about the future, rising before her as merely a maze of dead-ends. She was readying herself to leave the silent space on the verandah when a message intruded, materialising from emptiness, firm, categorical.

Your business here is finished.

She spun to look at the woman, who appeared oblivious and was leaning in the opposite direction towards a car reversing from its parking spot in front of the pub. Bec had never touched Lily before but instinctively, in a pleading gesture, placed a hand on a faded sleeve. The eyes that turned towards her were cloudy and the face showed some surprise. Bec's mind was playing tricks on her. She pulled back her hand and walked away.

As if there was an easy way to end the business of the man who pursued her. Her anger flared. It wasn't that simple. She could escape the town and still he would find her. She would never be done with him. She had run out of options.

It was her own fault. She had married young, blinded by her own needs, overwhelmed by his. He had seemed so full of promise, had done it tough growing up. She had been drawn by his potential and his certainty that she was the one. The steel trap snapped shut before she'd even seen it.

His behaviour had been erratic. Frequent disagreements had broken out with family members or colleagues, which he'd managed by refusing to talk to relatives, changing jobs or applying for transfers. Through it all she had been willing to trust he would stay behind an invisible line, where a passable explanation could be manufactured to make sense of his words and actions.

The only way such a balancing act could be sustained had been to divvy up her days into an ever-increasing number of silos, one for every time he raged or threw things, for every caustic remark he made so she would feel small. More to hold the many times he froze her out or stormed relentlessly to get his way. Rows and rows of silos, so many to build that in the end she barely had the energy to sleep or work.

In the weeks at Wyndham, with no need to run or fight, she had let them fall, let every last silo come tumbling down. He could keep the denial going if that's what he wanted. As for her, she would stand in the rubble and feel the jagged concrete and glass against the soles of her feet.

11

THE SWEAT RAN DOWN LILY'S back to the
pulse of the treadle sewing machine, as she drew
the fabric smoothly over the needle plate, leaning
forward to reach across her expanded belly.

When the machine arrived, Eddie had painstaking-
ly painted tall black letters onto a piece of timber and
nailed it to the front of the shop. 'Tailor and Outfitter'
was added beneath the sign for 'General Storekeeper'.

In the year that passed she had made steady earnings,
the machine whirring gently for long hours, stitching a
reputation for the quality of her garments and repairs
and the rapid turnaround times, though it was the way
she understood what looked best on a customer that most
inspired them to spread the word.

She had repaid her husband for the cost of the
machine in four months and it had pleased them both.
The baby would be here soon and the machine would
be quiet for her thirty days of zuo yue zi, spent resting
in bed. It would be different this time, without Mother
to attend in the difficult hours of birthing or to cook the
pig's trotters with ginger and vinegar to rebuild strength
and help the womb recover.

Chin Toy had a shop further up the street, selling

mainly cigarettes and newspapers. His wife Dorothy had visited Lily after the bulge began to show. She was older and already had two sons and a daughter.

'Send your husband when the time has come. I also have no mother or mother-in-law here and it has been a blessing to have the help of others.'

Lily was overcome by the kindness.

''Remember not to eat mutton or the baby may have epilepsy and jerk about like the teeth of a sheep as the animal chews. Also, have chicken broth every day.'

It was not Lily's place to tell Dorothy she had already experienced pregnancy, that she knew how important it was not to disturb the balance of qi through fear or anger, risking miscarriage or deformities. She had reduced her hours of work once the baby quickened for the same reason.

There was much to remember. It was necessary to avoid malign influences by keeping her thoughts kind and speaking no ill of others, especially by taking care not to say or do anything that might offend the ancestors. She no longer helped Eddie with heavy lifting in the shop for it was dangerous to do any demanding work that might disturb the position of the baby.

'I am relieved to have your offer of help, Mrs Chin Toy.' They were in the living quarters and she kept her voice low so Eddie did not hear as he worked behind the counter in the next room.

'I have been wondering how I would manage during my confinement when I must rest and my husband and I cannot eat together. It would not have been right for him to take care of me.'

'Please, you should call me Dorothy from now on.'

The arrangement lacked balance so Lily offered to sew for Dorothy's family to make it right. After a brief negotiation it was settled. She would make a jacket for Chin Toy and a dress for Dorothy's daughter.

Lily walked Dorothy out the front door of the shop to say farewell on the street, happy that serendipity had prevailed. As they passed through the shop she did not see the knowing look that flashed between Eddie up the ladder, stacking cans on a high shelf, and the wife of his fellow Cantonese shopkeeper.

Returning to her sewing she realised she had carried more worry than she had been admitting to herself. She did not want the birth to go wrong for want of an attendant, especially as the town's chief medical officer was not keen on helping anyone with coloured skin.

Eddie had made it clear it was not something he desired, in any case. She was in full agreement after he told her about the serious event that happened the year he arrived at Wyndham. The hospital, only a stone's throw up O'Donnell Street, was at the centre of the incident. The fact that it was so close to home seemed to have particularly unnerved her husband.

Eddie's friend Ah Too was a cook and had witnessed the crime. As he recounted it to Eddie, the doctor had left the hospital and gone next door to a room off the Post Office to join friends, as he often did, for his evening meal. He had arrived at the table drunk, with a snub-nosed 380 revolver in his pocket. When asked about the gun he had told the group he was using it to keep Aborigines from the hospital back yard.

One of the men had inquired if the gun was loaded. The doctor responded by raising it swiftly and firing at the tongue and groove partition separating the room from the Post Office. The bullet had gone through the timber, a window and into the operating room at the hospital. Ah Too retreated to the kitchen while the others persuaded the doctor to go onto the verandah. One friend immediately tried to gain control of the weapon while another ran to fetch the constable. Just then, Ah Too looked out from the kitchen. Before his eyes, the gun flashed and the doctor's dining companion dropped like a bag of wheat, shot through the heart.

Eddie shook his head. 'Such recklessness. If it had been me, I would have hung. Yet the good doctor only got two years in gaol with hard labour.'

He laughed so hard his entire body shook. 'The judge showed mercy because the medical man had been affected by the heat which, of course, would not apply to any other person in this town.'

The story had stayed with her. If that was the standard of behaviour then she was having no part in medical intervention.

The moon cycles passed smoothly as she settled into the later stages of carrying the baby. She made sure to finish outstanding orders by the end of the eighth month, allowing time to draw in energy for the birth. Bookings would not reopen for another month after that to ensure a full recovery. She remembered the many sleepless nights with Goot Song and was glad the meat season would be over, enabling her to resume work at a manageable pace.

Goot Song's spirit seemed to draw close in the final weeks of the pregnancy. Lily chose to interpret the girl's appearance in her thoughts and dreams as a sign of encouragement and hoped it was not because she sought to lure her brother or sister away.

She ached already to hold the baby in her arms, to nuzzle the soft flesh as she had her little girl, but the deep hurt at her earlier loss was sharper than her best shears, cutting off connection to the new life growing within. Dorothy visited from time to time as they made provision for the birth and confinement and was moved to offer encouragement.

'You will be a good mother, Lily. I see it in you, the love in your eyes and the way you carry your baby with such pride.'

Lily said nothing. She wanted to believe her friend but stumbled repeatedly over the reality that she had already failed one child.

———————•———————

Labour began as dawn stretched thin fingers across the ridge of the Bastion. Eddie went immediately to fetch Dorothy then, after shuffling from one foot to another for a few minutes, left the women to it and opened the shop, though it would be at least an hour before any customers were likely to appear.

After Dorothy examined Lily, she predicted the birth was some way off, giving her time to return home and organise her children for school.

'I'll be back soon. Keep walking up and down, it will help the birth along.'

Lily remained in the bedroom despite the build-up of stifling heat and in between contractions placed towels on a stool and folded extras in case they were needed. She heard Eddie ringing up the till as he began serving customers and soon after Dorothy reappeared in the doorway.

Not once did she cry out or scream, even as pain convulsed her body. By late afternoon she was exhausted and called to the spirits of her forebears for strength and courage, though it was the baby who seemed to will her to go on.

She heard Eddie's voice briefly at the door and Dorothy soothing in reply. At last it was time to spread towels on the floor and squat as Mother had taught her, one hand on the bed to balance, for the final push of the head down the birth canal. It was almost closing time in the shop when the boy landed, slippery, in Dorothy's hands with a rush of blood and amniotic fluid. Part of the caul was caught on his head.

He did not cry but rested in his mother's arms, eyes closed, wrapped in a towel, while Dorothy fetched water from the kitchen. Lily hoped the caul was a positive sign as she peeled it away.

Dorothy helped her to wash and change into a fresh gown then cleaned the baby gently from the top of his head to the tips of his toes while Lily watched on.

'Such delicate features. He has Mother's mouth.'

After Lily had settled comfortably on the bed, one arm curled around the boy, Dorothy ushered in Eddie. He was delighted to have a strong son and after Dorothy left decided a western name would be best. They called him George, a name with a solid ring to it, enduring as a temple bell.

Dorothy came and went as the days unfolded. Eddie occasionally entered the room for a few minutes when he had finished his work but for the most part she was left to her own obsession with the baby. Though the love did not flow as it had with her daughter, she marvelled at the tiny being breathing gently in her arms.

At man yue, the first month celebration, she left her bed, took a bath and washed her hair. George was dressed in new clothes, red as tradition required, and Dorothy and Chin Toy joined them as they presented him in reverence to the ancestors and gods, asking for protection and good fortune for their boy.

Their pleas must have been heard as the year that followed was one of the happiest Lily had known, the baby often in a basket at her feet, lulled to sleep by the purr of the sewing machine. When awake George loved to move, waving his hands back and forth, kicking his legs. He began to crawl earlier than expected and it was no longer safe to have him nearby as she sewed. Instead she rose before the boy woke, stitching in the cooler hours, then again when he had his daytime nap.

Eddie was proud of his son and Lily's heart softened towards him even more as she saw his genuine pleasure in having a family. Their evenings passed in quiet companionship while he reviewed the accounts and she sewed on jacket buttons or finished off embroidery on a dress, in the glow of a kerosene lamp.

Each day was an adventure for George and when he began to take his first tentative steps he giggled in delight at his own efforts. Mother could not leave the market garden so Lily took the boy to Darwin for a week to meet his grandmother. The acreage was a vast playground and George waddled up and down the rows, often falling onto his bottom, touching leaves, tasting whatever took his interest, moving happily from one lap to another between two pairs of protective arms.

When their time at the garden came to an end, Lily's sadness at farewelling Mother was quickly replaced by the joy of her son, delighting in climbing the ship's stairs on all fours, rubbing his hands along the worn railing on the deck, greeting passengers with his own mysterious language, and exploring myriad corners, shapes and textures of their temporary floating home.

———•———

It was insignificant, a month after their return, when the first locusts appeared in the air, darting right and left, diving swift as arrows into grass. By next morning the air was thick with them as they began landing in their thousands in trees and on ground cover, using powerful hind legs to jostle with each other for the best of the vegetation.

By late afternoon the slope to the water was a moving sea of dark brown. Inside the Fong kitchen Lily caught stragglers that jumped in the back door, tossing them out. Within an hour it was a hopeless task and she had no option but to slam the door shut.

The creatures had hatched with heavy inland rains, then as the land dried out had come with the wind hundreds of miles to the district, where the wet season had made the grass flourish. They crunched underfoot on the short walk to the Post Office and some flew up when Lily's feet disturbed them, forcing her to cover her nose and mouth with one hand.

For days, waves of insects methodically stripped every leaf and stalk in the town and surrounds, sparing only dense, tough foliage that grew high on sporadic bushes or trees, now small islands of green amid wasteland.

The locals talked about nothing else. No one dared slip between the sheets without checking first for rogue locusts, and woe betide any wife who added eggs to flour without scrutinising it first for a dark shape or two.

Tempers flared, for people were already dealing with the season's monsoon rains, windstorms and enforced isolation. Grazing lands, roadside verges, shade-giving trees, and precious gardens tended in back yards—all succumbed, and when damp ground dried from overnight rains, dust eddied into eyes and ears.

Lily, like so many others, thought the unwelcome visitors would never leave. Then one morning at dawn, a strong northerly came in and a billion tiny wings beat in unison as the locusts rose, thick clouds obscuring the sky, and left to find a new food source.

Looking back it was clear the plague was a bad omen, though it was Mother, of all people, who provided the first warning. Her letter had arrived on the *Bambra*, describing an influenza outbreak in Darwin.

'At least half the population have succumbed.' The speed of its spread had caught many by surprise.

'I stay out of the town as much as possible, sometimes sleeping overnight in the garden shed.'

Eddie was unloading their stock from the cart so Lily folded the letter, put it in her pocket and went to help him unload. He was grumbling about the delay at the jetty making him late to open the shop.

'They were three crew down because of sickness. Seems a passenger brought it up north from Fremantle when they last docked down there and it has galloped off faster than a prize horse.'

Darwin was a world away. Right now there was the pressing concern of Eddie needing to get the shop door unlocked and ensure there was sufficient change in the till. She thought no more of it until the end of the week.

George woke earlier than usual, coughing frequently, his breath rasping. He was almost weaned and only took the breast morning and night so she offered him rice water. He turned his head away.

She made peppermint tea, set it aside for an hour to cool then spooned it into his mouth often during the day. Twice she gave him juice squeezed from an orange to cool the hot wind moving through his body.

———— • ————

Next morning he was shivering, listless and still hot to the touch. He closed his mouth each time she tried to feed him and cried pitifully until she set him back down in the cot. All day and into the night she wiped his limbs and forehead with a damp cloth, in between fanning him. He lay motionless on his back, wet strands of fine hair stuck to his ears. Lily's hands were too busy to brush them away.

Soon after dawn Eddie came in with a bowl of congee to which he had added a few pieces of tofu. The consistency was thinner than the rice porridge she made, though the observation was irrelevant as she had no appetite. He made no comment about the congee left to one side and continued to sit with her.

'Get some rest. I'll look after him. I will wake you when it's time to open the shop.' He whispered it, as though speaking aloud would disturb his young son, might shatter the illusion that he was merely sleeping. She shook her head and he knew nothing would be gained by insisting.

He ran his hand over his son's hair, smoothing the fringe to one side, and stood to leave.

'Fetch me if there is any change.'

When he returned during his afternoon break she was sponging George and attempting to get him to take a little water, which dribbled from the corner of his mouth.

'I should get Dorothy. She may have advice.' For the first time since he met him in Mother's garden she heard the tremble of fear in his voice.

'No, she must not come. We cannot risk the health of her children.'

Eddie went up the street to Dorothy's back door, regardless, and called to her. When she appeared he stood at some distance while he explained the boy's condition and asked if anything further could be done. It may have been a trick of the heat, but her face seemed to melt and rearrange itself so that Eddie struggled to recognise the woman before him.

'Go to your wife, my friend. She is doing everything in her power. You must pray, for any assistance must come from others far more divine.'

On the third day the toddler's skin took on a bluish tinge and his breathing became laboured. Lily begged for him to be spared, praying for protection from the father she had never known, desperate yet unable to leave the boy's side to light joss sticks at the altar.

On the fourth morning the toddler no longer stirred. When she lifted the limp body to her chest his breath was shallow and slow, only audible by holding her ear close to his mouth. At some point there was a dawning, though she fought it with all her might, that he no longer breathed at all.

In that terrible moment she knew two things for certain. Never again would George smile. And she was the reason, for it was plain that she was cursed.

The knowledge of her culpability burned in her heart; a flame so hot it left only ashes. It silenced the scream that rose in her the next afternoon as the tiny white coffin was entombed by thudding soil.

As if to underscore her belief, others in the town became sick but George was the only child to die.

She was too numb this time to even stay in bed. She was one of the husks the grasshoppers had left behind, drifting this way or that in the forgetting of who she was.

It was Dorothy who, a month later, brought attention to the fact that her belly had swollen again.

12

BEC SLEPT FITFULLY AND WAS hungover with exhaustion as she stumbled through first light to the motel. The outline of the Bastion glowed as the sun signalled its ascent, the inevitability of which could not be ignored.

She had wanted badly to talk to Jo and Dave the night before, for another soul to know the danger she might be in. Yet every time she opened her mouth to speak the sounds refused to form, cottonwool against her teeth.

After dinner Jo went outside. Within seconds she began screaming. Bec and Dave ran to the laundry door, where Jo stood, shaking.

'Something big, alive, in there.' She pointed into the gloom.

Dave leaned in, waiting for his eyes to adjust in the dimness. A minute went by, maybe more. He began laughing.

'You've scared it.' He squeezed his sister's shoulder. 'It's beautiful. Check it out, Bec.'

She peered in. At first the only visible shape was the washing machine with its lid open, but as her eyes adjusted, a darting head with two eyes came into view, attached to a narrow body coiled around a bare beam.

'It's an olive python, probably a young one.' Dave couldn't contain his excitement. 'Saw a big one driving back from Kununurra a couple of weeks ago. The local cop had pulled over and was trying to get it off the road before it got run over.'

Dave took nearly an hour to coax it down into a pillowcase so he could drive it out of town to the edge of Parry Lagoons nature reserve. After he was gone, Jo was still skittish and Bec went to bed to escape her friend's nervous energy. She lay there for more than an hour, remembering the python, compelled by its beauty yet experiencing aroused instincts, the fear of snakes carried by generations all the way back to the beginning of human memory. She woke often and each time the python was fixing her with its gaze. By daybreak she was already up and dressed for work.

As she hauled herself up the stairs to the beer garden she remembered, with relief, that it was the week between shift changeovers for the oil rig and half the units were empty. It lessened the burden of bins, so she left for the tip much earlier than usual. When she returned Jack saw her park the ute and beckoned her into the office.

'The last delivery was short and I'm down a dozen bottles of spirits, mainly rum and whisky. I need you to finish early and do a run to the Kununurra pub to pick up some extras.'

'Won't they need it for their own customers?' She was stalling while she thought of a reason not to go.

'Nah, I know the publican. He can't give us all I was hoping for, but it'll be enough to get us close to when the next beer truck comes.'

'It'll take me two hours to do the round trip. I'll need

to leave at one, so I won't have time to do the pool or finish off the fridges.' She was counting on his aversion to physical work.

'I'll take care of that. Just let me know where you're at before you leave.' He handed her a map of Kununurra and she saw that the hotel was less than three blocks away from the police station.

At one o'clock she gave him an update on her progress and was given keys to the ute. As she reversed out she remembered Jo was on a day off and stopped at the house, where her friend needed no convincing to join the road trip. The travelling companion came at a price, though. Jo scooped up a couple of favourite tapes on the way out the door. Bec took a deep breath, steeling herself for two hours of Carole King and Split Enz.

They were barely under way when Jo began fiddling with controls on the dashboard. 'No air con, Bec. You didn't tell me that!'

The tray on the ute rattled and clattered. With the windows down, music was not an option till they hit the bitumen. Despite normal road noise resuming, the cassette player remained idle. Jo was uncharacteristically quiet.

'I'm thinking of heading home, making a fresh start.'

Bec glanced at the girl, who was staring straight ahead.

'Please don't say anything to Dave.'

The last thing Bec needed was the responsibility of being a sounding board. 'What's prompted this, Jo? That awful fellow?'

'To tell you the truth, I've been feeling aimless for a

while. Guess I thought if I found the right man it would all be okay.' She shrugged her shoulders.

They travelled in silence for a few minutes.

'It's smart to take charge and live life on your own terms.' If Bec had poured a teaspoon of sugar into her mouth the sentiment couldn't have come out any more saccharine. The hypocrisy needled. It was hard to bite back anger that flared at her own shortcomings.

'Yeah, I'm impressed with the way you're following your own instincts. It's helped me to see that I need to make changes.'

Bec swallowed hard and concentrated on the road, hot air whipping the side of her face as her passenger changed the subject and chattered on.

The Cockburn Range stretched like a fortress, high sandstone escarpments obscuring the horizon. The remainder of the country on either side of the highway had a desolate quality and she thought of Lily raising a family in such a hostile environment.

Bec had only her limbs to carry through each day of heat and dust and that was more than enough. The energy it must have taken for the Chinese woman to endure such conditions while raising a family and supporting a business was beyond her imagination. But then, her father used to say that you don't know what you are made of till you're tested. She had always understood that to mean that each person was capable of surprising themselves, but there were exceptions to every rule and she was the case in point.

Her father. She hadn't thought of him for a very long time. He would be older now. The stray grey hairs that showed up when Daniel absented himself would have taken over. She tried to picture her dad as he looked when she was a child. Tall and straight, he had thrown one arm around her mother's shoulders, pulling her in. The image of the pair wavered, returning to obscurity. It was hard to tell if it had been real or simply a compensatory fantasy.

Before marriage, she had travelled many miles after leaving home, watching fleeting views out moving windows, arriving and departing airports, train and bus stations, cycling country roads. She had discovered the world was vast yet nothing compared to the unfathomable depths within, where sinkholes lay in wait with shadowy pools of water, and one wrong step could leave you falling, forever falling.

Perhaps she and Lily shared the same need, to sense what was substantial and solid beneath them. Maybe that was the purpose of Lily's afternoon ritual, seeking the hard wooden chair against her spine in the way Bec needed the containment of work and its attendant routines.

It was an easy run to Kununurra and soon they were on the outskirts of town. Jo was suddenly full of energy and talkative, sparing Bec further rumination.

'Let's see if we can find a decent coffee. May as well make the most of our time here.' Bec was reluctant but she owed her this one.

'We can't stay too long, though, or Jack's going to worry about his precious ute.' She forced a laugh. They crossed the Ord River and followed signs showing the way to the main street, quivering in a mirage of asphalt and brickwork. She slowed near a café with a shady seating area out the front and parked nearby.

Bec suddenly felt self-conscious. She was still

wearing the same T-shirt and shorts in which she had emptied the bins that morning. She noticed that her sweat had dried into crusting stains, made worse by the recognition that, stripped of the shelter defined by the space between the share house at Wyndham, the general store over the street, the pub, all of which could be measured in footfalls, she was exposed.

Jo was already opening the café door when Bec glanced up. She froze mid-step and clutched at Jo's arm. 'Come on, I know a better place.' As she bundled her friend in the direction of the car, she could still see his profile through the glass, looking down, evidently studying a menu.

She swung the ute around and drove back to the highway then turned left along a small shopping strip straddling either side of the road. She didn't dare look at Jo, couldn't deal with the confusion no doubt visible on her face. They found a café, ordered coffee and cake then seated themselves in a garden area out the back. Their orders soon followed.

'Sorry Jo. Didn't mean to be so abrupt before. Think the heat's gotten to me today.'

Jo nodded and smiled, enthusiastically digging her fork into Black Forest cake.

'It's fine if you don't want to be up front with me Bec, but don't feel you've got to lie. I know when someone looks scared.'

She had cream on her top lip and Bec had the urge to point it out, maybe even pick up the paper serviette and rub it off, though it was Jo's unexpected insight she really wanted to wipe away.

'It's complicated, actually. A bit hard to talk about.'

Jo stopped eating and looked her in the eye. 'As someone recently said to me, the difficult stuff always is.'

They ate in silence, letting the coffees cool. The pressure was rising in Bec. She needed to start linking words, one to another, till she had a chain of them she could hold, a safety rail of sorts.

'I left my husband in Perth. He's a cop and now he's tracked me down.'

'Either he still loves you very much to go to those lengths, or …?'

'Definitely 'or', Jo. Let's finish up and get the grog.'

Several times on the journey back to Wyndham Jo started to gossip about happenings at the pub, then let each story tail off.

'It's okay, you know. I don't want to talk about him but that doesn't mean I want everyone around me to be mute.' Bec flung a grin at Jo and saw her relax. Soon she was nattering like nothing had happened, leaving Bec to focus on her own thoughts.

She had met her husband when she was nineteen. Within months he had wanted them to marry. She had suggested it was too soon, that they should take some time to get to know each other better.

'If you're not willing to marry me then I'll top myself.' He had said it in the full knowledge of how Daniel had died. Naively, she had supposed she had no choice, preferring to see it as a declaration of commitment. It had taken years of growing up to understand that, in fact, she had been claimed.

Soon after they married, her friends were subjected to forensic analysis. He was quick to exaggerate their flaws and sow doubt in her mind about their character or motivation. Before long she let them drift away and he had no need to trouble himself about it.

Her hands were sticky on the steering wheel. She glanced at Jo. It was strange that even now he could contaminate friendship.

When she dropped Jo at the house before returning the ute, she glanced across at the verandah out of habit. It was an empty space. Fifteen minutes later, the ute unpacked and the keys left in Jack's office, she hurried back up the street to the shop counter, feigning a casual stance.

'Haven't seen your mother outside today. She okay?'

'Some days she needs to rest. Thanks for asking.'

Bec covered her disappointment by cruising the shelves for something to buy, eventually settling on a couple of wooden spoons.

———•———

In her room out the back Lily lay on her back on the bed, listening to the voice of her young friend in the shop.

It was no accident they had been drawn together on the verandah weeks earlier. The spirits knew it was medicine for both. One on the solitary journey out of this world, taking solace from companionship with no demands, releasing herself little by little into forever. The other stalled, unable to fully enter the stream of life, yet called to Lily's side where she could at least touch the field of what lay beyond everyday sight and sounds.

Lily's mind travelled on a whim these days. The memories kept slowly unwinding, one after another, the flow of one person on her way to the inevitable end.

It had begun in earnest with the arrival of the young

woman, as though Bec had found a secret switch that set in motion the unfolding of many past sights, sounds, feelings, the markers of living. Her worn-out body ached. Soon it would not be needed, but she had come to see that first she must honour each curve of her life's road, leaving her free to let go.

She felt the weightlessness of her bones and flesh, as though she floated above the bed, even as she heard Louie's distant tone in the shop. Voices, sounds, none were now as vivid as the ones she remembered. She looked at the ceiling, the familiar walls, and as she did the surfaces seemed to draw forward and from the movement came an echo, faint at first, then unmistakeable.

It was the shriek that came from Ivy as she entered the world, in the room where Lily now rested. The girl had arrived caterwauling, as though she had a vision of her fate.

Such hopes Lily had held for 1925. It had been the Year of the Ox and she had yearned for the promise of steadiness that it carried, though it proved not to be a quality imparted to the new baby.

While Ivy's tiny face was similar in its features to Goot Song's, it was clear from the beginning that in temperament she was her own person. She could be fierce in expressing her needs and though Lily did her best to tame it, secretly she wanted to fan the flame.

She watched the girl closely as she grew and, unlike George, kept her nearby when she began to walk. Dorothy tried speaking in gentle terms about giving Ivy room to grow but Lily ignored her and continued on as before. Eddie was not so inclined to be kind.

'Stop wrapping cottonwool around the child. She

needs her own air to breathe.' To make sure, he had watched more diligently, and when he had been present she had loosened her hold on Ivy, at least until her husband's attention returned to matters of business.

———————•———————

Two years passed and it had been a relief that Ivy had survived beyond the ages of the two fated children. Lily was pregnant again, weary to the bone, though what can you do but get up and go on?

Late one afternoon she left the girl playing with her wooden pull-along dog in the open doorway. She needed a few minutes to finish the weekly dusting of shelves in the shop. The high-pitched screams that followed still echoed off the walls all these decades later.

She had left a bamboo steamer of pork dumplings on the table and forgotten the water set on the stove to boil. It was not the steamer that caught Ivy's attention but the sound of the water and the shine of the pot handle.

Ivy had tipped the pot to one side, water scalding her left shoulder before it splashed across the floor. Eddie came running with a customer behind, but Lily got to the girl first and began stripping off her clothes. She shouted at the two men to get out, waving them away furiously. Eddie looked shocked by his wife's behaviour but left.

Shame will do that, give you a big voice.

The skin was already blistering across her toddler's shoulder and down the upper part of her back. She kept crying and screaming and wanted to be held but there was no time to soothe her. Lily sat her on the back step and poured dish after dish of cold water over the burns, forcing herself to continue despite her daughter's distress.

After she had carefully smeared on the red ointment Chin Wang Hun, with its soothing lobelia, myrrh, frankincense and sesame oil, Ivy's screaming reduced to an exhausted whimper. Lily covered the burns with strips of soft muslin and only then could she take her in her arms and rock her.

The toddler was in shock and slept little because of the discomfort but next morning Lily could see the ointment had helped with the swelling. She boiled water, cooled it and despite Ivy's protests washed the burns gently then applied a thick coating of honey then fresh dressings.

The skin eventually puckered and healed, though Ivy was permanently marked, as was her mother, carrying the stain of guilt. What woman does not suffer when her child is in pain, would rather bear it herself than her little one? Yet she had been the cause. She had hurt her own child.

———·———

Later that year, to Eddie's delight, another son was born. A daughter and son had already died and a second daughter was disfigured. She could not help but wonder in what way she would prove inadequate for the care of this boy. They called him Joe and perhaps her husband experienced a nervous sense of the future, for he immediately began planning a China trip so the boy could receive the blessings of extended family.

They left the following year just as the wet season started, for eight months away, which would coincide with New Year celebrations. Three-year-old Ivy, her blunt fringe cut short, was required to have her own documentation giving exemption from the dictation test. The scars on her shoulder were noted as a distinguishing feature.

They sailed on the liner *St Albans*, bound for Hong Kong. Lily marvelled that it was almost a century since one of the earliest steamships made the world's first big ocean crossing, from its home in Ireland to New York. The *Sirius* had run out of coal and the crew had to burn the cabin furniture and even a mast, though eventually they made it, purely on steam power. The *St Albans* was also Irish, built and launched in Belfast, but it was one of the new breed of steel ships that were far bigger and more reliable, for which Lily was grateful.

Steerage berths for Chinese passengers were on the main forward deck, far from berths for Europeans. Eddie spent much of each day playing mahjong with a group of men he knew from Darwin, relishing the freedom of recreation. Lily, meanwhile, resolved to keep Ivy and Joe inside as much as possible.

Despite fearing typhoon conditions, she was reassured when the weather remained largely calm and began taking the children out of the cramped cabin onto the deck for an hour each morning. It did not ease her fears, for they attached themselves to the prospect of disease or drowning or a myriad of other concerns that exploded in her head, fireworks spraying darkness everywhere.

The time with Eddie's family passed in a blur of vigilance that wore her out. The baby was always in someone else's arms and Ivy ran wild in the rice paddies near the rammed earth house in Qiao Ting village, where they stayed with Eddie's youngest brother, his wife, their three children, and Eddie's elderly mother.

Lily enjoyed meeting her husband's family and learning more about his early place in the world. She was pleased, though, as the date of their return drew closer and with it the prospect of being back in charge of her own routine. The anticipation of departure was aided more than a little by the way the house merged seamlessly at the back with the pig pen, occupied by two smelly, grunting inhabitants.

One morning, about two weeks before the end of their visit, she was tidying the sleeping platform that had been provided for them, while Joe slept in a wicker basket positioned in a shaft of sunlight coming through the open doorway. It was still early when she heard an unfamiliar voice. Eddie's brother had left at first light to work in the fields and his wife and their children had gone to the market, insisting on taking Ivy with them. Eddie went outside to greet the stranger. They spoke for a few minutes in low voices.

When he returned he leaned heavily against the door frame while his eyes adjusted to the dusky light inside. 'Come away outside so we can talk, Lily.' He gestured towards his mother, dozing at the table, and went back out into sunlight. She followed.

'I have some news.' She heard the kindness in his voice and stiffened.

'Is it Mother?'

'I am sorry to say that it is.'

He explained the circumstances twice before she could allow it to sink in. Mother had collapsed on the side of the road as she made her way from the market garden to her customers. She had been struck down by a bleed in her head.

'But when?'

'Just after full moon, a week ago.'

Mother had dropped to her knees under the weight of all she carried, while her daughter had been separated by an ocean, not even aware that such an essential pillar had crumbled. In her mind's eye she saw the baskets falling from Mother's shoulders, suspended in the moment before they scattered ripe mangos, eggs, vegetables in the dirt. Mother lying there, soil on her white shirt, hands still gripping the bamboo pole.

The reality struck Lily like a blow. She had no concern for what the neighbours might think, falling into her husband's arms, sobbing loudly against his shoulder. When she stopped crying, she went quiet. She remained that way for the remainder of their time in the village, even when her husband's sister-in-law gave her white iris flowers to wear in her hair while they sat an overnight vigil to honour Mother.

Late into the night they lit more incense and burned joss paper as spirit money, though Lily knew it would not compensate for the absence of an only child at the coffin in Darwin.

The loneliness that assailed Lily as a young wife without husband and a mother without child had been hard enough to bear. This was different, confusing her bearings, leaving her marooned in the flash flooding of an inland sea.

Though she had not seen Mother for more than a year, they had written regularly and more than that, she had relied on the gravitational pull of the woman from whom she had come, circling in her orbit as the moon around the Earth. The departure of Mother left far too much empty space.

They returned to Australia on the *Changte* with about two hundred other passengers, mostly Chinese. Lily longed for the sight of Thursday Island, where their documents would be processed for re-entry to Australia, taking her ever nearer to Darwin and the moment when she could properly attend to Mother.

Within hours of reaching the island the captain announced that after the ship berthed, everyone would be detained on board for an extra day.

She and Eddie immediately knew why. One of the cooks in the steerage galley was Chinese and had shared what transpired. While the ship's name meant 'long life', it had not been so for one of the passengers. Late at night, an Englishwoman in her forties had kissed her adult niece goodnight then left for her own cabin. She had been seen minutes later, going overboard in the Basilan Strait as the vessel steamed through the islands of the Philippines.

At Thursday Island, passengers were restless with the desire for travel onwards to home. Police came aboard and began interviewing the crew and any passengers who may have been in the vicinity of the handrail where the woman had disappeared.

As the officers inquired about the circumstances, it did not surprise any of the Chinese passengers that witnesses were encouraged to the view that it was probably an accident due to disorientation or poor eyesight.

Had they bothered to ask Lily she would have set them straight. White skin, yellow skin, women were their own kind. Regardless of origin, circumstances or race, they knew there was a price to pay for wanting more. She clutched baby Joe as she stood on the deck. It was hard to live with only the one foot on the rail.

By the time they disembarked in Darwin, Mother had been gone for almost three weeks. Lily was disturbed by the prospect that she had been buried in a grave for the destitute.

Fortunately, she had underestimated the respect Mother had earned as a producer, supplier and wise Chinese elder. The Chinese Association had taken charge in Lily's absence, ensuring the farewell was conducted in the proper way. A feng shui master was consulted in choosing her final resting place, on a gentle slope off to one side of the cemetery, away from the flood-prone area. Nanyin musicians had led the coffin from the ceremony to the grave.

Aside from repaying the association for burial costs, there was little Lily could do and that did not help the mending of her heart. The only comfort was that Mother would remain buried in Australian soil, unlike many others, their bodies interred and returned to the country of the ancestors.

Mother had been clear years earlier about her wishes. 'On the roots of the tree rest falling leaves. I will be a new tree and it will be your duty to tend my spirit and when the time comes the grandchildren will take over. I don't want you shipping my bones back to China.'

Although it was not Ching Ming, the tradition- al time to tend graves, Lily went to the cemetery as the sky thinned ready for dawn, hopeful that the parting of darkness might open the way to the heavens. She placed a burner on the unmarked plot, setting fire to paper money, then incense. The sweet smell caught in her hair as she said prayers, laying out ripe mangos so Mother could eat, placating her so she would not become a wandering spirit, looking to inhabit a living person to find rest. She promised to return once a stone marker had been arranged.

The family sailed for Wyndham a few hours later. There had been the loss of a husband, a daughter, a son and now, Mother. It was the end of a cycle, and in the natural way of things, what was supposed to arrive was a beginning of some kind. Back in her own home she waited in anticipation, yet all she sensed within and without was dead air.

DISRUPTION

Oppressive heat and humidity,
maximum temperature 40⁰C.
Dry season likely to break in a month.

13

S HE SAW HIM COMING THIS time. As Bec exited
the ute at the rubbish tip, he strolled from the
shade of a nearby tree. It was just like him to use
the power of surprise, throw her off-balance.

'Bit rude not saying hello in Kununurra yesterday,
Bec.' His smile stretched far too wide.

'It's really up to me what I do or don't do these days.'

She refrained from turning to see where the council
workers would be but then realised, with a jolt, they
were on the truck doing the town's weekly household bin
collection.

'You need to be more careful, Bec. I could report you
for stalking.' He laughed.

That tone, she knew it well, a light-heartedness laced
with poison only evident in the aftertaste.

At the same time he seemed relaxed, different, as
though the spring inside him had uncoiled in the weeks
since they had been apart. In his eyes she saw the man
she had married, while the familiar tilt of his head spoke
of the shared history in the years they'd been together.

As if reading her thoughts, he smiled. 'There's too
much to throw away. We could give it another shot, start

over. You can come back to Perth when you're ready. I'm not going to pressure you.'

She was leaning into his words as they called up memories of the known, the familiar, the certainties that had been abandoned for the void in which she now lived. Wife, journalist, competent woman.

The truth of it struck her suddenly, a sucker punch of all the loss she had kept at bay. The force of it made her falter. He saw it and didn't attempt to touch or steady her but left the space for her to be with her reaction. At least that was what she believed in the moment.

'I can't even think about that.'

The morning upended all the heat it had gathered since dawn onto the two figures near the pub ute.

'Come into the shade for a minute.' He gestured towards the shelter of a nearby flame tree and she followed him towards it. There was no sign of his hire car.

'Look, if you want to stay on and keep things open-ended while you work out what to do, maybe I could take the van back to Perth.' The suggestion was casual, his face still relaxed.

'That way, if you want to get back together, we don't have to stay there. I could pack our crates back onto the roof rack and we could meet somewhere new, start afresh.'

She had no instinct about what to do, how to respond to him. The future was a vortex that swirled up from the hardened ground under her feet and drew all thought or desire into its empty centre. The past offered no place to inhabit and the woman who once lived there had faded, a visitation from a dream forgotten a day later. She no longer strained to find her.

Maybe he had changed, too. He'd been taking his time trying to convince her to leave, not in her face, not forcing like the old Glen.

It made sense, she supposed, for him to take the van. At least it resolved the issue of driving a vehicle that technically was not hers. Maybe it was a good idea to release it, consign it to the past. It was a final anchor and without it she might sense a rising tide and let it take her to a new destination, or maybe she would continue the routine that kept her suspended, preserved in the glass jar of Wyndham, and that would be okay, too.

If he had the van, perhaps he'd be more likely to leave. She could hand it over and see if that worked. It was a chance she would take.

They stood close together in the small circle of shade thrown by the stunted tree. He looked into the distance, only the side of his face visible, the drag of something weighty like sadness in his eye. He had suffered, that much could be seen, and in the suffering she no longer saw him as a threat. She would get the key to the van. He could take it.

She beckoned towards the cabin of the ute. 'Hop in. I'll take you to the van.' She didn't bother asking what had happened to his car. He'd have an answer ready and it wouldn't be worth the breath she would waste with the question.

As Bec gunned the ute onto the main road, the thought of him taking the van and driving out of town, returning down south, worked on her as though she had tossed back a couple of glasses of wine. The closer she

195

got to the house, the more buoyant her mood grew, the taste of liberation already on her tongue when she pulled up on the verge and brought the ute and trailer to a rapid halt.

———— • ————

Lily had finished a light lunch and shuffled outside to sit under the reach of the corrugated verandah roof, while the heat danced, fiendish in its footwork, on the road and up on sandstone outcrops of the Bastion. She settled on the wooden chair in the shade, pressing against its back, bringing her hands together on her lap, thumbs touching.

Most of what she saw these days was a blur and although others felt sorry for her, something she recognised without them saying it aloud, the fact of it was no cause for concern. In her world, the hard edges had been rubbed away, giving everything a pleasing softness, even the dusty motel ute pulling up opposite.

Her young friend was busy in the mornings, but her afternoon visits had become a highlight of the day. She thought she saw two people exit the ute, then decided it was part of the unreliability she had come to expect from her eyesight.

It was a gift, the gratefulness for what she could see and the acceptance for what she could not. How many times, as a younger woman, had she wished for the power to avoid seeing what was in front of her, especially in the years after Mother died.

———— • ————

Soon after the first anniversary, she had recognised the

familiar changes in her body. Trying to ignore them was futile and within days of the ninth moon cycle Willie arrived without fuss. He seemed to understand that it was best to make minimal demands of what little energy his mother had, settling easily into a feeding and sleeping routine and thriving with little encouragement from Lily.

Despite being close in age, Joe was fascinated by his baby brother, while Ivy was a natural nurturer, ever ready to fetch whatever Willie might need.

For his part, Eddie was delighted to now have two sons, though the echo of the third reverberated between husband and wife, especially in the quiet moments.

They should have been remarkable, peaceful times. The business thrived. The baby grew strong. Ivy excelled at school. Willie, once he learned to speak, was happy to entertain himself, curious about every discovery of a new plant, insect or bird.

Yet Lily remembered little except the stiffness that assailed her when she realised, three years later, that another baby was on the way.

By now there was more time needed to cook, clean their living quarters and clothe the children, and she still took whatever sewing commissions she could manage. The only time she felt alive was in the rat-a-tat rhythm of pedalling the sewing machine. She rarely ventured into the shop to help Eddie and as they ate in the evenings, if he felt she had drawn away from him he said nothing, though he would touch her sometimes as she slept, to reassure himself that she was living skin and not a spectre.

Lily herself wondered some days if she was even alive. It was as if she walked and worked in a time between times, where the past was barricaded and what lay behind the door of the future was more than she could bear.

It was into this becalmed period that the great wind roared, at first quietly gathering itself up over waters off Java, evident only in a few thunderstorms that drew streaks of cumulus cloud into their centre. Squalls broke onto the surface of the Timor Sea and were pushed by wind speeds that increased during the day then fell away to almost nothing overnight, in a divine game unobserved except for a few Indonesian fishermen far from their home ports.

In the Cambridge Gulf, where the sea floor dropped more than twenty-five fathoms in places, whirlpools and eddies began to seethe between narrow underwater gorges, disturbing the occasional giant stingray seeking to rest or feed on the seabed.

Updrafts of heat and moisture began to form long bands that spiralled inwards. As they turned ever tighter towards the centre of the low pressure system, gale-force winds turned cyclonic. The whirling mass, by now rotating clockwise to form its own engine, started driving towards the northern coast of Western Australia, looping back on itself a few times, gaining intensity before continuing its onward trajectory.

An unsuspecting fleet of about thirty pearl luggers, each with a crew, divers and shell-openers, all up nine or ten men, were first to see the fury coming, as the ocean surged and tall waves rose ever faster. Working out in the gulf, far from their home port of Broome, they were fishing for pearl shells, intent on making up for income lost during the cyclone season. Each year, ports down the

Western Australian coast to Onslow were choked with masts as a hundred or more luggers laid up to wait out the danger period. A month later, they were out on the open ocean, unprepared for a freak cyclone.

As the seas continued to rise, the luggers made a run for shelter in one of the many creeks along the shore but were far from safety when violent headwinds struck, forcing them away from land. The men worked desperately against the offshore gale, trying to keep their flimsy vessels upright, despite knowing it was hopeless, that if they lived it would be through a mercy beyond any puny human effort.

Far away at Wyndham, the morning was proceeding predictably. Eddie had taken delivery of new stock, much of which had been on order for regular customers, so he had been busy at the cash register. While he made small talk and served at the counter, a weather warning was telegraphed through from Perth and the postmaster dispatched a delivery boy to relay it around the town.

No sooner had the message gone out than light winds accelerated, turning sheets of dust to sandpaper, blasting the street, stinging the faces of those still hurrying home. Within minutes, the temperature dropped about forty degrees. Eddie rushed from window to window, nailing a wooden screen across each before locking the front and back doors.

He joined Lily and the children in the kitchen, alert for what was to come. They did not have to wait long. Suddenly, a rush of wind battered the building with the high-pitched scream of a caged beast hurling its might against its walls. The children huddled close to their parents.

Willie, almost four, began crying and pushed under his mother's arm, which she automatically lifted to pull him against her round belly. Ivy's eyes were wild but, aware that she was five years older, she gripped her hands together and remained silent. Joe, though only seven years old, understood his responsibility as the eldest son and when his father offered reassurances that they were safe, that the willy willy would blow over, he nodded wisely and ventured: 'Of course it will'.

Outside, chaos continued. The telegraph service was already a mess of downed poles and wires in several places along its route to Derby. It would take linesmen on horseback, leading pack mules laden with equipment and materials, at least two months to render it operational again.

Along the creek behind the meatworks, trees snapped like pipe stems. Throughout the port and town, fences smashed and sheets of roofing iron, wrenched from outbuildings and houses, spun upwards. One piece of iron slammed from thirty feet in the air with such force it sliced into a jarrah beam on the side of the jetty.

The *Bullara* had docked the evening before from Fremantle and the vessel swayed and lurched at the wharf, though the captain was unconcerned. His ship had survived a cyclone at sea two decades earlier with only the loss of a funnel, and as he monitored the conditions he was confident she was safe moored in the curve of the inlet.

No sooner had he made his assessment than a sharp tidal surge gripped the steamer and shook it. The shorelines snapped with the crack of whipcords, loud even against the howl of the wind. The ship's stern swung out into the inlet as the bow strained on two forward hawsers that barely held, while the captain rushed to organise men to reinforce the ropes.

In O'Donnell Street, white ants for months had been working their way into the main beam of the police station. Against the onslaught the entire roof gave way, with little resistance, and whirled skyward.

The Fong building shook and strained. The family heard little above the banshee wind but they felt every thump as objects were flung onto the roof or against the walls in an attack of such ferocity that even Eddie feared for their lives. For almost an hour their dwelling shuddered until it seemed to Lily, finally, it would hold. At that moment, she heard a deep groan issue from the front of the shop, followed by the unmistakeable tearing away of a structure, as swift as ripping apart a piece of cloth along the grain.

The timber door adjoining the shop buckled inwards. Eddie shouted at them to get down and cover their heads as it flew open and thumped against the wall, the handle punching through the pine lining. Eddie and Joe pushed the table across to jam the door shut, straining against the force that threatened the building's timber frame.

The pounding and the deafening whine of wind continued for another ten minutes then, without warning, stopped as though a switch had been thrown. Eddie stood, ready to go outside and survey the damage. Lily plucked at his sleeve. 'Not yet. It might not be over.' The stillness seemed more unbearable than the noise because its meaning was uncertain. It got to Eddie and he opened the back door and slipped out.

Voices could be heard shouting on the street and

among them was Eddie, calling to his family that it was safe. They filed out into the yard then stopped as one at the sight before them. Upturned drums, torn trees, unrecognisable debris had been scattered indiscriminately. One tree remained standing but was studded with several iron bolts, lined up neatly as though fired from a gun.

Eddie came up behind them, stabbing a finger towards the inlet.

'That's most of our verandah there, in the water.'

A hump of corrugated iron and a crooked beam, looking for all the world like a drowning sea creature, were all that was visible above the surface.

'Others have not been as fortunate.'

They joined him in looking up the street, where backyards were strewn with tangled bits of timber, broken glass, vegetation stripped from trees and even an upended table, missing two legs.

Lily tried but she could not see that any good fortune had come their way. It seemed to her that the spirits must be greatly disturbed to have sent such a storm.

Just before dark, the State Shipping Service vessel, *Koolinda*, limped into port with twenty-five Japanese and Chinese crew members, rescued from three luggers abandoned out on the ocean. The remaining twenty-one luggers had ripped apart, their timbers scattered across the sea, along with everyone on board. The captain had tried to divert from his usual route to search for almost one hundred and fifty missing men, but it had been impossible. Some of his female passengers were still crying, nerves jangling from the distress of the pearlers, the chaos of wind, and wilfulness of ocean.

The willy willy had disturbed something in Lily, too,

and she had her own impossible search. It was clear that the woman she once had been was gone, and there would be no point in attempting to seek her out. The knowing did nothing to quell the desperation to find a sense of solid ground within.

While Eddie set to work restoring order, including retrieving what he could of the verandah, she became jittery as the pregnancy reached its final stages. Even while she carried out her household duties, she had longed to be elsewhere without knowing where that place might be.

———— • ————

Seated at her vantage point in the shade, a dull throb in her shoulders, Lily recognised the same dislocation in her young friend. She turned her head a little in Bec's direction, neck refusing to yield in the way it once had. If only she could pour all that was needed into the young woman's heart, soften it, open it again to the pulse of eternal energies. But she could not, it was a power she did not have.

Power, a strange word for an old woman to roll around in her mind. Yet she had known it in the animal instinct of the birthing hours.

———— • ————

The familiar sensations of labour had begun. Lily had finished cooking the evening meal and while waiting for Eddie to finish up in the shop, prepared the bedroom. Dorothy would be getting food for her own family, so she was in no hurry to summon her.

'What is it, wife?' Eddie was looking at her an hour

later, as she doubled over at the table. The urge to push was so strong that Lily was unable to give a reply. Eddie did not wait for one.

'Get Dorothy, Joe. Hurry!'

Ivy pulled Willie to her side, cuddling him as Eddie helped their groaning mother out of the room.

Dorothy arrived soon after, panting, with a dusting of rice flour on her skirt from the batter she had been mixing to steam for wrapping beef cheung fun. One look at her friend and any thought of rice noodle rolls was completely forgotten.

She hurried Eddie out of the bedroom and closed the door. Lily leaned on the edge of the bed and let herself down to squat.

'No pushing. Let me check where the baby is first.' Lily could only nod, with all her breath channelled towards blocking the overwhelming downward urge while Dorothy kneeled to examine her.

'Gentle breaths. Let the baby ease itself out.' She turned to gather the towels from the stool.

Dorothy barely had time to get to her knees when Lily leaned forward onto her hands. She felt about to break. Dorothy shifted position then paused momentarily as her friend swallowed back a deep grunt. In one more breath a baby girl arrived in a rush of blood and amniotic fluid, shooting into Dorothy's hands as though the tail of the cyclone swept her into the world.

Soon after, Ivy managed to sneak into the room and was overcome with joy and anticipation of a sister to share her bed, ignoring the blood still on the baby's face as Dorothy began gently washing the newborn.

The older girl's energy grated and Lily pushed her

away more roughly than she had intended, before turning her face to the wall.

'It'll be okay, you'll see. The love will come,' Dorothy whispered as she lowered the small bundle into her mother's arms. The baby opened her eyes and looked to Lily, but as she looked back at the infant all she saw was its blank face full of hollowing need.

It took her back to the afternoon when she sat with Mother in the market garden as it pulsed with abundance and fertility, learning to weave with bamboo grown for the purpose near the tool shed. She had not applied the correct tension as she looped the strands over and under the spokes to work the frame. Next morning, when she loaded the completed basket with freshly picked tomatoes, the bottom sagged apart and the skins punctured on gravel spread along the path, making the tomatoes unsaleable.

She felt, again, the anger at herself and the wastefulness of her endeavours.

That evening they named the girl Sue, in honour of the teacher from whom Eddie had learned English when he was newly arrived in Darwin. Later, while the family slept, Lily stared into a burning candle and saw that it was not the birth that caused the final threads within to snap but the sight of another small, open mouth.

———— • ————

Within weeks, Lily took to walking in the early morning and late evening with the baby tied to her chest, pacing in an endless circle from the kitchen, across the foreshore road and down towards the water. If any of the children tried to walk with her, she barked at them in a voice she barely recognised and sent them inside.

In any case, the children had long since been discouraged from straying near the water's edge. It was common practice for residents in O'Donnell Street to scatter leftover chicken or beef bones and other food scraps on the muddy edge of the inlet. Crocodiles were older than dinosaurs, surviving through a knack for adapting. One of the old ones feeding at the meatworks blood drain had worked its way upstream in search of a more varied diet. At dusk it slid silently from the dark water and back, leaving soft marks to dry in the mud, the only sign of its wide belly full of daily offerings.

Each day, Lily walked with purpose yet went nowhere, trying to deter the thoughts spiralling like screws into the soft timber of her soul, biting deeper as they turned. Her younger self had considered Mother's views a little harsh but now she saw that the older woman had been right. The unfolding of life could not be prevented and the fact that it did not seek Lily's cooperation was of no consequence.

She went on because she saw no other way, rising at dawn, performing her tasks efficiently as usual, avoiding customers in the shop. She sent Ivy to the Post Office to collect the mail, so there could be no unexpected greetings or questions that might agitate the calm waters on which she floated, causing her to sink. And if there was no rejoicing and only the weight of responsibility for the two living sets of sons and daughters? Well, the punishment was her due.

Such a strange time it was, looking back on it. Though she walked, talked, tended children and home, honoured the ancestors as a good wife and daughter must, it seemed that she was vapour, lost to the world of substance.

She prayed daily to be at peace. As she watched the white smoke rise from the incense to carry her pleas to Mother, to any ancestors who might help, the months continued their relentless march onwards and no indication came. She began to understand she was alone.

───── • ─────

By late October, the build-up to the wet season was already fraying tempers and temporarily unhinging some of the locals. The slightest exertion sent sweat rolling down faces and the back of clothing, which delighted flies gathering around eyes and across damp shoulders. The temperature climbed and humidity rose rapidly. Vivid sunsets heralded rolling black clouds, the darkness soon split by spears of white lightning dashed onto the water.

As Lily worked her way through each day and cared for the baby, she felt the pressure grow. It was in the air and in the barometer of her blood.

Late one afternoon, with the sun hovering in the western sky and the evening meal prepared, she put on her straw hat and walked out the back door. Eddie would be in the shop for another hour and although the older children were home from school, Joe had gone up the street to play with the Chin Toy children and taken Willie with him, while Ivy was at the kitchen table practising her letters.

Sue was strapped to Lily's chest, dozing in the heat as she usually did when her mother paced. The air was heavy and Lily was forced to slow her steps as she left home and walked towards the water. She reached the line where desiccated grass faded into cracked, dry soil above the high tide mark, before it merged into grey sludge, then water-logged mud.

A line of bent mangroves with twisted roots threw patches of shade towards her and she found the one where she always turned, where her footprints from the previous day still marked the dust, footprints she had left in all the days before.

She spun on her heel and returned to the back door, glancing up to see Ivy's outline as she bent over her schoolbook and worked her pencil, then turned back towards the water. When she reached her patch of shade, the one she felt was hers because she had earned it in all the days of pacing and surviving, her feet stuck fast.

She rested her eyes on the silvery pattern, thrown down in defiance of the sun. The infant's head was resting on her left breast and Lily heard a soft sound as the little one stirred, then went quiet again. The baby was physically vulnerable but growing up as a girl and gaining maturity as a woman would only deliver a different kind of helplessness. The inevitability of it was a force that gathered up Lily's past and rolled it forward in a stream of images that laid out the future for the girl.

Out of nowhere, a sea breeze found its way from the coast to the woman standing motionless on the edge of the inlet. The hot air began to move. It took on Lily's restlessness and carried it off. Relief washed through her.

A shadow shifted against the breeze, close to the water's edge, and if she saw it she had no desire to examine the movement. Her feet began to rise and fall of their own accord, purposefully, steadily, across the last strip of dry grass and onto the oozing grey sludge.

The baby must go with her, she did not doubt it because the little one was bound to her, not by the length of cloth tying her in place but by the breadth of her dependence. It would be a kindness to Eddie for it to happen this way. He would save face. He could tell the policeman that she did not see the crocodile, that it was an accident.

She was possessed by the idea. It moved her feet forward. One step, two steps, another, more. Her hips strained with the dragging weight of the baby, but she made no attempt to reposition the girl higher on her chest.

A mangrove kingfisher startled and flew out from a nearby canopy with a string of sharp screeches. It swooped towards her, flashing sapphire blue tail and wings against a bright white belly, then at the last minute veered up and disappeared towards the burning sun.

The mud was a welcome of velvet around Lily's toes, soft and gentle. In a few steps it became smooth cotton sateen sliding across the tops of her feet, giving way to fine silk brushing her ankles, the touch of royal fabrics she rarely had the opportunity to sew and never to wear. The pleasure drew her on, an inviting flow of sweetness.

The water ahead was alive with bouncing light, glittering as though the silt-stained brown of the inlet had been swept clean. It beckoned with a promise of purity. In the distance a dog barked, then a male voice shouted and the animal was silent. A steady hum of human activity drifted over the water from the direction of the meatworks.

If any of the sounds reached Lily, there was no indication. Despite the baby slumped against her and the mud sucking at both heels, she was weightless like the birds, flying free in a place where burdens were smoke rising to the heavens. The hard colours of the sunburnt landscape no longer ached against her eyes but yielded to hues of blue, pink and gold.

She felt her body slip away as the colours drew her on, towards the sparkling path of light thrown down by the sun as it slid to the west, where it would be extinguished.

All around was air and she was but a wisp of gossamer floating towards the pull of the water, all thoughts yielding to the brightness ahead.

She was at the water-logged edge when her elbow was seized, jolting her back inside her rib cage.

'Mama, mama.' Ivy's voice was urgent, firmer than a nine year old's should be.

'It's not safe. Come back, mama.'

For the briefest moment, Lily thought all three could wade in. Instead, she turned instinctively towards the fear in her older daughter's voice and began to follow her home.

Ten feet away, in dappled light, a pair of eyes floated on the surface of deeper water and watched it all.

14

S UE LIKED TO CHATTER, AND at more than
two years old, gathered words like a fledgling
took worms and insects into its beak. She named
what she touched and saw, pinning objects and people
to points in space and time as though it was a compen-
sation for the mother she could not bring to ground. She
was first onto Eddie's lap if he paused on a chair in the
kitchen and would slip through the door to join him in
the shop if he left it the slightest bit ajar.

Eleven-year-old Ivy and nine-year-old Joe were
patient with Willie and Sue as they did their household
chores or played in the dust out the back. It was Sue,
though, who most sought to have their attention, toddling
from one to the other while six-year-old Willie seemed
to accept whatever was offered by way of interaction and
ask for no more.

Eddie rarely stopped by her sewing machine, so when
he did one Wednesday morning, she stopped pedalling
immediately.

'Should we go to tomorrow's memorial service for
Matron?'

Lily paused, struck by the unusual circumstance of her
husband not only asking for her opinion on an important

matter but also suggesting she might accompany him to a community event.

'Will Dorothy and Chin Toy be there?' They might know if Chinese residents were welcome at the gathering. Matron Irwin had been one of the first taken by dengue fever when it reached the town a month earlier. A no-nonsense former war nurse, she was something of a friend to the Chinese population. She had grasped their reluctance to attend the hospital and more than once had slipped medicine to an ailing adult or child.

'They are unsure, which is why I am speaking to you.'

Lily, hands either side of the sewing machine needle, stretched the fabric to ensure no folds would be fed across the stitching plate. The thought of a social occasion, let alone something as formal as a memorial service, was cause for dread.

'Then perhaps we should stay home.'

Eddie nodded and the matter was settled. He retired to the shop and she rolled the flywheel and pressed the treadle with her right foot to set the machine whirring again. The fever visited Wyndham and other far north towns every decade or so but this time it had knocked only on doors at the Three Mile. The unfortunate Matron had nursed patients who lived there.

The dull beat of the sun continued as it did each year in June at the centre of the dry season, when the heat governed in a dictatorship, prescribing when and how much work could be done; requiring townsfolk to cease all movement in the middle of the day.

Eddie kept the shop open as usual at one o'clock, leaving a bell on the counter so he could eat then doze on a bench out the back for an hour or so, yet still be alerted if a hapless customer needed attention.

Willie and Sue squatted to play half-heartedly with a ball in the shade, rolling it back and forth while their father napped. Lily happened to look out the door just as Sue folded forward then fell sideways onto the dirt. She went to her daughter, ready to scoop her up and take her inside for her daytime sleep, but as she leaned down she saw the telltale lace of the fever rash tracing along capillaries on her arms and cheeks. The girl whimpered and pressed her hands against her temples, then balled her fists into her eyes as Lily called to Eddie and carried the toddler to her cot.

'Get Dorothy.' Lily was harsher than intended, propelled by panic.

As Eddie hurried off, Lily placed the back of her hand on the girl's forehead. She was burning. She stripped off the toddler's clothes then poured water into a basin and dipped a cloth in it, bathing the small body repeatedly in the hope of cooling her down. At first Sue lay unmoving in the cot, but by the time Dorothy arrived she had begun thrashing on the mattress and crying pitifully.

Dorothy took the cloth from Lily and continued wiping the little one down. 'Get a cup,' she ordered Lily. 'You must keep her drinking.'

Lily stared at her restless daughter, unable to move until Dorothy gripped her arm. 'Do it now, my friend.'

Within the hour Sue had begun vomiting, and although Lily continued to offer water, any that was swallowed was not retained for long enough to be of any benefit.

Eddie assessed the situation from the doorway, addressing Dorothy.

'You must go home. If a mosquito bites her and then you it is too great a risk to your own family.'

She nodded in reply and sought to reassure them as she departed.

'She's a strong girl. All will be well.'

Soon after dark, Sue fell into an exhausted sleep. Lily felt the girl's forehead and could tell the fever was abating. Relieved, she climbed on the bed to get some rest.

Eddie was awake. 'The worst is over,' she whispered.

The room was still dark when she woke to the animal sound of her daughter vomiting while groaning in pain. When Lily reached out to the girl she felt the heat come off her before her hand even touched the forehead. It was then she realised the fever had not ceased but had drawn back only to assault the toddler with greater force.

The vomiting continued till dawn when Sue's breathing became rapid and she stared at the ceiling, wailing as though she saw through it to the souls of all wrongdoers, roaming eternally in anguish. Eddie lifted her up, pacing with her in his arms while the sheet was changed then, with the girl back in the cot, Lily resumed sponging her down and attempting to trickle water between her lips.

When Ivy woke, she took the cloth from her mother's hand and begged her to go to the kitchen and eat. Reluctantly, she agreed. Eddie, on his way to open the shop, placed a hand briefly on Lily's shoulder and left.

She began spooning cold rice into her mouth, not because she wanted it but because she needed to keep up her strength. She recalled how listless Sue had seemed in the previous couple of days, yet she had not thought to check if anything was wrong. The rice was sticking to the back of her throat.

It was then that Ivy called out in alarm. When Lily stepped up to the cot, a pool of bright blood stained the fresh sheet. Sue was bleeding from the nose.

All day she stayed by her toddler's side, cleaning up, fanning her, dribbling water into her mouth, speaking in soothing tones. The bleeding came and went. When Sue became restless again late afternoon, she sang the children's favourite song in soothing tones. 'Bright moon, shining on the ground. Little Shrimp be good and go to bed and sleep …'

Sue turned her face towards her mother, eyes still closed. The song had several verses and Lily, encouraged, sang them all then started again. The toddler seemed more peaceful and her temperature had eased, so Lily tried tempting her with a slice of watermelon, rubbing it against her lips to no avail.

By the end of the next day, the child had still not eaten and was taking only occasional sips of water. Her breathing had become more strained. Lily sat up with her through the long night, stroking her hair for hours.

At daybreak, she instinctively gathered Sue into her arms and found she was not asleep but unresponsive. Her daughter remained warm and still breathed but Lily felt her spirit pulling away, already departing. Overcome, she buried her face in the side of the girl's neck and begged her to stay. Eddie entered the room soon after and together they watched Sue draw a shallow breath that was her last.

A flood rose up from deep within Lily, overflowing in one long shriek. Even when the children came to the door she could not hold it back, drawing in breath only to release the same sound again. They watched, fearful, as she continued to hold the toddler's body, to weep, and to pray with a ragged voice that Mother be the one to meet the girl and guide her with comfort and reassurance in her new state of being.

When Eddie tried to take the small, fevered frame, Lily slapped his hands away, shouting 'no, no, no,' not caring that it was unseemly. Joe's eyes were wide, never having seen his mother's anger unleashed. Ivy leaned against the door jamb and sobbed into the sleeve of her blouse. When Eddie shepherded the others into the kitchen his daughter refused to budge and he left her there, a mirror image of her mother bowed under the burden of her tears.

Lily had no way to know if Mother would accompany Sue in the realm of the afterworld but she felt, without a doubt, the older woman's presence at her own side, a whisper in her ear even as she held her little daughter's sweat-wet body. It carried an exhortation, urging her to fall to her knees and grieve, and grieve some more if it was not done, then to rise and walk on. It was only what generations of women before her had done; it was what a woman should do. She wept anew for all that a woman must carry.

A day later, she was not at the cemetery so was spared the sight of shadows at the open mouth of the grave as they swallowed the small coffin, and the swarm of flies that followed as it was lowered. Eddie had made sure she stayed away, arranging for Dorothy to be with her.

It was clear to Dorothy, seated opposite the distraught mother in a chilling circle of silence, that she was beyond reach. She could not know that out at the cemetery, under the searing sun, Lily's spirit was quietly slipping over the lip of the grave and down to rest on her daughter's body, even as the gravedigger began shovelling in orange soil.

It had been slow, the smothering of any fire that remained in Lily. There was no shame, no sense of failure this time. She was beyond such feeling, for it would be a sign that she still had capacity to recover.

Mother had been the one to rise and walk on. It had been the older woman's destiny, but it did not mean that it was the path fate had laid out for the daughter. She felt the chair's stiff seat beneath her and could not comprehend that she would ever lift from it and stand.

It was hard to remember the weight of it now that she wore so many years, her body stretched thin, opening in places to let in the light. Lily lay on the bed in the cooler air of evening and let the material matter of bone and muscle be gently drawn up and away.

Something was coming, she sensed a shift happening beyond the room, the shop, the town, beyond even the sky. The ancestors were almost ready, the way had been prepared for whatever would be required of her, though her heart was certain it would be in the service of her friend.

Lily knew the signs, saw the pressure rising. A time for choosing was approaching for Bec, as it had once come for her, and afterwards nothing would be the same.

The Earth had turned, the moon rose and fell, the sun was its usual bullying self, and the days had been all one for Lily. More than a year had passed since she last held Sue in her arms when it became evident she had not bled for two months. It was no surprise, for her life force had continued to ebb, leaving her blood unwilling to have release and risk losing what little aliveness infused it.

'Are you sick, mama?' Ivy, now twelve, was helping prepare breakfast while the boys slept and her father was at the wharf to fetch the latest consignment.

'I am well, daughter. Wake the boys. It's time for everyone to get ready for school.' Seven-year-old Willie was already coming through the bedroom door, rubbing his eyes, saving Lily from the prospect of further questions.

Later, with the three children off to school, satchels on their backs, she wondered what had prompted Ivy's question, for she was always mindful of her responsibilities as a wife and mother. However badly she wanted to curl up and let the despair take its course, tasks and routines in the household went on as usual.

When Eddie returned, she helped with unloading the dray and shuffling boxes into the shop, so she was later than usual in settling on the stool in front of the sewing machine. As she pedalled, her mind blessedly opened like a quiet pool on the bend of a river. She rested there as she did most days, the only time in her waking or sleep when she truly let go, her hands and feet drawing out the energy that at other moments turned back on her as though the ancestors stood in a circle, each with a stick to strike her.

Her thoughts turned again to her daughter, tall and knowing in ways that Lily herself lacked. Mother had passed on her strengths but Lily had let them slip through her fingers and they had flowed to Ivy, who had the good sense to recognise and grasp them. Like Mother, Ivy had a way of seeing beyond the surface. Where others saw sky, Ivy saw limitless worlds. When birds or animals called or cried out she understood if it was in friendship, alarm or pain, and when a person presented the mask of politeness, Ivy saw through it to the soul that hid inside.

If her daughter had asked such a question she had seen a change in her mother, even if she had no ability to name it. And then it struck Lily. What Ivy sensed was as clear as the tremor in steamy air signalling the approach of the monsoon winds, when the elephant ear wattles on the rocky slopes of the Bastion, the grey box trees out at Marlgu Billabong, flatback turtles in soft mud near the mouth of the gulf, every creature on land and in the water began opening to the promise of the fertile months.

The signs could no longer be ignored. Another child had begun growing in her womb. Lily stopped pedalling, her feet poised on the treadle, her breath stilled, then hit the palm of one hand repeatedly against the side of her head.

In the days that followed, Ivy began spending less spare time in the shop with her father. She had been an enthusiastic apprentice, learning how to talk to customers, do stock orders, reckon the takings; to note when certain goods were running low and occasionally ring up purchases on the cash register. Now she stayed by her mother's side, making tea, fetching spools of thread from the cupboard, cleaning up after meals.

'Ivy, have you changed your mind about having your own shop one day?'

The family was sharing bowls of sticky rice and water egg, cooked in chicken broth to the consistency of custard. Ivy looked at her father in surprise. She had chopped the scallions, beaten the eggs for steaming and cooked the dish for the first time, under Mother's supervision. When Father addressed her she was expecting praise for the meal.

'No, Father, I have not.'

The girl looked down at the chopsticks she was using to mix rice with the edge of the water egg, willing the exchange to end. Joe, beside her, took the opportunity to get his father's attention. 'There is no school tomorrow. I'm helping make a billy cart with some boys in my class. Would you have some rope we could use for steering?'

Eddie's eyes lingered on his daughter for a moment longer.

'I cannot waste new rope on a billy cart.' Joe's hopeful smile faded as Eddie swallowed a large spoonful of the water egg. 'Though I can probably spare a length of the cord I use for lashing supplies to the dray.' Joe grinned and thanked his father. The family continued eating and Eddie held his tongue.

A few hours later, as he lay beside Lily in darkness, he spoke quietly so the children in the next room could not hear.

'I know it is the way of each generation, and it is the proper responsibility of a daughter, but she is too young to be caring for you in this way.'

'I have not asked her to do so.'

Lily turned her head away and nothing more was said, though she remained awake for some time, remembering the way worry lines had dug into Mother's face after they had returned, penniless, from Canton to live in Darwin. The fear, not tempered by Mother's reassurances, had slid on its belly as a rat might squeeze under a door. She had heard it sniffing about, smelled its rank breath.

It was still there as she fell into sleep, the sensation of ground shifting beneath her feet in knowing Mother was shaken by her challenges. The memory had released its hold by the time she woke and began her daily tasks.

Mid-morning, she took the jacket and matching vest from a man's suit to the chair near the back door, where the last slice of shade clung on before it crossed to the front of the shop. Unlike the suits commissioned by locals, mostly in linen or tropical worsted cloth, this one was a special occasion outfit in worsted wool for a meat-worker returning soon to cooler temperatures.

The fabric was warm across her lap as she hand-stitched three buttons down the front of the jacket, lining up each one to a buttonhole, stopping frequently to rub the damp hand holding the needle across a scrap of old towel looped around her opposite wrist. She had moved on to the vest when she noticed the quickening, the baby making itself known.

Within seconds, the air was disturbed by the flurry of rapid wings. A flock of Gouldian finches landed as one on the lowest branch of a young snappy gum about twenty feet away, their coloured feathers bright against the white bark of the limb and leaning trunk. They faced her, as though waiting, and she dropped the sewing onto her lap.

For the first time in many years, she thought of Grandmother, her skin translucent on her bed-ridden body as eternity entered, shrinking organs and tissue. In a rare lucid moment the old woman had spoken of birds that came in large numbers to wait outside the home of the dying. As a child, she had slipped out of the bedroom and gone to open the outer door, where she had waited and watched all afternoon.

Now, she watched again.

Was she to die soon? If so, there was no fear for herself, but she could not bear it to be another one of her children, another dusty grave where she knelt in the dirt and wrestled with the urge to begin digging for the child buried below.

It is a new life. It must be properly valued.

She heard it as clearly as if someone stood beside her in conversation, though it was not a sound made by the vibration of vocal cords. It landed within, resonant in its own way, a message carried by the finches, winged messengers of the ancestors. The birds remained in a line, heads scanning rapidly this way and that, occasionally chirping or shifting a few steps, but always facing her.

Their arrival was discomforting, stirring the inertia of her malaise. For the first time since the realisation that she was pregnant, she allowed herself to know what was under way beneath the skin already stretched like a drum. Alongside the pulse of her blood was a fainter rhythm, barely perceptible, the heartbeat of a tiny being, perhaps with a face, already growing limbs, working on shaping ears and eyes and fingernails, holding on despite any distance or denial she mustered.

She saw Ivy's face, alert and shining in all the watchfulness of recent weeks, and the sadness that stretched tight around her daughter's mouth, where once had been a ready smile.

More finches began cheeping, their calls rising to a higher pitch, urgent, noisy.

A gust of hot wind shook the eucalyptus leaves as a pair of crows, feathers blue-black, landed nearby. The finches peeled away from the limb in swift twos and threes and disappeared. The crows thrust blunt beaks into the soil, snatching what little seed remained, so close the whites of their eyes were visible. They flew into the canopy, gave a brazen string of sharp caws, then were gone.

In the silence that followed, she understood what she must do. Whatever effort must be summoned, however long it took, she must find a way to care for the baby and spare the daughter growing old before her time. As if in response, there was a fluttering once more below her ribs.

————— • —————

The children would be home from school soon so Lily began clearing the table where she had finished cutting out grey serge pants for the last customer she would take on now her pregnancy was nearing its end. Eddie had been tired lately and she wanted to be sure that his evening meal was not delayed.

She heard a man speaking to him in the shop, though the drawl was muffled by shelves of tinned goods on the other side of the wall. Eddie must have dropped a box of stock on the counter, ready to unpack, for there was a dull, sharp thump and the man stopped talking.

'Missus, missus.' The shouting was urgent.

She hurried into the shop. Eddie lay crumpled at the foot of a stepladder, his customer red-faced, leaning over him.

'He was getting me a set of spanners from that shelf. Then just like that, he was on the floor.'

She knelt beside him. Though he was dazed he was making futile attempts to sit up, pawing at the floor with his right hand, trying to get purchase on the boards with his right boot.

'Easy, easy mate.' The man had his hand under Eddie's arm, steadying him as he dragged the shopkeeper upright, into a sitting position.

The fall had changed the familiar contours of her husband's face, and in its drawn countenance Lily saw the toll of his seventy and more years. She brought a chair over and they helped lift him onto it but he was unable to sit unaided.

'I'll get the doc.'

The customer fled, leaving Lily kneeling on the floor using her arms and torso to prop up Eddie.

Soon after she heard Ivy and the boys chatting as they straggled home from school, down the path beside the shop.

'Ivy, come and help, and shut the shop door on the way in.'

The left side of Eddie's face sagged and his left arm hung unnaturally straight. At the sight of it, Ivy froze momentarily before following her mother's instructions, supporting the good arm while Lily manoeuvred her shoulder under the useless limb. Together they hauled the small-framed man a short distance, then paused to catch their breath, before dragging him without stopping into the next room.

'Keep going, keep going,' Lily urged until they were beside the bed.

Ivy, buckling under the strain, lost her hold and her father pitched forward onto the mattress. She burst into tears.

'It's okay, Ivy. All will be well. Your father is a strong man.'

Lily rolled Eddie over and lifted his legs onto the bed. He was trying to extend his right leg and arm to help but his awareness of the paralysed left arm and leg was causing agitation. His eyes were wide with shock or terror, Lily could not tell which.

'Put a pillow under his head, daughter.'

She found other small tasks for Ivy, sending her out to the kitchen, keeping her in motion tending to the boys, hoping it would calm the girl. Meanwhile she sat by Eddie, trying to thaw a mind that had frozen, so she could decide what to do.

The doctor knocked within the hour and Lily felt she had no choice but to let him in. By then Eddie was lying still, eyes closed. She could not tell if he was sleeping or unconscious.

Was it her husband's death the birds had come to foreshadow? The idea curled reptilian around her throat, making it hard to maintain a calm voice as she shooed the children outside.

'It's a bad business. He fell, I understand?' Lily nodded.

Doctor King flicked the switch on a small torch and began lifting Eddie's eyelids to examine the pupils.

'Have there been any signs that he's been unwell? Tiredness, confusion, difficulty finding words …'

Though Lily was on edge about having the doctor in her home, he was new, having arrived in Wyndham two weeks earlier, and rumour had it that he was showing no aversion to treating a patient with skin a different colour.

'More tired than usual, yes. It has been a busy time in the shop.'

It was worse than that, she thought, shivering. There had been at least three times in the past week when she or one of the children had been speaking to Eddie and his eyes had glazed over. Afterwards, he had not known anyone had spoken. Several times in the evenings, as she watched him tallying debit and credit columns in the shop ledger, he had squinted and held the accounts book at arm's length, struggling to focus on the numbers.

Eddie had dismissed her concerns. 'Just a little dizziness, that is all.'

The doctor finished his examination and ushered Lily out of the room.

'Your husband has had a stroke. There is little I can do for him. The main thing for now is to encourage him to swallow fluids, mainly water, but if possible a little soup.'

He studied his shoes and paused.

'If he becomes conscious, you must massage his limbs often, particularly the ones affected, and encourage any movement. If you do so, he may well recover at least some of their use.'

Some of their use. Lily swayed a little as the doctor snapped shut his brown leather bag then steadied herself for his farewell, but he was not finished.

He seemed to understand it was not appropriate to have eye contact and instead, held his bag tightly and looked out the back door where the boys huddled, forlorn, on either side of Ivy.

'I feel it is my duty to tell you, Mrs Yong, that many patients do not survive a stroke of this magnitude. I am sorry to say that those who do are often in need of round-the-clock-care.'

He left then, hurrying towards the hospital where he would request a briefing on medical supplies from the Matron and make himself busy with lists for replenishing the store cupboard, to wipe from his mind the thunderstruck faces of the Chinese wife and her flock of dependent children.

15

BEC PARKED OUT THE FRONT of the house and rushed from the ute, calling over her shoulder to her husband as she went down the driveway.

'I'll get the key. I just need to get a few personal things out of the van before you take it.'

She shouted to Jo as she slammed the back door, but her friend had already left for work. Window shades were down in the kitchen and dishes were draining on the sink. The wall vents were half-closed and the stale air in the hall was thick like a curtain she parted to reach the bedroom. In the rush for work that morning she had left dirty clothes on a chair and the bed unmade, expecting to sort it out later. Without thinking, she bundled the clothes into a laundry hamper in the corner, smoothed out the sheets and quickly tucked them in, then began looking for the keys.

It had been a while since she'd used the van and the keys were not on the stool she used as a bedside table. They were not in her handbag, either, or in the pocket of the shirt she had worn when she'd last gone to Sheryl's house. He would be getting impatient by now. She was debating going out to tell him she was still looking when she picked up her backpack and began going through its compartments. Nothing. She shook the pack, just to be sure, and heard the jingle of metal. The keyring had worked its way into the worn corner of the main section and she had almost missed it. Relieved, she hurried from the room.

When she stepped back out he was already at the sliding door of the van. She unlocked it. The door dragged a little as she pushed it open and in the haste to climb in she forgot how far it was necessary to bend, banging her forehead on the roof lip.

The van was in shade from the house but heat from the morning sun was trapped inside. Her hands were sticky as she dragged a plastic crate from under the bed platform. She pulled out a battered colander that had belonged to her grandmother, as he climbed in the driver's door and began adjusting the seat. She was checking another box for shoes when she suddenly realised there was no longer anything in the van she desired. She pushed the box away and stooped to get out.

He was leaning over the passenger seat, looking in the glove box.

'Where are the rego papers?'

She glanced up. 'They should be there.'

'I can't see them. You sure?'

She was ready to be rid of him. She opened the passenger door and perched on the edge of the seat, pulling out a box of tissues, the van's manual and service record and, beneath it, the registration papers.

She turned towards him, her right hand balancing the tissues on her lap and her left extended with the papers. For a moment she was puzzled. Something in his hand prevented him from taking the documents. In the instant it took for her to understand, he snapped the handcuff onto her left wrist and lunged across to attach the other cuff to the door handle.

With one sweep of her head she saw Jo had left the laundry door ajar again and hoped the python had not returned. Further along, washing hung stiff on the line. The back door to the house was wide open. Out the front, the keys were still in the ute. Bec gripped every detail around her, clawed at it as though she could, through an act of will, remove herself from the van, be outside it.

He slammed the door beside her with the lock on, went around the nose of the van and got back behind the wheel. As the engine rumbled to life she began screaming and wrenching with her trapped fist.

He drove onto the street in a spray of gravel and headed towards the Three Mile and the highway out of town. She waved frantically at any oncoming vehicle and yelled for help as they passed the occasional pedestrian, but it was as though she had become invisible. The more agitated she became the calmer he grew.

'You're wearing yourself out, getting worked up for no good reason.' They had reached the open highway.

'What? I don't know what you think you're doing, but you've kidnapped me.'

He smiled then.

'Bec, really. You've been up here in the heat too long. You're getting delusional. We're just taking a nice drive and I'm keeping you safe. We don't want you getting confused, then jumping out and hurting yourself.'

A sliver of sun hit the steel confining her wrist and jerked a circle of reflected light across the dashboard. She shook her head as if to dislodge what he'd said.

It was all flooding back. His belief in his own words was rarely dented by the world coming at him. It was the fender buffering the image he cultivated of himself, protecting him from the knowledge of his darkness. She had come to understand, over the years, that he needed it to survive, that something had shattered long before she met him. He had abandoned any chance of healing to embrace self-preservation, whatever the cost.

Two realities were colliding in her brain, one in front of her eyes, a van speeding down the highway with her chained to it, and the other pressing at her from the figure behind the steering wheel. She strained to stay with the sensation of the handcuff digging into the bone on her wrist, to the irrefutable truth of it.

He did this, bent what she saw and heard out of shape until she doubted herself, until anything resembling truth got shredded and hung, tangled, from whatever story he concocted in the moment.

No one would believe her. Always it was this. How could she hope to explain the man he was in private when he peeled away the mask of charm, the veneer of unruffled efficiency in his job. There had been no bruises, no evidence she could produce. He was careful about that.

He would have primed his colleagues, been the devoted husband. It was obvious now. Would have said he was worried about her mental health, that she was showing signs of cracking under the strain of the anaesthetist's death. There had not been one single spontaneous move on his part in recent weeks. He had been deliberate with every step he intended to take.

She sank back in the seat and focused on her

breathing, fighting to withstand the panic cascading through her. It threatened to sweep her away, rushing fast like the asphalt coming at the windscreen. The awareness of the way it engulfed her drove the terror to greater intensity. She feared her heart would seize.

She braced against the seat. She would not give in to the fear, must hold herself together, stop the splintering of self.

She cast around in her mind for something steadying and immediately Lily was there, on her chair in the shade. She imagined the peaceful face, the resolute body, and the way it felt to sit there with her elderly companion, solid yet eternal. The panic remained but she could turn away from it to the memory of Lily's force field of calmness, to the sense of breathing it in, sharing what permeated the space around the elderly woman without either of them saying a word.

The van lurched around a dead wallaby and the thrust of the steering wheel sent her rocking from side to side, yet still she sat on the warm pavers out the front of the shop. The dread was circling as they hurtled down the highway, but at least for now she was no longer dissolving.

Soon after, he pulled the van off the road and got out. She allowed herself to believe that the calm she had recovered had somehow touched him, brought him back to reality. He walked purposefully to low scrub and parted a couple of bushes, lifting out a blue coolbox. He carried it to the van, dumped it in the back then strode off, returning with a bag slung over his shoulder, his hands balancing a cardboard box of cans and packets of food. The third time he returned, each hand carried a large jerry can of water.

'It's a long trip. We have to look after ourselves.' He flung the sliding door shut.

'This is ridiculous. When we get to Perth, I won't stay with you. You can't keep me locked up. Life is not going to be the same as it was.'

'Of course it's not.' He said nothing more.

They had already passed the turn-off to the Gibb River Road and were continuing south. At the highway junction near Kununurra, a sign pointed to the right—west towards Broome on the coast, from where the highway skirted the iron ore mines of the Pilbara and the towns that serviced them. Then it swung south to follow the edge of the Indian Ocean till it eventually rolled into where she had started, in Perth, the place where he seemed to think they could start over.

He ignored the turn-off and drove on. The disbelief unleashed a burst of nausea that bubbled up, burning her throat before she swallowed it down. He had a plan and it was not about Perth.

———— • ————

Back at Wyndham, Lily dozed for a while in the heat and when she opened her eyes, a bulky object was in full view opposite, drawing her attention. Something about it was familiar, yet at the same time disturbing for no reason that could be fathomed.

She could make out the form of it, heavier at the front than the rear, and then something else attached beyond that. She remembered then that the motel ute and trailer had pulled up much earlier. Occasionally Bec had

233

stopped there for a few moments on the way to or from the tip but had never left it parked there for so long. A feeling took hold of her, the unwavering certainty that it should not be there. Something was wrong.

She lingered on the chair for much longer than usual, drifting in her mind. Soon she felt herself walking down a long road and as she walked she met the curve of the Earth. Though the road bent to it, she walked straight on into nothing except air. In the lightness of being she searched for her companion, but the young woman was not there.

Lily sensed her, far off, in a place of danger. What was a frail, old woman to do? She summoned all the learning gathered in her many years, took a momentary pause then called without sound into unearthly vastness, crying out for the woman's kin to protect her.

This was the moment, she knew it. The ancestors had prepared her for it. It was the purpose for the weeks of connecting, the weeks of sharing strength with her companion. Lily focused her thoughts and poured all the energy she could gather into the call.

Louie came out from behind the shop counter to check on his mother and saw she seemed to be napping, head slumped towards her chest. He went to wake her so she could return indoors out of the heat, but something stopped him mid-stride. He left her undisturbed and resolved to bring her in under the ceiling fan a little later.

———— • ————

Bec had no idea if they were heading up to Darwin, further south to Alice Springs, across to Townsville on the east coast, or if her destination would be, instead, a shallow grave along a lonely road.

Such stupidity. She'd been kidding herself she understood him, could manage his moods. She had convinced herself she had found a rulebook of sorts, that even he had limits. She had foolishly trusted in it.

He was volatile, throwing barbed words in her face or flying into a rage at the smallest slight. He would go cold and uncommunicative for days to punish anything he decided was a transgression but then would be conciliatory, sometimes remorseful, and the man she had married would reappear.

His behaviour was his dirty secret and it had become hers, too, when she signed the wedding certificate years earlier. She had understood implicitly that it was now her responsibility to keep it hidden. A contaminated covenant sealed with a kiss.

His shame became her shame. Each time he called her useless, ranted because she dared have a different opinion to him, made her pay with a hail of criticism when she had success at work, the thought was there, that she must be defective or lacking in some way to be treated with such contempt.

In the past year, though, her ragged scrap of self-esteem has been torn down to almost nothing and when you have little there is a lot less to lose. She had begun, involuntarily, to take an occasional stand, to challenge or answer back.

She hadn't realised it might lead to this, being held captive on a road trip to who knows where.

She should have seen it that Saturday, months earlier,

when they argued about his insistence they spend their savings on a high-end stereo.

'That's our emergency fund. Let's wait till we can afford it.'

Suddenly, the argument was no longer about a new stereo system.

'You don't get to say what I spend my money on.' He sneered.

'It's my money too. And my name also on the account, so legally I do get a say.'

'Don't be ridiculous, Bec. All this talk about legalities. I am the law.'

Her brain had slipped a gear, clicking lightning fast into the wrong groove, where it slammed to a halt.

'Oh, you're such a big man.'

The words had jumped out before she could stop them and the disdain in her voice dripped through the deathly pause that followed. She knew immediately it was a mistake, that the worst thing she could do was humiliate him.

He had just replaced rusted screws on a second-hand table collected earlier that morning and the electric drill was in his hand. She saw his arm coming up to draw back and instinctively ducked to the side. The heavy drill had velocity as it flew towards her head, barely missing before it cracked onto the floor, the bit gouging out a chunk of carpet and tearing through the underlay to the concrete base.

She had dropped the subject immediately. It had been another incident she'd been willing to pretend had never happened, or at least willing to collude with the pretence.

She snapped out of the memory. It was futile to waste

energy retreating to the past when she needed her wits in the present. She sat bolt upright as the van ate up more kilometres.

They were approaching the turn-off to Lake Argyle, where country occupied by the Miriuwung Gajerrong people for at least forty thousand years had been submerged to create an irrigation scheme. Native grasslands were now a lake bed; hills and ranges had been stranded as islands. She felt the creep of the water as it covered the plains. She was a valley floor with a crush of water bearing down.

The van was running smoothly down the highway. She had filled the tank when Jack first paid her and had barely driven it since. It could cover about four hundred and fifty kilometres on the remaining fuel, propelling her hours away.

He drove on. Soon after they crossed the border into the Northern Territory, with only a peeling welcome sign to mark it. The panic was rising again. Perhaps she could engage him in conversation, get him to give something away about his plans.

'So where are we going, then?'

He gave her a withering look. 'What is it you want from me, Bec? I've done so much for you, but it's never enough.'

She swallowed. This was nothing new. He often convinced himself he was the victim.

'I just thought, if we're having a road trip, it might be more enjoyable if I know where we're headed.'

'Even though you reckon you're a prisoner?' The harsh voice.

'May as well make the most of the drive, I guess.'
She was keeping it low key, hoping to sound friendly.
'Well, you'll just have to wait and see.'

RECLAMATION

Warning of flash flooding for rivers and low-lying areas, with 100-170 millimetres of rain expected.

16

I T WAS JACK, OF ALL people, who was the first to recognise Bec had disappeared.

He bailed up Jo in a lull between drinkers in the bar.

'Seen Bec? The ute's not back.'

Jo was incredulous. It was at least two hours past the usual time her friend finished the tip run.

'You need to look for her. She could have had an accident, for all we know.' She glared at him.

He wasn't impressed that she had delegated the responsibility to him but he nodded in agreement, mainly to save face. He went to his car, parked in front of the last row of units, one of which was his home. The vehicle was barely out on the street when he caught sight of the ute.

'What the hell's she playing at.' He pulled up in front of it, still grumbling aloud. Through the driver's open window the keys were visible in the ignition. He'd give her a good earful about that when she answered the door.

At the front entrance, he knocked. In the ensuing silence he surveyed the street, seeing the Chinese shop-keeper's elderly mother, a shrunken little woman, out the front of the store. He ignored her and knocked again. When there was no reply he began shouting.

'Bec, are you there? It's Jack.'

After several failed attempts to get a response he went down the side of the house.

The back door was wide open, the house dim inside. When he leaned in, the air was stale and he heard blowflies banging against the kitchen window, trapped behind the lowered roller blinds. It set his teeth on edge.

'You home, Bec? Just wondering if you're sick or something …'

It didn't take Einstein to know what his employees thought about him, that he was devoid of feelings or compassion. Somehow, though, it had not occurred to a single one of them that he was successful at running hotels because he had good instincts. And now they were working overtime.

He sensed in the deadness of the house that she wasn't there, that she had been gone a while, though he had no idea how or where.

He left the door as it was, spun his car around and returned to the bar. Jo had just finished pulling a beer and had two more punters waiting to order when Jack grabbed her arm.

'Out here,' he jerked his thumb towards the beer store and she followed.

'The ute's at your place but she's not there and come to think of it, neither is her van. Ring Sheryl and see if she knows anything. Use the office phone.'

The punters in the bar were shouting for service and he left to quieten them with a few schooners.

'No, she hasn't said anything to me about a trip.' Sheryl was holding the phone against one ear and removing an earring with the other, while kicking off her shoes.

'I saw the ute outside your place on my way home. Thought it was a bit unusual she was so late getting back from the tip run.'

She'd assumed her friend had dropped in home for something that had been forgotten, immediately putting it out of her mind because all day she had been getting up the courage to ring her daughter and stand in the rejection when the girl likely refused to speak to her. She'd hurried home to catch her as soon as school was out, before Saffie went to hang out with friends.

'Maybe Bec's sick.'

Sheryl's mind was still on her daughter, so she was flummoxed when Jo began to cry.

'What is it, love?'

'Jack's already checked the house. She's not there.' Jo blew her nose.

'The other day, when I went with her to Kununurra to get the spare grog, she saw her husband and she was dead-set scared. She didn't want to talk about it either.'

Jo braced herself for Sheryl to do what she usually did: offer reassurances in her motherly tone. Instead, there was a brief pause.

'I'll be there in a minute.' She left home, forgetting to remove the other earring.

The two barmaids waited in Jack's office while he fetched Kieran, ignoring her protests about needing to finish cleaning shower bays in the units and head off. He set her to work behind the bar, pulling a clumsy beer. He was red in the face when he returned.

'We need to call the police.'

Sheryl held up one hand. 'Hang on, Jack. I don't know that's a good idea. If it's her husband, he's a cop and you know how they stick together.'

'Yeah, well we don't even know if we need to report her missing. There's always the possibility she might have just taken off. We've got no proof she's lost or anything's happened to her.'

His rational response set Jo off. 'Don't be ridiculous. It's a sure bet. She's hardly the unreliable type. Besides, what have we got to lose in assuming she's been taken against her will, other than a bit of embarrassment?'

'There's more at stake than embarrassment.' Sheryl looked shaken. 'She might have felt she needed to run. By alerting his mates, all we're doing is setting the dogs after her.'

'So, we do nothing?' Jo was beginning to crack.

'Look, he was here at the pub last week and she was pretty rattled when she saw him. Maybe she's seen him again, panicked, and headed off in the van under her own volition.'

'She'd phone one of us, let us know. She would be aware we'd worry.'

Sheryl had to concede that one to Jo, remembering how Bec had risked stopping, even as she fled from her husband in Perth, to let her boss Andy know she had gone.

Jack was insisting the police be notified, but Jo was not listening. She picked up the phone and began punching in the numbers for Dave's workplace. Sheryl was still debating the best course of action with Jack when the aviation centre answered Jo's call. She heard the voice on the other end of the line and although she had met the receptionist, all she could see was the face of the woman who had come to her aid when she had run from the lake at Kununurra.

Bec was trying to keep track of time. The sun had begun its descent and was burning her arms and thighs through the windscreen. She ached with thirst and the inability to formulate a plan.

He spoke as though he was continuing an existing conversation. 'There's likely to be cattle roaming and wallabies on the road now it's getting close to dusk. We'll stop at Timber Creek, find a good spot to camp along the Victoria River.'

He smiled at her. 'I reckon I can catch us a nice barramundi for dinner.'

He was back to pleasantries. It was surreal. She jerked her arm with the handcuff, deliberately hurting her wrist to stay present, not disappear into the cosy, familiar fog in her mind. There was a line running through her centre and on one side was a hollow log in which she could curl up, feel woozy and safe, and on the other was a madman saying sane things while he kept her prisoner.

She had to stay in touch with the madman if she wanted to save herself.

He would be planning to refuel at Timber Creek. She was sure of it, and sat rigid in the seat, barely glancing at the vivid red escarpments fencing out the sky. She ran through every move he would have to make to buy petrol, going over it repeatedly to identify a moment when she might get help. It was likely to be self-serve so maybe when he went to pay she could get the window down and scream for attention.

They were close to the town and she was on high alert when the van slowed and turned left off the highway, causing her to choke back a gasp. A blue sign flashed by and she glimpsed the letters spelling out the location. Policemans Point. In other circumstances she might have laughed.

A dirt track snaked back and forth until it reached the Victoria River, where the land pinched the water into a narrow channel that flowed swiftly before spreading out into shallows at the wider reach near the parking area. The place was deserted. He drove the van off to one side, reversing so that its nose was facing in the direction they had come.

'I'll try casting with a lure when it's getting dark.'

Surely it was fanciful that he had exercised the foresight to bring a fishing rod. As if to answer, he clambered from the driver's seat and walked around to the sliding door, shoving it open. From the bag retrieved earlier in the day, he pulled out a couple of T-shirts, an old towel and, finally, a neatly folded fishing rod. Contorted as she was to see around the headrest into the back of the van, the lungful of surprise made her cough.

He held it aloft in a triumphant gesture, as though to underscore the fact that he was capable of anything. Another time, without the handcuff imprisoning her wrist, she may have sought to find a more generous inter-pretation of the gesture, that it was a simple expression of anticipation at the possibility of throwing a line into the river. But it was all the times of manufacturing benign explanations for his behaviour that had led her here, chained to a sweltering metal can, about to pass out.

He unlocked the passenger door and she reached across with the uncuffed hand and pushed it open, ready to slide out. The damp skin on her thighs stuck to the vinyl seat and she had to rock forward, lifting one leg then the other, before she could pry herself loose.

She was on an awkward lean as she got both feet on the ground, exiting backwards with her left arm still trapped. He held up a saucepan with some water poured from one of the jerry cans. It was almost hot enough to make tea but she gulped it down regardless.

'You could unlock me now. It's not as if I can go anywhere. Besides, I need to pee.' Her voice summoned the compliant self that was most likely to get a positive response.

He smiled, all teeth and no eyes.

'Don't take me for an idiot, Bec.'

He carried the heavy coolbox to a shady area beneath low-growing acacias, out of sight of the track. When he returned to the van he unlocked the handcuff from the door and attached it to his wrist before half-pulling her into the shade.

The handle of the coolbox was securely attached to each end of the solid body and he flipped it back out of the way and pushed her down so she sat on the lid. Then he removed the cuff from his wrist and with a deft flick, snapped it shut around the handle.

'Go ahead and pee. I'll move you and the coolbox to a clean spot in a minute.'

If he was intending to debase her, he was succeeding. She had seen farm dogs chained to their kennel with more dignity than this. He walked away with exaggerated steps, as though emphasising that he was a considerate man, giving her privacy. She winced, but there was no choice. Her body had its own needs.

After about fifteen minutes setting up his fishing rod, knife, and a fold-up chair that was kept stowed in the van, he came back. He had taken his time, she could see that, and it was all part of letting her know she was at his mercy. She stood and followed the coolbox as he moved it ten metres or so towards the river.

She resisted the urge to struggle. The only weapon she had to defend herself was the inside knowledge of how he worked.

He was always more relaxed when he believed he was in control, and she needed him to have complete confidence in the fact that he was. Her only hope would be that in kicking back a little he might make a mistake. She had to believe she would last that long.

17

L ILY SHIFTED CAREFULLY ON THE chair, not
wanting to move inside where it might be cooler.
She sensed she must keep watch, hold the connection to Bec while keeping her own instincts tuned and
her heart open.

It could take a lot to crack open a closed heart. There
could be pain in doing so, but good pain.

She closed her eyes for a moment and rested. As she
did, the image of Bec she had been holding close began
to shift and reshape itself. At first she did not recognise
what it had become, until she saw she was looking
at another woman, small, defeated. That woman was
herself.

———— • ————

The afternoon had been fading fast when Ivy came to
stand beside Lily.

'The boys are hungry. What should I cook for them?'

Lily withdrew her hand from Eddie's arm, which she
had been holding in the hope of feeling even the slightest
response. He was in his day clothes for want of any
decision about how they could be removed to get him
into a night shirt. The challenge of changing him had

kept her thoughts occupied, far better than fretting about a future as a second-time widow left to support three children and another one who would hurry into the world soon enough.

'I'll go. You sit with Father. Talk to him, it might help.'

She glanced back as she left the room. Ivy had dragged the chair closer to the bed and was already murmuring softly about tasks that would be waiting tomorrow in the shop, as though her father might sit up at any moment and give an opinion or provide instruction.

At the table, Lily slammed the chopper onto the wooden block, cutting the last of the Cantonese sausage into pieces before using the large knife to slice leftover cabbage, bok choy, a few shallots, dried mushrooms and ginger. She tossed it all in the hot wok for a few minutes then spooned the steaming food into bowls and left Joe and Willie eating.

She sent Ivy to have her meal, while she tried again to spoon a little water into Eddie's mouth. It dribbled onto the neck pillow. She fetched a towel and lifted his head carefully to cover the pillow and protect the buckwheat hulls inside. He murmured briefly and she waited for several minutes but he made no further sound.

It was only when the kitchen had been cleaned and the children were asleep that she risked a glimpse into the future. It was a terrifying place. Dust gathered in the shop, the door closed; a vulnerable baby squirmed in her arms; the sewing machine sat, useless, in the corner. The faces of the three older children were tense and scared, while the home reeked of destitution.

She must keep a disciplined mind. Better to shut

herself of from the hardship to come, which made the present unbearable.

Sitting with Eddie, hoping for a word or two, perhaps a sign that he would stay, she sensed the presence in the room of those who had gone, circling the bed, saying his name. She was sure of it.

Though it was not the way to demand particular outcomes, she prayed fervently, bargaining for his life as a fishmonger might haggle for wares at the seafood market.

'We need him here. Please spare him. I will do better.'

It became a mantra, the words on repeat as darkness deepened outside and in each of the houses, lights were extinguished as inhabitants retired for the night.

Her mind roamed in the dark, searching out shadowy corners where doubts and concerns gathered like dust balls. She was struck by the idea that she had not gone to tend Mother's grave the previous year on Tomb Sweeping Day. Perhaps it had disturbed her spirit in the afterlife, leading to disruption.

There was also the matter of the Jade Emperor, ruler of heaven and Earth, giver of mercy, the one who sees through the character of each person and rewards or punishes them according to what he finds. The statue had been at the centre of her household shrine since Mother gifted it on the occasion of her first marriage. Weeks earlier, she had been cleaning with an unfocused mind and it had slipped from her hand onto the wooden shelf, cracking one piece from a foot. Would this not anger the deity?

So much worrying, it wore her out, and by midnight she was slumped over the side of the bed. She was asleep, she was awake, she was neither; out of her body and watching over the scene. She saw a tiger stir at the base of her spine. It stretched powerful limbs, one by one, then sprang up. As it did, energy rushed through her and she sat bolt upright, wide awake. Her throat opened and the energy continued upwards, lighting up her mind.

The aliveness frightened her at first, quivering in muscles and the marrow of her bones, an inheritance that she understood immediately was not hers alone. It came from something far larger, flowing from an invisible realm, threading through one generation after another, leading to her, a simple woman seated on a wooden chair, experiencing hard times. She was no longer alone but joined to all the lives that had gone before, to the ancestral knowledge gathered by every woman and man in her family line.

She had imagined she was the one in charge of her life, that she owned any small stroke of luck that had come her way, and more importantly, had created every misfortune and cause for grief. She had been foolish.

She saw how so many of her people, known and unknown, had strived, hungered, crossed oceans for a new life, birthed babies and given their lives in creating a story much larger than just one, a swelling story that surged within her.

The ancestors had not visited for Eddie. It was so clear, now. It was her name they had called, seeking to break through her defences and wake her up to a greater possibility.

She had been trapped by the past. She had let it happen, succumbing again and again to the lure of surviving and the easy inertia that accompanied it. She had been willing to flounder in the mud because it asked nothing of her.

In her ignorance, she had failed to grasp the central task of her life, though Mother had done her best to show it in the months and years they spent together; Mother, who knew it was not something to be conveyed by mere words.

It had been right there in front of her the whole time, in every fold of cloth she worked as a seamstress. It called to her every time she unrolled a new bolt of fabric. It was there, even as she shook out cream linen obtained a month earlier and stroked its surface, smoothing it in readiness to craft the double-breasted suit for the new headmaster. A fresh smell had risen up, of the far-flung corner of Europe where the flax had been grown, and it kindled a thrilling promise held in the weave.

She had been particular in specifying the type of linen, in the same way she gave careful consideration when making any orders for cloth. It could take many weeks to be sourced and freighted. Once it arrived, regardless of its quality, she was obliged to work with it the best way she could, understanding how the warp engaged with the weft, cutting with care to avoid wastage, marking out the correct shaping and adjustments with tailor's chalk so the fit was perfect for the customer.

It was essential to strengthen the edges where there would be hard wear and to stiffen what needed to lie correctly. So many small acts were needed to honour the spinners, dyers and weavers who, together, had called forth the cloth she sliced, shaped and stitched into its new incarnation.

At the age of nineteen, however, she had begun to

resist the fabric of life, denying the efforts of all that infused it and would continue to shape it in unseen ways.

She had confined herself to the smallness of her own contribution, had strained against the warp, resisting its natural form, forcing where the weave was not created to go. When it did not conform to her desires she had retreated from what had been supplied.

In the half-light from the candle she studied the misshapen lines of Eddie's paralysed face, resolving to keep praying for the full return of her husband even though she understood he might be dying.

Then she vowed, with every strength and skill she possessed, to cut and stitch whatever cloth she was to be given, and in doing so to open to that which she could not know through touch or sight.

That night Lily was restless and had not long fallen into a deep sleep, when at first light Eddie began to stir. He tried to talk, though it was the sound of a drowning man with a mouth full of stones. He seemed to swallow a little water when it was offered and she preferred to think he had, even when it trickled from the corner of his mouth.

When the children woke, she gathered them around her in the kitchen.

'We all need to help Father till he regains his health and strength.' She summoned all the conviction she could as she spoke, yet the three faces looking back were full of alarm.

'What should we do?'

It was Ivy who recognised they stood in the eye of the storm, as they had the afternoon the willy willy arrived, and there probably would be worse to come.

Lily addressed her daughter first.

'Today you will go to school as usual, except when the final bell goes, you will tell the teacher you are not returning. You are the one who best understands the workings of the shop, so tomorrow you will open it for business. I will help where I can.'

Ivy nodded and Lily saw, in the one simple gesture, her daughter pass from child to adult.

The boys were stiff and silent, hair uncombed, still in their night attire, looking through the open doorway at the fragile man who had replaced their father. She needed to give them a semblance of certainty and it would not come from false promises about Eddie.

'Education is important to Father and me, therefore I want you both to keep going to school.'

When Willie began to cry Joe reached over to place a hand on his shoulder, leaning in and briefly touching heads. At the sight of it Lily fought the urge to gather them both in her arms and sob uncontrollably, for she knew if she did that the stitches she was placing with great care might loosen and their lives would fall apart again.

'I will prepare a roster. Willie and Joe, when you are not at school there will be extra jobs to do. It will make a great difference.' She spoke in more tender tones.

It was Joe, the thoughtful one, who asked the difficult question.

'And Father, when will he be well again?'

'Only the gods can know, and in the meantime we will give him good care. The doctor says he may be up and about in a few weeks.' She had not intended to lie and hated herself for it but could not bear to cause them further disquiet.

'Go to Father at least twice a day. Talk to him, it will help him find his way back to us.'

Willie's face crumpled and he covered his eyes with his arm.

'That's not him, though.'

The seven year old's chin wobbled and he began to keen from behind his arm, the lament rising in pitch till it rebounded from the ceiling.

Lily went to him, standing at his back, pressing hands to his upper arms as reassurance that all was not lost.

'His form may seem different for now, but his love and loyalty remain untouched. We must remember that.'

After the children had left for school she tried feeding Eddie congee mixed with a dash of sesame oil and juice from grated ginger. The smell seemed to reach him but when she attempted to spoon a little into his mouth his teeth did not open. She added more water and mixed it to a loose paste and this time he swallowed a few small spoonfuls. His eyes were open and they held fast to Lily's as the spoon went back and forth from bowl to lips. The concern radiating from his pupils seemed more potent than the sun, already causing the sheets of roofing iron to expand and chafe against the rafters above.

'You've had a fall, but you'll be better soon.' She put down the bowl and spoon and reached across to pat the hand that still had movement.

He strained as though trying to rise, urgent sounds issuing from deep within him, but his mouth could not marshal them into any coherence and all that came out were ugly grunts. His eyes had shifted to her belly and she knew what he was trying to say.

'We'll keep the shop going until you are well again. Ivy is ready and I will help. While we may not keep it up to your standard, we will not fail you.' A faint pressure from his hand gave the reply.

'You must rest, husband, and eat and drink so you grow strong again.'

He relaxed against the pillow and as she left him a knock came at the back door.

'How is he?' It was Dorothy, her voice low.

Lily stepped outside. 'I am trying to remain hopeful.'

'Oh my friend, a new baby here soon and an invalid to care for.'

All the panic Lily suppressed seemed to be rushing through Dorothy's veins and it left Lily feeling unexpectedly calm.

'Pray for us, and especially Eddie.'

Dorothy took a deep breath. 'Yes, of course.' She paused till she had regained control.

'I have spoken to Chin Toy and he is in agreement that I will come to help for an hour each week-day afternoon. At least until …'

Her voice tailed off before the sentence ended. Neither woman sought for it to be completed.

Dorothy's assistance in the afternoons, preparing food for the evening meal and giving advice as a fellow shopkeeper to Ivy, meant Lily could begin massaging the limbs on Eddie's left side. Almost a week had passed and though he sounded like a man speaking underwater, they could understand some of what he expressed. When the doctor arrived unannounced Lily saw on his face the surprise that his patient had not deteriorated. It spurred him to action.

'We must try to get him up.'

Lily moved to grasp one of Eddie's arms but the doctor stopped her immediately.

'Not in your condition.'

She was left a helpless bystander while the doctor and Dorothy dragged her husband's frail body into a sitting position.

Eddie had extended his right arm to help prop himself up, but the left one hung heavily at his side and threatened to topple him with it. The doctor asked Lily to bring over the wooden chair and he slid Eddie onto it.

'Do you have a towel? We will tie him to the chair so his muscles can learn again how to balance.'

It seemed to please Eddie to be in a seated position and though he was exhausted after an hour, needing to return to the bed for rest, he took a little more food at lunchtime. With detailed instructions given by the doctor, Lily ignored her own weary body and the baby kicking to begin an exercise program for her husband.

Each morning after breakfast she moved his arms and legs, bending and stretching the muscles and flexing the feet and hands. Ivy helped her mother get him onto the chair before opening the shop. After he was back on the bed and Dorothy had arrived, Lily worked his limbs again.

As the days passed, Eddie seemed more able to keep himself upright and his right arm and leg strengthened. One afternoon, Lily and Dorothy managed to get him into a standing position, providing a broom handle for him to lean on with his right arm while they supported him, Dorothy holding his paralysed arm and Lily behind. When he tried to walk the left leg dragged and he was unable to take his weight on it.

After Dorothy had departed Lily went out the back door and crossed the foreshore road to the nearest tree to lean against thick bark. Goot Song, George, Sue. They could not be saved. She looked up into the spreading branches, each one depending on the trunk to supply life-giving water and nutrients. Ivy, Joe, Willie, the baby, and now Eddie. She could not allow herself to fall over just because the wind was gusting through her load.

———— • ————

Late that night, she woke to familiar gripping pain and knew she would likely have another baby by dawn. She woke Ivy and while the girl ran up the street, nightie flying under her old school cardigan in the haste to fetch Dorothy, Lily left Eddie in bed and lay towels on the floor in a corner of the kitchen.

It was not an easy birth. The baby was in no hurry, as Sue had been, preferring to cling to the wall of the womb and leave Lily to do all the work. The minutes and hours collapsed in on themselves in the hardness of the floor, the convulsing pain, the sweat that mixed with tears, salty in her mouth.

As the sky became lighter Dorothy went to Eddie and helped him with the bedpan, but needing to be with Lily, did not try to move him to a chair. She woke Ivy and set her to making breakfast and feeding her father.

Still the baby did not come.

The boys woke and though Dorothy tried to shield them from the sight of their mother, bent over, face strained and slick with exertion, it was some minutes before Ivy could get them dressed and lead them out the door to the Chin Toys' home. As she walked them up the street there was nothing she could say for comfort, so she took the hand of each, gripped firmly and gave them something sturdy to hold.

Back at the living quarters behind the shop, Lily was deep in the stage of labour where the veil over the world thins. Through it she could glimpse the states of life and death merging in a timelessness that had no past or future, no beginning or end, but remained entire in the one field of endless possibility.

She was her body and yet she was more than her body, and the baby was not of her but part of a greater unknown that encompassed the kitchen, the town, spreading out to rivers and oceans, the country of her forebears, the spinning planet. On and on it went, to the sky, the moon and sun, into the space between the stars and more, so much more, and she went out to it, wondering if she might ever return.

'Push, Lily. Push with all your might.' Dorothy's voice broke through, commanding, urgent.

This would be the final baby. The certainty of it came looping out to Lily, a rope thrown out on a tossing sea, and she caught the end of it and gripped on tight, let it pull her back to the arms of her friend, supporting her as she squatted and grunted.

'Keep going, the head is close.'

Dorothy helped Lily lean onto cushions so she could be free to guide the baby. One push later, the blood-streaked body slid out and his mother let free a long gasp, her head falling back in relief. The room was suddenly still and quiet.

From the bedroom Eddie began calling, one low sound rising to a higher note before a pause, then the sequence repeated. Though Dorothy was lifting the scissors to cut the cord she could tell he was saying her name.

'It's a boy,' she announced to both parents. Eddie stopped his noise and the room was silent.

None of the babies Lily had birthed before had been soundless when they arrived. She lifted her head and struggled forward to see if he lived. As she did, Dorothy stood with him, wrapped in clean muslin, and lowered him into Lily's arms. The baby lay there, wide-eyed, dazed and gently breathing.

Once the afterbirth arrived, Dorothy fetched cool water and sponged Lily's face, arms and legs then fetched the undergarment already lined with strips of old towels. Leaving her friend more comfortable, she went to Eddie and helped him shuffle to the edge of the bed, then half-pushed and pulled him onto a chair she had dragged close to the bed, securing him in place with the strip of cloth Lily had made for the purpose.

In the kitchen, she put the baby in the crook of one arm and with the other, helped the exhausted mother up from the floor and into the bedroom. With Lily and the baby settled on the bed, she stood before Eddie and bowed her head.

'May your son be blessed and may he live as long as Mount Nan or at least for one hundred years.'

She left after promising to return later in the morning.

Eddie stared at the boy, a smile on the right side of

his mouth. It was not convention for the father to share the same room, but Lily was only too aware that conventions failed to cover such a situation. There would be no observing of man yue. It was too much to allow Dorothy to help with the children as well as Eddie, for she had already done more than any friend should.

She was a daughter, inheriting responsibility for respecting ways that had been important for thousands of years, keeping the flame of identity alive as People of Tang, descendants of the golden age in imperial China. Now, the traditions Mother had taught her were bending and breaking, reeds bowed down by the storms blowing through her days.

The necessity of change saddened her, but as she gazed at her newborn's face and fragile hands, seated beside a crippled husband, under the reign of relentless heat, burdened by the need to make a living so they could all survive, what she felt above all was purity of love.

The headwaters dammed for so long had burst, perhaps under the pressure of all that had come to pass, and love flowed in a natural way she had not experienced since first seeing Goot Song. It came from a boundless source, wrapping itself around the newborn as he slept peacefully in the curve of her hip, cradled by her arm.

'With your approval, I would like to call him Louie. It was the name of a man who worked with me in the tailor shop in Darwin. I am told it means famous warrior.'

To her surprise, Eddie managed a nod for the first time since his fall.

'Strength and independence will be necessary.' She was not sure if she was saying it to the baby, her husband or herself.

Two weeks later Lily took the mair dai from the cupboard, and with Louie curled in the sling against her chest, walked in the hot air of mid-morning to the hospital. She was shaking and anyone passing could be excused for thinking it was because she was far too soon from her confinement to be walking in the heat.

Lily was anxious for other reasons. In all her time at Wyndham she had never dared go into a white domain. Oh, they were blind enough to the colour of her skin when they needed her to sew their suits and dresses, but their sight was miraculously restored should she, or any of the Chinese population, need their assistance.

The natives, too, were not welcome at the hospital and had their own poorly resourced place, built out of sight on the edge of town only a year earlier. She had been in the Post Office and heard with her own ears the previous doctor's views, expressed to a visiting official.

'The colour question here is very strong. They are not wanted in the town'.

She ignored her apprehension and went to the hospital anyway. It sprawled along the base of the Bastion with its back to the rock monolith. The nurse who answered the bell stiffened when she saw the mother and babe.

'What is your business here?' The woman's head tilted back. At such proximity the hair in her nostrils was visible.

'I need to see Doctor King, sister.' It went against everything Lily had been taught but she forced herself to raise her eyes and meet those hovering above the starched uniform. Much depended on what happened next. She must not be cowed.

'He's running late today and still finishing his round, so he won't have time to see you.' She began to turn away.

'The doctor has attended my husband. He will want to hear what I have to say.' The nurse heard intrigue in the statement, possibly something scandalous. She hesitated.

'He knows you?' The question was followed by a searching stare at Lily and then the baby.

'He does. I will wait, but perhaps it could be in the shade.' The resolute tone left no room for debate. The nurse stepped back and gestured Lily towards three or four cane chairs lined up in the shade on the first of a series of long verandahs. She dragged a chair to one side, away from the window of a nearby ward and the eyes of patients or staff.

'Your name?' She barely waited to hear the reply.

'I will inform him you are here. It will be up to him to decide if he will see you.' She was haughty again and swept off in a decisive fashion intended to restore her authority.

As the morning rolled on Lily watched the edge of the shade move across the timber boards in front of her feet, getting closer to her chair. As the sun neared the midday position, the baby began stirring to be fed and with his slow waking came an urgency to get back to Eddie. She was rising to leave when Doctor King appeared.

'Your husband, he is doing well?' He showed none of the nurse's hostility.

'He has gained some use of his body but is unable to

walk more than a few steps. It is the matter for which I seek your assistance.'

When the doctor nodded Lily pressed on.

'I wish to obtain a wheelchair for him. It would make it easier to care for him and would mean he could assist our daughter in the shop. I will pay, of course.'

The doctor pondered the request and in the long pause that followed, Lily began to doubt he would help.

'We have none to spare here. However, it occurs to me that the hospital in Darwin has surplus wheelchairs, once used by men returning from the Great War. They're replacing them with newer models. I could make inquiries on your behalf if that's acceptable.'

Within the month Lily had paid a small fee, mainly to cover freight, and a wheelchair arrived. It was a challenge to unfold and when she did the first inspection showed brown stains in long streaks across the cushioned base and padded back. The chair was cumbersome, with a wooden footrest protruding awkwardly at the front. It moved on what appeared to be four pram wheels, but she was thankful to see it had spring suspension, should Eddie need to be taken outside. She could make new covers for it and perhaps provide additional padding for comfort.

Getting him back in the shop would aid his recovery. She was counting on it.

18

A S THE SUN DROPPED LOW in the sky, Bec watched her captor take his fishing rod and walk towards the shallow edge of the water, staying back far enough to scan for crocs. Soon it would be dark. At any moment it might be too late to slip away.

She had been straining to hear the first rumble of any approaching vehicle, and although a few times she'd convinced herself that someone was coming, not a soul materialised.

It occurred to her, as she desperately willed a camper to arrive, that he would have found a way to get around the regulations. Doubtless his handgun, the standard issue Smith & Wesson with the blue steel barrel, would be hidden in the van.

She did not want to be this woman, trapped in a remote area without a soul knowing her whereabouts, had fought to keep that self at a distance from the minute he'd driven out of Wyndham. Despite the effort, the vulnerable woman had come down the highway, along the track, and now met her at the point where her wrist, radiating pain, was secured with the handcuff.

The stripping away of any pretence that it might be a

sick game, ending at any minute, was a jolt. It knocked the breath out of her.

He was silhouetted by the fading rim of the sun as he flicked his lure into the river and turned momentarily towards her, despite the cover of scrub between them, raising one hand as though to acknowledge he knew she was watching.

The gesture galvanised her. She removed the coolbox lid and took out the bag of ice, a carton of milk, a dozen eggs, cheese, other packets and bottles, emptying all the contents quietly and with no sudden movement that might attract his attention. There was no plan, except for the understanding that she would need to stay near the river for access to water. The Victoria was renowned for its big freshwater crocodiles, and it likely had salties too, but she would not allow her mind to consider what might wait out of sight.

Emptied out, the bulky coolbox could be lifted with some effort but had to be wrangled vertically to take the pressure off the cuff, where only a stiff hinge separated it from the opposite side encircling the handle. She set it down momentarily and stuffed a block of cheese into the pocket of her shorts, then hoisted the coolbox back up and lurched deeper into the bush. She began working her way downriver, the load making progress much slower than was needed.

He would likely expect her to loop around and head back three kilometres to the town, so she must go the other way. If she hid out for the night, she could leave the river at first light and get to the highway, along the section where it swung closer to the river. It would mean walking across open savanna beyond the flood plain.

She couldn't risk being seen walking on the highway but there had been a sign for a side road to the rubbish tip. Surely someone from the town would eventually show up if she crossed the highway and got herself there.

The coolbox rubbed against her hip with every step and the skin underneath the handcuff was rubbing raw, but she forced herself on for what seemed an eternity, though in reality she had covered less than a kilometre when the bush petered out.

A short stretch of yellow spinifex offered no cover and she lengthened her stride, ignoring sharp spikes drawing blood on her bare legs.

The day's heat radiated up from the ground, hitting her in the face as she crouched to push under a stand of stunted eucalyptus, limbs sagging low. One snagged the corner of the coolbox and snapped her sideways, sending her falling awkwardly in the dirt. The moulded plastic collided with her left eye and she lay where she fell for a minute or so, dazed, before crawling out and continuing to flee.

He probably had a torch and would have no difficulty tracking her. She needed to get into the shallows of the river, where footprints would be quickly washed away. She shivered as she remembered. It was Dave who had told her that crocodiles mostly fed after dusk.

It was almost dark. Clouds of mosquitos were biting her arms, face and ankles, drawn to the smell of sweat. With both hands balancing the weight of the coolbox she had no choice but to let them feed on her. She went towards the river and took a breath at its edge, then slid down on her bottom, landing with water around her feet.

It was up to her calves as she waded awkwardly,

feeling her way along the bank. The light was fading faster in places than others. She startled when a long shadow appeared nearby, followed by another. Adrenaline triggered a mad scramble away. When she glanced back, breathless, rows of them were visible in a pattern on the water and it was a relief to recognise it was only a patch of ripples from the current.

The river in its dull brown had absorbed the day's sunshine and its temperature gave little relief as she tracked along its edge, holding the coolbox and the panic close to her chest. Night took over, and in the blackness she paused as her eyes adjusted.

Over her shoulder she thought she saw a torch beam flicker towards Policemans Point. She froze, ears trained on the fading calls of birds and the river gurgling past her legs. It was foolishness to focus back there; what mattered lay ahead.

Mud pulled at her sandals, each step requiring concentration to remain upright as she found a foothold in the washouts, small holes and rocks of the riverbed. The mosquitos continued to bite but she hardly noticed as she listened intently to the water lapping against the bank, ready for any change that might signal she was being stalked by enormous jaws.

She imagined giving in to the exhaustion and pushing out into deeper water, letting the coolbox fill and take her down without effort or struggle. The image of sinking, the sense of growing impossibly heavy, filled her with dread. She had to get out of the river and head inland.

She bent and gulped several handfuls of muddy water then scrambled up the bank on her knees, using the coolbox for traction on one side and scrabbling at the soil with the free hand to pull herself forward. Once out of the range of crocodiles she collapsed onto the ground, weak with hunger.

It was then she remembered the block of cheese and tore it open with her teeth, breaking off a couple of large chunks and eating hurriedly. It restored her a little and she ignored the itching of insect bites and bone-deep aching of her body to get back on her feet and keep walking.

It was impossible to see more than a couple of metres ahead. Shapes emerged and at the last minute were low branches that whipped her face, or a boab trunk looming forward, sometimes a boulder, to navigate. She kept her back to the river, or where she thought the river was, and looked to the stars for a sense of direction. When she could no longer carry the weight of the coolbox she lay on her back beside it, resisting the need to sleep, and raised her eyes to the sky.

High above, the glittering arc of constellations began to sing into the night, one long low note issuing from the biggest stars, joining with a silvery sigh from small ones in clusters. It was barely audible, the celestial symphony, but the lights pulsated and as they did sound seemed to vibrate in time. It played on, to no one but her, and soothed by it she dropped into sleep.

Darkness was thinning when she woke and she guessed it was two or three o'clock. She broke the remainder of the cheese in half and chewed slowly as she waited for the first light of dawn, when she might get a better fix on the likely location of the highway. Mud had dried and encased her lower legs and she scratched and rubbed at it to free the skin.

He would be furious that she had evaded him. The

thought of his rage turned her stomach and she began to tremble, as she had so many times. She willed herself to stay calm and her thoughts turned again to Lily and the palpable peace the woman radiated, with such reach Bec could still feel it hundreds of kilometres away. For a brief moment she could believe she would find safety. It was a fleeting sensation but it counted for something, she knew it.

The horizon was forming as she raised the coolbox, positioning it above her left hip to keep it from the bruised areas of her chest and belly where she had fallen hours earlier. The handcuff's narrow hinge meant the only way she could use her left hand was to maintain tension where the steel rubbed her wrist. The band of skin was weeping, lined with dirt, and already attracting flies.

As she began to walk she saw Lily's face, then Jo's and Sheryl's. Her mind was roaming. She thought of her mother for the first time in weeks and saw the loss undisguised by the ironed dress she wore and the flattened voice. The faces of the women stayed with her as she reached the start of the open grasslands. Perhaps she was hallucinating, but if she was she didn't want it to stop. It was a comfort of sorts, as though she were a child again, walking in the thick grey of morning fog, yet aware that the mountains and sky were still there.

The sun had risen and was already blistering the back of her shoulders and neck. If she hadn't gone too far from the section of river that curled in close to the highway she should make it to the road in the next hour or so. With the cover of scrub behind her, the blue of the coolbox jarred against the faded yellow of the grasses and rust red of dirt and rocks. She shielded her eyes with the free hand and scanned the scrub but there was no sign of him. It could not be ignored, the thought that if he hadn't followed her on foot then he was pursuing in the van.

The highway was a danger. She stood, paralysed, looking back towards the river, yet unable to go forward. It was then her ears caught a familiar sound, barely perceptible but building to a low whine that rose for a minute more then faded. It was a siren call, the cry of truck tyres along a sealed road. She began stumbling towards it.

———— • ————

He had not slept all night. At first he had searched the perimeter of the parking area and found her footsteps heading downriver, but he didn't see the need to follow them. She would struggle carrying the coolbox and would be back, though it was just like her to make this a big drama.

When she failed to reappear and it had been dark for an hour or so he cleaned the barra he had caught and took his time cooking it on the gas stove then eating it with his fingers. He left the food she had dumped where it was.

At first light he'd head to the highway and cruise up and down. She had either continued downriver or had looped around and gone east towards town. Either way she was heading for the highway and would be easy to spot in the open surrounds after leaving the strip of trees along the riverbank. If she wasn't there he would have no choice but to return and search for her on foot. It served her right if she hadn't had the sense to stay out of reach of the crocs.

———— • ————

An hour of walking and Bec had made slow progress across the rough ground, pockmarked by clumps of grass. The weight and bulky form chained to her was harder to carry than the evening before and she knelt every now and then to set it down and rest.

Without a hat the sun was relentless, burning her neck, arms and legs, but she walked on steadily, buoyed by the sound of regular traffic in the distance. Gradually shapes came into view, seeming to float across the land, tall ones that were trucks and lower vehicles, probably sedans and utes. Then something else in-between, that might be a flash of green.

She dropped the coolbox, its mouth facing up, and fell with it, head down to wrap her body around as much of the blue as she could. A sharp stab shot up through her arm but she ignored it, waiting a minute or two before raising her head to check the highway. There was no sign of the van.

She would collapse under the hot sun if she stayed too long in the open, yet there was nothing to gain in returning to the river. She stood with her load and walked on, keeping attention on her feet to avoid holes, rocks, snakes, or a glimpse of something on the highway that she might not wish to see.

Though the traffic noise had become more distinct, drawing her on, every footfall was a drain on whatever energy remained. It was unwise to stop and rest. She might not have the strength to lift a knee one more time. She slowed instead, to look ahead and reckon how far it was to the road.

To her right, above the thin ribbon of road, a wedge-tailed eagle rode the thermals, wings spread wide, effortless as it searched for the previous night's roadkill of kangaroo or maybe a solitary northern quoll. It was the first of its kind that she had seen for years. The dry season was lingering although it was early November, and it must be hungry if it was willing to risk the traffic to feed on carrion. It soared back and forth over the one area, where the highway rounded a corner and disappeared behind a low hill.

She lowered her eyes and looked to the left. It was a mirage, surely, the figure emerging from the distance in a halo of quivering air and growing bigger by the minute. It walked towards her, less than a kilometre away, at a steady but measured pace. The gait was familiar, arms stiff by the sides, holding in fury or whatever might be set to boil over.

Instinctively, she began to hurry towards the sporadic traffic, where there might be a chance to attract attention.

He was mocking, laughing in her face when he caught up.

'You outdid yourself this time.'

For a split second she thought she might shove him with the coolbox, force him to back off. She opened her mouth to say something angry but almost immediately closed it. The heat buzzed in her ears as he unexpectedly reached out with a small key and unlocked the handcuff.

'You're a mess. All your own fault. This can't go on, Bec, we need to get to the van.'

As the coolbox dropped to the ground, the buzzing faded to a thrum and then a whisper, dissolving into certainty that she must not let him take the lead. She walked on, full of purpose.

'You keep doing this, making it worse. If you were

prepared to be reasonable, we could work this through.'
He roared the final words at her back and when she didn't
stop, ran to catch up.

Neither of them noticed clouds that had been
brooding on the horizon, massing ever thicker as the
morning progressed. They hid a storm system that within
minutes broke free in a squall line and began moving
rapidly towards them.

Ahead of the squall, lightning flashed, the air around
it exploding, sending shock waves reverberating as
thunder. Bec heard it crack in the south-east but did not
break her stride.

He was close now, the heavy smell of his sweat
overpowering.

'If you don't stop and do as I say, it will be your
fault.'

The gun barrel jammed against her spine as he
grabbed her shoulder, spinning her around. The rumbling
in the sky behind them grew louder.

She swerved and shook off his hand then faced the
highway again, the air sizzling with electricity. As if in
response her body surged with energy, feet not limited by
gravity to the ground but powered forward as though by
the charge thrown from approaching thunderbolts.

She would do it this time, she'd never felt so certain
of it. There was no longer need for compliance or resistance. She was gloriously free; she had been free all
along.

Inside her bones, even as she dodged clumps of
spinifex and drew closer to the highway, the marrow was
rising. Any chaos she'd once felt was coalescing into
new blood cells generated in all the hours with Lily, in

the days with her friends. She walked on while the cells tuned themselves to the storm, tiny transmitters signalling stronger than her fear, urging her forward.

There were no guarantees how this would end. There was no sense she would be safe, no awareness of any particular action to take. She walked, listened, trusted, and that was enough. She understood, at last, the peace that emanated from her elderly friend.

Though the rumbling grew louder and the wind flung handfuls of soil upwards, she had no desire to look back, steadfastly focusing ahead.

So it was that she did not see the helicopter land a hundred metres away. She heard a voice shouting into the edge of the squall, felt the first drops of rain on her face, the shift of pressure in the atmosphere, then the words echoing and dispersing into nothing.

In the confusion, thunder rumbled, and above the sound came the unmistakeable smack of a gunshot.

She reeled to the ground face-down, chin snapping hard, forcing teeth through her tongue, and lay still while blood filled her mouth and she waited to die. A whirl of wind blew grit and hair into her eyes and she shut them, feeling her body embrace the contours of rock and grass stubble.

It was done. It was all done. He could take no more from her, she could let go.

A hand brushed hair back off her forehead but her eyes were unable to open. The rain began pelting the side of her face.

'Bec, it's over now. It's over. You're okay.'

It was Dave, helping her sit up. Her body was an

empty sack and she almost fell back to the ground, steadied only by the arm across her back.

What she saw, as she opened her eyes, was a khaki-clad stranger kneeling over a dark shape spreadeagled nearby.

She choked back blood and threw her hand in front of her mouth, fearing she would vomit.

'The cop, he shot him?'

The answer was slow to come.

'No, he did that himself when he saw us land.'

Dave was grateful she was too shocked to ask further questions. He didn't want to tell her what he saw from the cockpit as the helicopter landed, her pursuer, slow and deliberate, raising his pistol and pointing it at her re-treating back.

It was only when the sergeant opened the chopper door, drawing his own firearm, that her husband had turned the pistol on himself.

———•———

In the Fong kitchen it was late morning and Louie had taken time from a quiet patch in the shop to make tea for his mother. He poured it from her special clay teapot and left it on the table to cool a little.

'It's near your hand.'

He spoke out of habit, though often she did not hear, gently tapping her shoulder to be sure she understood. As he turned to leave her hand lifted and found his arm, brushing down to his fingers, which she squeezed. She was smiling.

It was pleasing, he thought as he returned to the counter, that the tea had made her so happy today.

Though Lily was half-blind and hard of hearing she did not need those senses to know that her missing friend had been delivered from whatever confinement had imprisoned her, eased into a greater self than could be found within the limits of one person's power or independence.

There were those who were birthed, lived, then died without allowing the experience of the beyond to touch them. Others were more fortunate and were born once, then, when the time was right, were birthed again into a world where the mystery of the unseen danced with the seen, and men and women bowed their heads in reverence to the meeting of both.

She had been late coming to her true birth. So many times before then it would have been a consolation to know that life could be trusted, that an inheritance of invisible forces was a source both within and around her.

19

EDDIE'S INITIAL IMPROVEMENT HAD PLATEAUED in the second month and Lily blamed herself. There was never time to exercise his limbs and massage them as often as she should. She cooked the evening meal, fed the baby while Ivy and Willie washed the dishes, then sewed till midnight. After that the baby woke her to be fed and Eddie sometimes needed a bedpan.

In the shop, Ivy was doing well for a girl thrust early into responsibility. She served customers, arranged stock and with Dorothy's help learned to do the orders, but the task of keeping the ledgers and managing the finances fell to Lily, as did some of the heavier lifting when new supplies arrived.

The wheelchair was a blessing, at least for Lily. She could get her husband to the toilet during the day and move him between rooms. It had not occurred to her that for Eddie it might also be a curse.

The day of its delivery she and Ivy helped him to shuffle three steps from the bed, and with Eddie bracing his good hand against the steel frame, they lowered him into the seat.

The back was adjustable and the combination of

a small tilt to it and two armrests meant he had better stability. They no longer had to tie him in place and there was dignity in that, though it was not enough for the boys to interact with him as they once had. Unless Lily requested them to hug their father or assist him they kept their distance.

The first day he sat in it for a couple of hours, Lily only pushing him from the bedroom to the kitchen, letting him take some time to get used to it. Over the following week he became more accustomed to the chair, spending more of the day in it. Lily even dared push him outside early one afternoon, leaving him near the back door for fresh air and the chance to look around.

He could feed himself now, so after the boys had left for school she could attend to baby Louie while her husband ate. Afterwards she wiped his chin and mopped up spilled congee from his shirt.

'We will go into the shop and perhaps you can be of assistance to Ivy.' He gave no sign of a reaction.

Ivy was serving one of their regulars as Lily pushed the chair into the shop. The customer tipped his hat in Eddie's direction.

'How are …?'

The man faltered as he saw the answer to the unfinished question in the sagging left side of Eddie's face and the foot that turned in. He stiffened.

'Good to see you, Mr Fong.' He was already at the exit by the time he had finished his attempt at courtesy.

Lily pushed the chair alongside the counter then turned it, positioning the back against the wall so Eddie could survey the room.

'Hello Father.' Ivy spoke as a parent might talk to

a worried child. Eddie began to make strained sounds, though he quieted when Ivy rubbed his good hand.

The town had emptied out the previous week. The meatworks' picture gardens had screened its last outdoor movie for the season and except for a skeleton maintenance crew, workers had boarded the diesel motorship, *Kangaroo*, for the return to Perth.

Ivy busied herself on a shelf behind her, straightening boxes of painkillers and foot powders, amber bottles of antiseptic and tins of salve, while Lily made as though she was returning to the kitchen. Instead, she remained near the door, out of Eddie's line of sight.

A few minutes later the school administrative officer leaned her bicycle against the outside wall and came in at a clip for writing paper, pens and a typewriter ribbon. She complained to Ivy about Education Department delays in sending quarterly office supplies, engaging in vigorous conversation to avoid acknowledging the frail man sitting in the wheelchair. As she left Eddie began to groan, forcing sound out through his mouth while shaking his head.

'What is it Father?' Ivy bent down in front of the chair. Eddie began thumping his right fist against the armrest. Ivy placed her hand on top of his to stop him hurting himself.

It was too much for Lily. Her husband was clearly overcome with shame, humiliation or a sense of being useless; quite probably all three. She went immediately to the chair and began pushing him back to their quarters.

'I think that is enough for today.'

She said it with her head turned towards Ivy and when she looked back at her husband he was hunched forward, shoulders shaking. In the kitchen she stood at his side, not intruding by trying to touch him, and waited as he let the tears fall, using the only thing he had available to express his distress, a guttural, wounded imitation of a voice.

It cut deeply to hear him cry with such abandon. She had allowed herself to forget his essence, driven by her desire to make things the way they had been. He was a proud man, an independent man, and she had brought him face to face with everything he no longer was as the head of the family, as a father, a businessman. It had been cruel.

'I will not do that to you again. I promise.'

He continued to shudder, chin on his chest.

———— • ————

Although it was only June, the dry season had become unusually sultry in a month where they could confidently predict clear skies. Late one evening, as rain began pattering on the roof, even Willie was surprised.

'Why is it raining?'

'Because it is.' Ivy, tired after a day on her feet, was in no mood to discuss the weather.

'I expect it will stop soon.' Lily spoke in soothing tones.

Within an hour the deluge hammered down, drowning out any possibility of conversation. The family gave up and went to bed early.

Lily lay awake for a long time. This town never ceased to surprise her with its freak weather, though a winter storm was a new experience. She got out of bed, lit a lamp and took it into the shop, checking that the windows and door were secure.

The soft light of the lamp shone out the window, where a ceaseless wall of water gushed off the edge of the verandah, blocking any view of the street. She dared not open the door in case the waterfall was spilling across the pavers and might rush inside. The door was a tight fit in its frame; Eddie had made sure of that for cyclone season. She rolled up a towel and jammed it against the bottom just in case. Satisfied there were no leaks, she checked the kitchen and back door then went back to bed.

Drifting off to sleep was impossible with the assault continuing overhead. The rain seemed to scream in her head. She lay still, hoping the water was rushing unimpeded to the inlet, relieved that Eddie was sleeping.

It eased a little in the early hours of morning, when she finally dozed off, but was still loud on the roof as she started the day.

'Perhaps there is no need to open the shop for now, Ivy. No one will be about.'

'All the more reason, Mother. If someone is that badly in need then I should be there.'

Shortly after ten o'clock, Ivy put up the sign saying the shop was closed for five minutes and risked the short walk to the Post Office for mail. She was full of news when she returned, shaking her umbrella out the back door.

'Waterfalls are pouring down the Bastion. I've never seen it like that.'

The combination of high tide and rain had flooded Wyndham racecourse, out of town on the edge of the salt pan, and water was sweeping almost five miles inland in places. The Ord River was banking, overrunning the Ivanhoe Crossing, and cutting off cattle stations to the east.

'Three trucks left for Hall's Creek late yesterday and they had a terrible time. One was bogged for hours. They've all had to come back to town. Five and a half inches of rain, the Postmaster says.'

Flushed after so much news to share, Ivy returned to the shop. A loud shout followed.

'Mother, come quickly.'

Lily, with Louie in her arms, opened the adjoining door to see water streaming down shelves on the wall behind the counter and Ivy standing paralysed.

'Get as much stock as you can away from the water.' At the sound of her raised voice, the baby began to cry.

She left Louie in his cot and ran out into the rain. There was no time to get a coat. At the side of the shop she saw the gutter overflowing. Her clothes were soaked, already clinging cold to her frame.

She ran through the front door of the shop, ignoring Louie's screams, and got the ladder. Ivy had begun saving what goods she could.

Lily was angry at herself. She knew it was important to clean the gutters regularly. Eddie had been diligent about clearing them and ensuring the downpipes were not blocked. In her haste, Lily failed to position the ladder properly and it wobbled in the soft ground, flinging her from the fifth or sixth step into the mud. She lay on her back, rain stinging her face, overcome by the storm.

The scream that sought to come would be a waste of effort sorely needed. She pushed upright without bothering to wipe mud from her hands, repositioned the ladder under the gutter and climbed it, scooping out handfuls of leaves that had matted with soil until the blockage was cleared.

As soon as she had changed into dry clothes she helped Ivy sweep water out of the shop. The rain stopped late morning, disappearing as suddenly as it appeared, and the sky was clearing as they tallied the damage. A quarter of the stock was water-stained or too damaged to sell. It would be a difficult month, with suppliers to pay and no ability to recoup the costs.

Ivy was inconsolable.

'We will manage. Have hope.'

Lily left her to cry alone in the shop. A storm needed release. After all that had happened since her father's collapse, Ivy needed to let the tears run their course.

She took her time settling Louie, and when she returned to the shop her daughter was composed and stacking the last of the spoiled stock into a crate. Together they opened the shop door.

———— • ————

News travelled fast the next day. The pilot of the mail plane, with a passenger on board, had attempted a landing at the aerodrome earlier that morning but the Dragon's wheels had dug into the soft ground and it had flipped. No one was injured but the plane was extensively damaged.

Joe and Willie wanted badly to see it and even though it was a long walk, well past the Three Mile, Lily gave them permission.

After they left she thought of nothing else but the

plane at the airfield, stuck on its back, silver wings useless, like her husband, caught in his own mire.

It was time to face it. He would never again work in the shop.

———·———

The night dragged its feet through the hours till dawn and she rose from bed at first light to shake it off. Later, with the children at school and Ivy at work, she positioned the wheelchair near the open back door so Eddie could have a change of view. She watched as the baby, now four months old, suckled quietly, full of faith that his needs would be met, that there was good in the world and it would come to meet him.

All night she had tried to resist the new understanding, yet even the son curled in the curve of her arm already embraced it. She had been wrong to believe she could force destiny to the path she wanted for herself or anyone else. She had been arrogant. Her husband's pain had been the result.

The process of living was confusing. She had attempted to fulfil the requirements of responsibility, as society and tradition determined, and found its limits. She had appealed to the ancestors to save her, to shape circumstances to her personal wishes, perhaps even to reward her, though they had not bent to these desires. She had tried retreating from what was demanded of her.

Yet only now, with a legacy of grief, with dependent children and an invalid husband, was it clear how to be in the proper place of relationship with one's life. It had seemed so complicated, yet in reality it was extraordinarily simple, a matter of trusting the guidance that came and learning to allow the pattern laid down, even when the purpose did not seem clear.

Her husband might die in the coming months, might live like this for years or grow ever weaker and more in need of care.

Whatever was to happen, all was unfolding as it should, within a much vaster picture than she could ever see. She hugged the thought close as though it were the baby, feeling it, remembering the shape of it, the potential contained in its form, for the times when the struggle to show up in her own life seemed too great.

Old Grandmother in Canton had a saying that, as a young child watching on, had made no sense. *Love the house with its crows on the roof.* It had taken a lifetime to understand what it meant. The good, the bad; the wanted, unwanted, they were not hers to choose, only to love however she could.

The sun was higher now, had come into its own to command the day. The familiar tilt of her husband's head was outlined against the brightness beyond. He was not a burden but deserving of respect and acceptance for who he had become. If she stopped treating him as an endless set of tasks, if she stopped pushing him to be what he could not and began to meet the person, then perhaps his sons would too.

She thought she heard the rising and falling melody of the finches and went to the doorway, standing to look over Eddie's head, but the branches of the nearby tree and the ground beneath it were empty. She smiled just the same, then leaned down to show the boy to his father.

20

T HE HOUSE FELT TOO QUIET after all the fuss Bec had been through, though she could hardly complain when she was the one who'd encouraged the silence.

She barely remembered the first interview conducted by Northern Territory detectives at Kununurra, after an overnight assessment at the hospital. The second interview, a few days later, was prolonged and painful.

In a break, she had gone down the corridor to find a toilet. The local sergeant was coming the opposite way and in his stare she saw the accusation that she had pushed their colleague over the brink, made him lose his mind. His mouth was hard. He looked ahead, passing her with no acknowledgement.

She had sat in the cubicle and sobbed; a fist balled up against her mouth so no one could hear.

Later, Sheryl had driven her home, barely speaking on the journey, understanding it wasn't a time for words. The smallest sentence could be a battering ram against the eggshell holding her friend together.

She had waited while Bec showered and dressed in fresh clothes, discarding the borrowed jeans and shirt from the police lost property bin. Dave was away and Jo was on duty behind the bar so she stayed to cook a simple omelette, though she doubted her friend would eat it.

'Here, take this.' She handed Bec a tall glass with cold water and two aspirin.

'I don't have a headache.'

'I know you don't, but I can tell you're in physical pain.'

The dressing on the ulcerated wrist had been removed for the shower and Sheryl studied the circular wound as Bec swallowed the tablets.

'Oh hon, that looks bad.'

Bec slammed the glass onto the kitchen bench and pushed a palm near Sheryl's face.

'No, don't. Don't you dare do that. I do not want sympathy from you or anybody else.' She ran off towards her bedroom.

Sheryl ate the omelette rather than waste it, taking her time cleaning up in the kitchen. When Jo still hadn't arrived home, she sat quietly on the back doorstep to wait. She had not wanted to leave until there was someone else in the house.

———— • ————

Bec heard Dave knock at Jo's door down the hall and call her name, then the murmur of voices before the house was silent again.

She remained in her room. She had assured Dave and Jo that she was okay with them hosting the party at their house.

———— • ————

289

'Ready?'

Jo left the suitcase unzipped on the bed. She would have time to finish packing in the morning, but for now she had the farewell do.

'Pretty much.'

Dave sat on the end of the bed while she fiddled with her hair in the mirror. A few days earlier he had signed another twelve-month contract, after which he'd be set up for good jobs back home, carrying a substantial record of hours in the air.

'I'm sorry you're not staying but I get it. There's nothing here for you now the adventure's worn off.'

She wiped wet eyes. 'It's more than that.' He leaned in, waiting for her to finish.

'Sheryl and now Bec … they're good people and yet bad things have happened.'

He pulled her to him, hugging her briefly. It was tempting to fall into big brother mode, to offer a platitude, maybe about how the two women were strong and would work it through. Best to zip it.

'I thought I'd come here, stay a year or so, then everything would be clear. I'd know where I was going with my life and get on with it.'

'Oh Jo, I hadn't realised you expected to find answers here. So why are you going home now?'

She got a tissue from the bedside table and blew her nose loudly.

'Because it's time to stop hiding out.'

He hugged her again then went to the door.

'Come and give me a hand when you're ready. I'll get the glasses and drinks sorted if you take care of the snacks.'

They had arranged a nine o'clock start so the party would still be in full swing at pub closing time, when the bar and kitchen staff could get away.

Hazel and Kieran were the first to arrive, blowing in the front door at the same speed that saw them swoop into the motel units for the daily clean. Next were the school headmaster and his teacher wife, as well as a couple of nurses from the town's hospital, all friends Dave had made as part of giving himself conversational opportunities beyond the beer and hangover talk on rig worker trips.

He opened wine brought by the guests and poured it into glasses, then fetched a beer from the ice-filled bath. Jo had put out french onion dip and crackers on a tray with cheddar cheese, a wheel of Brie, and a bunch of grapes, and was emptying packets of cashews, potato crisps and cheese puffs into bowls.

Dave flicked on the oven ready for the frozen mini pizzas they would heat once the drinks had flowed for a bit. He'd check in on Bec, take her some food later.

She heard the tide of conversation rising and falling, mostly muffled but with the occasional loud laugh or exclamation. Glasses clinked. Dance music grew louder.

Bec remained on the bed, her back propped against the wall. She was a slate wiped clean. Every feeling, every thought had been shocked out of her body. Even the shame. It was a miracle that she still functioned. She had watched herself get out of bed, return to work, eat some food that had been offered.

Yet into the stillness within, a faint stirring had begun.

———— • ————

Despite Dave's best efforts to keep it down, the volume coming from the boom box kept returning to full throttle and by the time Pete, the new kitchen hand Brodie, Leonie and Sheryl straggled in just after midnight, most of the guests were dancing.

Jack turned up soon after, putting in an obligatory appearance.

Dave was fishing out a few beer labels floating in melted ice in the bath when he saw Bec go down the hall towards the party. Despite the music continuing, he heard the hum of conversation drop away.

It had led news bulletins across the country, though mercifully names had been suppressed initially till the husband's family could be officially notified. She had stayed quietly in her room for much of the first week while the town talked about nothing else. It was her awful time in the spotlight and Dave couldn't help thinking about Lindy Chamberlain's trial by media. Just as well Bec hadn't known her turn would come.

The first day she returned to work he had watched her from a distance, when he turned up at the car park to collect rig workers for transfer to the chopper waiting at the aerodrome. She was carrying a bin in the direction of the trailer bay, her feet seeming to glide, barely touching the concrete pathway.

She seemed such a whisp of air, if he'd reached out

a hand it would have passed through her. He resisted the urge to disturb her by calling out a greeting.

He and Jo had attempted to provide opportunities for her to talk about what had happened but she had shut them down. They'd resorted to offers of meals or, given the van was impounded for forensic purposes, outings for a swim, barbecue or picnic. Every suggestion had been rebuffed.

Dave had reined in Jo's need to get through to Bec. He had seen it before, in his colleague after the failed mountain rescue, the way a trauma could blow out every nerve ending so there was no choice in the early days but to withdraw and protect the rawness.

He picked up a few stubbies and returned to the party, distributing the unmarked beers. Jack was taking advantage of the lull in conversation to make a farewell speech for Jo.

'One of the most cheerful workers I've ever had.' The remark landed as a criticism of the other pub employees, who gravitated together in a corner of the room, exchanging surreptitious nods and eyerolls.

Oblivious, Jack pressed on, finishing with a toast that was met by a rousing cheer and the chaos of many hugs for Jo, interspersed with appeals for her to keep in touch.

Afterwards, the crowd slowly thinned until only Dave and the pub staff remained. Jack went over to Bec, and as he did Sheryl stepped up beside her in what seemed like a protective stance.

'Actually, Jack ...' Sheryl was now in front of him, the others nearby holding their drinks but despite varying levels of inebriation, falling quiet as they sensed change was coming.

'I'm handing in my resignation too, effective from the end of next week. I'll give it to you tomorrow in writing.'

Jack jerked his head back as though Sheryl had slapped him. 'But, but why? I thought you were here for the long haul.'

She smiled. In his shorts and up-to-the-knee socks he looked every inch a schoolboy.

'I don't believe I need to give you an explanation, but for what it's worth I'm going back down south to be with my daughter.'

Jo gave her a hug. 'Oh, that is the best news, Sheryl.'

'Yes, whatever it takes, I'm sorting it out.' It was a whisper only for Jo.

As the hubbub died down from Sheryl's announcement, Jack drew Bec off to the side.

'I had a phone call late this afternoon, a woman with a message for you. Says she's your mother, she wants to talk and can you ring her.'

Bec brushed him off without explanation. She turned back to the others. 'While we're at it, I've also got an announcement. I get the van back in ten days or so and I'm going to leave then, too.'

She turned to Sheryl, then nodded in Jo and Dave's direction. 'Sorry to drop it on you. I've only just decided.'

The news was met by a semi-circle of conflicted faces.

'Geez, at this rate I'll be running the pub on my own!'

The remark failed to attract any sympathy, forcing Jack to flounder towards a veneer of graciousness. He thanked the three women for all their work, then promptly left.

Jo couldn't contain her concern any longer. 'But where will you go, Bec, what will you do?'

'Who knows? I'll find out by going, won't I?'

She went to sit on the shop verandah for the first time since Sheryl had driven her back from Kununurra. Each previous afternoon, she had walked home in the same fashion that got her through the eight-hour round of duties at the pub, looking neither right nor left, eyes down to avoid sympathetic looks or worse, judgement.

It was a familiar feeling. She had run from it once before.

Shame had a way of consuming all it touched. The shame of knowing her brother would rather die than confide in her, seek her help; of dealing with a community where people pointed fingers, chose to blame the living. Here it was again, leaving her fragile. It swelled a little more with every breath, a balloon of bad feeling pushing against her rib cage.

It felt way too public to be sitting with Lily, but she couldn't leave early the next day without honouring what had passed between them. Her mentor had spoken little in the months at Wyndham, had looked in her direction so few times she could count them on the fingers of one hand. Yet she had been the one to open her eyes to the deep waters that flowed beneath daily life.

It would have been easy to couch it as mystery, to see it in the mystical terms promoted by new age gurus, yet it was more palpable than that. Bec had experienced it, felt it as a real force, despite having no way to parcel it up.

The lack of definition didn't matter, in fact it was

probably the point. What mattered after everything that had gone down was that she had a new source of strength and the trust that she wouldn't lose it. What had been barely noticeable at first had, since the decision to leave town, grown into a certainty.

In Bec's hands she held a box, carefully wrapped in red paper. She did not want to inadvertently cause offence in giving the present to Lily, so went into the shop to discuss it with Louie. When he heard what it was he seemed pleased, though gave a gentle instruction. 'It's customary to offer a gift with both hands.'

'Thank you. Your mother is an extraordinary woman.'

'More than anyone could ever know. She has enjoyed your company also.'

Bec took one look around the crowded shelves and was turning for the door when he called out.

'By the way, don't expect her to open the present, at least not until later. In her time, it was considered impolite to open a gift immediately.'

On the verandah Bec took up her familiar position, the gift on her knees, as the sun began to slide towards the west, the weight of its heat taking it down.

Lily looked towards her, dipping her head in a barely perceptible nod, the only sign she was pleased to see her young friend again.

Occasional customers hurried from scorching cars into the cooler reaches of the shop then soon departed. One or two waved but most stared pointedly at Bec then ignored the pair. Neither of the women noticed.

'I have something for you, Lily. It is precious to me and the only way I can possibly show you how much your company has meant.' Bec looked up at her elderly friend's restful face.

The son, waiting for the next round of customers, leaned out the door and glanced their way. He saw the two figures, each leaning a little into the private space between them. He quickly withdrew and went back behind the counter.

Bec rose to her feet and with both hands placed the box in Lily's lap. Uncertain about touching her companion, she held it there until the wrinkled hands came up to cradle the gift.

'I was given the set of dolls as a child and it was much later, on a museum visit, I learned they came from your tradition, from the Song Dynasty, when nesting boxes became popular.'

Bec paused. Lily probably couldn't hear most of what she was saying, which was a good thing because it sounded like an encyclopaedia entry. Without thinking her hand went up to rest against her heart.

'What you've given me, I will carry always with gratitude. Matryoshka means mother.'

Bec stopped speaking, for it was difficult to find any way to express what she felt about Lily and the woman's place in the world, the sense of her energy radiating out like the rings on Saturn, influencing much that lay beyond Bec's power to comprehend. Though she did understand one thing. It had saved her.

They sat together in a shared communion, the gift in Lily's hands. Bec wasn't sure how much time went by, but at some point she reluctantly stood.

'Goodbye, dear friend.'

That evening, under the fluorescent light that had long since replaced the oil lamp, Lily unwrapped the box and removed the gift from its tissue paper. She found the join around the centre of the first doll, without needing her son's assistance, and gently prised it apart. As each doll opened she held it in the palm of her hand, wrapping fingers around to feel its shape and weight, allowing each to reveal its layer of truth.

She placed the dolls one by one on the table, and as she did her heart became lighter.

She was the large doll, carrying at her centre all the versions of herself that had come before. There would be no more, for her time of growing was at an end. All that was needed had been gathered within, and all that was not had found release. Her young friend, precious companion as the journey neared its end, had more versions of herself that were yet to come.

Lily sank back into the armchair, at peace. The ancestors were coming for her. She saw them hold hands, circling above. She sensed Bec, too, now understood she was not alone, that her ancestor spirits would come when they were needed, to urge her on.

Bec had finished packing the van by seven. With the sun already stealing over the Bastion she was keen to get on the road and get in as much driving as possible before the heat intensified. Jo and Sheryl had left town already and it was down to Dave to give her a hug and wave her off.

'Let us know how you go, and where. I mean it. Jo and I want to stay in touch.'

She got in the driver's seat and turned the key. The engine came to life.

'I'm not good at lingering farewells.'

She laughed through the open window to cover her discomfort, blew Dave an exaggerated kiss, and drove off before the tears came.

The rattle of the van along the gravel road no longer had the noisy rhythm of a familiar friend. It bucked and shuddered, as though all the strange hands taking finger-prints, photographing its innards and loading it onto a tow truck had made it jumpy. She decided she would sell it at the first opportunity after the coronial inquest, when the question of shared finances could be settled.

The mudflats and salt pan seemed smaller as she crossed to the main part of town. Perhaps the mangroves lining the waterway had inched closer to the road overnight while she slept.

She passed the supermarket and the final string of houses, glancing out of habit down the street where Sheryl had lived. There was no desire to slow down and do a final lap.

Beyond the town boundary the van picked up speed on the silver highway. The air was already fierce as it buffeted her arms and face through the open windows. When she reached the intersection with the Gibb River Road she swept past, continuing along the Great Northern Highway.

As every kilometre disappeared in the rear-view mirror, Wyndham fell further behind, was becoming the past, leaving a vacuum where the present moment was arriving, renewing itself after days and weeks of stagnation. In the heat, veins were plumping on the back of her hands, sunglasses sliding on sweat down the bridge of her nose, but they went unnoticed.

What held her attention was the line of low hills gliding by, running one into the other, obscuring a continent so vast she was the merest speck on its surface. She held onto the insignificance of herself, the relief of being humbled, of becoming no one. A truck roared past in the opposite direction, and when the wash of air nudged the van it was exhilarating to feel the tremor.

On the approach to Kununurra, she surprised herself by speaking aloud.

'It's time for me to listen.'

She leaned towards the open window, and with all her might screamed the words into the wind, hoping they would carry to Lily, the one person who would understand. The steady hum of tyres on hot asphalt was all the confirmation needed.

An idea began to form. She would take her time, let herself heal a little as she went south, through the red desert to Alice Springs and across the South Australian border. From Adelaide she would work her way towards the coast then go east, would keep going east until she found her way to the family farm, to her mother and father.

It was time to reclaim what had been lost to her, and perhaps, to them.

She had no illusions about how it would be, no expectations of redemption. Sometimes pain just hurt. She needed to let it cut clean.

ABOUT THE AUTHOR

Anna Housego has always been fascinated by the currents that ebb and flow in us and in our lives, bringing strength or creating havoc, depending on how we meet them.

A former journalist, she has worked in a range of jobs, from roustabout at a frontier pub to political adviser, and for two decades was a freelance communications consultant. The storytelling gene comes from Irish ancestors. Growing up in a wilderness town full of eccentric characters switched it on.

She lives a long way south, on the island of lutruwita/ Tasmania, off the south-eastern corner of Australia, close to her two adult children and their families.

Crows on the Roof is her third novel.

www.annahousego.com

@annahousego

@annahousegoauthor

ALSO BY ANNA HOUSEGO

The Way to Midnight

One Small Life

Made in the USA
Coppell, TX
04 December 2022

87833389R00180